Praise for

'A writer who has created a world of her own – a world
...trophobic and irrational which we enter each time with a
... of personal danger ... Miss Highsmith is the poet of
a... rehension' **GRAHAM GREENE**

'Highsmith is a giant of the genre. The original, the best, the
g... sly twisted Queen of Suspense' **MARK BILLINGHAM**

...nks of comparing Miss Highsmith only with herself; by
...er standard of comparison, one must simply cheer' **AUBERON**

...th was every bit as deviant and quirky as her
... heroes, and didn't seem to mind if everyone knew it'
..., *DAILY TELEGRAPH*

...on is that when the dust has settled and when the
... f twentieth-century American literature comes to be
... story will place Highsmith at the top of the pyramid,
... place Dostoevsky at the top of the Russian hierarchy
...s' **A. N. WILSON,** *DAILY TELEGRAPH*

...he greatest modernist writers' **GORE VIDAL**

...ses most of her books with a feeling that the world is
...ngerous than one had ever imagined' **JULIAN SYMONS,** *NEW*
...*MES BOOK REVIEW*

...eliciting the menace that lurks in familiar surroundings,
...e's no one like Patricia Highsmith' *TIME*

VIRAGO
MODERN CLASSICS
628

© Jerry Bauer

Patricia Highsmith (1921–1995) was born in Fort Worth, Texas, and moved to New York when she was six, where she attended the Julia Richman High School and Barnard College. In her senior year she edited the college magazine, having decided at the age of sixteen to become a writer. Her first novel, *Strangers on a Train*, was made into a classic film by Alfred Hitchcock in 1951. *The Talented Mr Ripley*, published in 1955, introduced the fascinating anti-hero Tom Ripley, and was made into an Oscar-winning film in 1999 by Anthony Minghella. Graham Greene called Patricia Highsmith 'the poet of apprehension', saying that she 'created a world of her own – a world claustrophobic and irrational which we enter each time with a sense of personal danger' and *The Times* named her no.1 in their list of the greatest ever crime writers. Patricia Highsmith died in Locarno, Switzerland, in February 1995. Her last novel, *Small g: A Summer Idyll*, was published posthumously, the same year.

Novels by Patricia Highsmith

Strangers on a Train
Carol (*also published as* The Price of Salt)
The Blunderer
The Talented Mr Ripley
Deep Water
A Game for the Living
This Sweet Sickness
The Cry of the Owl
The Two Faces of January
The Glass Cell
A Suspension of Mercy (*also published as* The Story-Teller)
Those Who Walk Away
The Tremor of Forgery
Ripley Under Ground
A Dog's Ransom
Ripley's Game
Edith's Diary
The Boy Who Followed Ripley
People Who Knock on the Door
Found in the Street
Ripley Under Water
Small g: A Summer Idyll

Short-story Collections

Eleven
Little Tales of Misogyny
The Animal Lover's Book of Beastly Murder
Slowly, Slowly in the Wind
The Black House
Mermaids on the Golf Course
Tales of Natural and Unnatural Catastrophes
Nothing that Meets the Eye: The Uncollected
Stories of Patricia Highsmith

THE GLASS CELL

Patricia Highsmith

Introduced by Joan Schenkar

virago

VIRAGO

This paperback edition published in 2014 by Virago Press
First published in Great Britain in 1965 by William Heinemann Ltd
First published in the USA in 1964 by Doubleday

A CIP catalogue record for this book
is available from the British Library.

ISBN 978-0-349-00495-2

Typeset in Goudy by M Rules
Printed and bound in Great Britain by
Clays Ltd, St Ives plc

Papers used by Virago are from well-managed forests
and other responsible sources.

MIX
Paper from
responsible sources
FSC® C104740
www.fsc.org

Virago Press
An imprint of
Little, Brown Book Group
100 Victoria Embankment
London EC4Y 0DY

An Hachette UK Company
www.hachette.co.uk

www.virago.co.uk

To my dear cat
SPIDER
born in Palisades, New York,
now a resident of Positano,
my cellmate for most of these pages.

INTRODUCTION

2.30 a.m. My New Year's Toast: to all the devils, lusts, passions, greeds, envies, loves, hates, strange desires, enemies ghostly and real, the army of memories, with which I do battle – may they never give me peace.

Patricia Highsmith, 1947

Well, she's back.

Just when we thought she'd settled down to a quiet Afterlife, too.

But here she comes, The Dark Lady of American Letters, frowning and smiling and blowing her smoke rings of misdirection at us through the slow, insidious pull of her novels on the gravitational field of modern fiction.

She's back and she's putting the frighteners on again.

Oh, it's Patricia Highsmith all right. I'd know those cloven hoofprints anywhere. She sidles into your sentences, hacks your *aperçus*, drunk-dials your dreams. Scatters her props and propensities all over your imagination, then shatters your sense of self with her secret plans for sharing: 'What I predicted I would once do, I am already doing[;] that is, showing the unequivocal triumph of evil over good, and rejoicing in it. I shall make my readers rejoice in it, too.'

Here are her maps, her charts, her obsessive little lists. Her art-loving psychopaths and lovesick stalkers. The minds marred by murder, the ambitions cleft by failure. The ice-cold blondes, the amnesiac alter egos. The beer-stained, tear-stained love notes on napkins. The traces of blood at the corner of her smile.

An outsider artist of gravelled gifts, savage talents and obsessional interests, Mary Patricia Highsmith (1921–1995) wrote some of the darkest, most delinquently original novels of the twentieth century. She is responsible for inserting an adjective ('Highsmithian'), a proper name ('Tom Ripley'), and a phrase ('strangers on a train') into the language, but her best books are still corralled in categories which cannot account for their depth, their dazzle or their direct attack on her readers.

'Crime' and 'suspense' are the classifications to which her work is most often relegated, but her novels and short stories splay across genres, interrogate genders, disrupt the idea of character and offer the most thorough anatomy of guilt in modern literature. Patricia Highsmith isn't a crime writer, she's a *punishment* writer.

Born in her grandmother's boarding house in Fort Worth, Texas, rooted in her family's unreconstructed Confederate past, raised in Greenwich Village when it was 'the freest four square miles on earth', Pat Highsmith was a paradox from birth. She was both 'legitimate' and 'born out of wedlock' nine days after her artist mother divorced her illustrator father. She grew into her contradictions.

High art was always her goal, but in the 1940s she had a secret seven-year career as the only woman scriptwriter for Superhero comics.* Proustian in her innumerable love affairs and desired by many, she brought a headsman's axe to all her relationships. She

* It was Pat's anonymous writing for comic-book superheroes and their mild-mannered second selves that gave her an early (and unacknowledged) opportunity to explore her affinity with alter egos and double identities. 'My obsession with duality saves me from a great many other obsessions,' is how she put it.

'worshipped' women, preferred the company of men and cloaked her narrative voice in another (but not exactly opposite) gender. She is as unconscious a 'gay male novelist' as Ernest Hemingway, and as gifted an anatomist of male sexual anxiety as Norman Mailer. Murder was always on her mind, and she usually confused it with love.

'Murder,' she wrote, 'is a kind of making love, a kind of possessing,' and nearly every Highsmith novel is organised around the reverberant psychologies of a homicide. Although love was her lighthouse and she lived for its illuminations, she couldn't live *with* it. So she killed for it over and over again in her writing. A Freudian in spite of herself, she murdered her fictional victims at Greenwich Village addresses where she made love in life.

At twelve, Pat knew she was 'a boy born in a girl's body'. At sixteen, writing was for what she *wished* would happen: she turned her urge to steal a book into a short story about a girl who steals a book. 'Every artist,' she said, 'is in business for his health.' At twenty-one, her focus was fixed: 'Obsessions are the only things that matter. Perversion interests me most and is my guiding darkness.'

Her turbulent love–hate relationship with her erratic mother sundered her psychology and spawned all the Noir bitches in her writing and most of the heart-broken blondes in her bed. Her sentiments for her mild-mannered stepfather were simpler: she wanted to kill him and said so. She grew up to occupy both sides of every question.

In adolescence, Pat began 'double-booking' herself with *cahiers* (notebooks) for her novels, short stories and essays, and with diaries for her love affairs with the beautiful, intelligent women who were her Muses – and the few good men who were not. These lifelong journals – like conjoined twins arising from the vapours of her youthful fascination with doubling – embezzled each other's materials, rehearsed her obsessions before she published them, and gave her the opportunity to renew her vows to the only lasting love match she ever made: the union that joined her intense rushes of feeling with her compelling need to commit them to paper.

At twenty-nine, she published her sensational debut novel, *Strangers on a Train* (1950). The 'deal' at its dark heart – an anonymous exchange of homicides – set up the quintessential Highsmith situation: two men bound together by the stalker-like fixation of one upon the other; a fixation which always involves a murderous, implicitly homoerotic fantasy.* *The Price of Salt* followed in 1952, and its richly figured language borrowed elements from *Strangers* and subdued them to the subject of requited lesbian love – the only 'crime' Pat left out of her other fictions. Published anonymously for forty years, *The Price of Salt* (now reissued as *Carol*) sold hundreds of thousands of copies and made its author uneasy all her life.

Highsmith's industry was staggering. Five to seven neatly typed pages of finished fiction rolled from the platen of her coffee-coloured 1956 Olympia Deluxe portable typewriter each day, followed by book themes, articles, lists of every description, short-story ideas, and four or five personal letters in her oddly impersonal prose. Her thirty-eight writer's notebooks and eighteen diaries were written in five languages, four of which she didn't actually speak. She drew, she sketched, she painted; she made sculptures, furniture and woodcarvings. The simple savageries of gardening – who lives? who goes to the compost pile? – appealed to her American Calvinism, and she took up her secateurs with a will.

Out of her great divide (and in the acid bath of her detail-saturated prose), Patricia Highsmith developed a remarkable

* Alfred Hitchcock's wonderful (if skewed towards normality) film version of *Strangers on a Train* (1951) revived his directing career. Raymond Chandler, on the other hand, said that working on the film script drove him crazy.

image of an alternate Earth: Highsmith Country. Its shadow cabinet of homicidal alter egos, displaced guilts, and unstable identities convenes in permanent session in the Nightmare Alley just behind the American Dream. And the deep psychological partitions its citizens suffer (as they count up their culpabilities or slip into measurable degrees of madness) come from its author's unblinking examination of her own wayward tastes:

> I can't think of anything more apt to set the imagination stirring, drifting, creating, than the idea – the fact – that anyone you walk past on the pavement anywhere may be a sadist, a compulsive thief, or even a murderer.

Pat's Suffolk period was the first creatively settled interval in her long, strange European expatriation. And England was ready for her. She had loyal English publishers and agents. Francis Wyndham's crucial survey of her dark materials (part of an extended review of *The Cry of the Owl* in the *New Statesman* in 1963) had provided the public with an elegant introduction to her work: '[T]he reader's sense of satisfaction,' he wrote, 'may derive from sources as dark as those which motivate Patricia Highsmith's destroyers and their fascinated victims.' London-associated writers as diversely distinguished as Julian Symons, Brigid Brophy, Graham Greene, Arthur Koestler, Sybil Bedford, and Muriel Spark admired her writing.* And *The Two Faces of January* (1964) would win the CWA's Silver Dagger Award in 1965.

But it was love alone – and in a magnitude she hadn't yet experienced – that brought the talented Miss Highsmith to Suffolk. In late 1962, domiciled in America, but travelling widely

* Muriel Spark adopted Highsmith's favourite cat, Spider, the dedicatee of *The Glass Cell*, when Highsmith moved to England from Italy. Spider, Dame Muriel said, 'brought a bit of Patricia Highsmith with him'.

and restlessly, Pat fell in love ('like being shot in the face', is what she said – still mixing up love and murder) with a cultured, attractive, solidly married Londoner. Obsessed by this woman 'as never before' and so 'killed by pleasure' that she couldn't continue the novel she'd started about a good man wrongly imprisoned (*The Glass Cell*), Pat 'cleared her complicated decks' in America and made her way to Europe and thence to Suffolk, to be nearer (if not closer) to love's inspiring shocks.

Stalking her London romance – but keeping her distance from it, too – Pat wrote most of *The Glass Cell* (1964) in Positano and Rome, and then revised the manuscript extensively in Aldeburgh. Finally, in 1964, she settled in Earl Soham in Suffolk in what had been two country cottages, now knocked together as one dwelling: Bridge Cottage.

The double structure of Bridge Cottage suited her psychology as much as the ambiguities of a love affair with someone else's wife suited her temperament. Lush productivity and plain prose were the results, punctuated by an invigorating volley of complaints. English weather, 'dreary' English pubs and too-infrequent meetings with her English lover encouraged her natural negativity, but only an English Christmas could raise it to the level of simile: 'The holidays here exhaust one, creeping through closed windows like a poisonous gas,' she wrote, sounding just like a Highsmith character.

In fact, Pat was having a better time in Suffolk than she admitted. Enlivened by her new surroundings, she very quickly began to write *A Suspension of Mercy* (1965), and then found a collaborator with whom to plot out a possible television script. She made fast friends with Ronald Blythe, at work on his Suffolk book *Akenfield*, and they gossiped for hours and toured the Suffolk churches. And James Hamilton-Paterson, future author of *Gerontius* and *Cooking with Fernet Branca*, won her heart by walking out on her when she burst into tears. 'I don't blame him,' said Pat, who would have done the same thing herself, 'give him my love.'

Although each of the three novels Pat completed during her Suffolk period was set in a different place (New York, Suffolk, Venice), Highsmith Country is their one, true home.* The first of them, *The Glass Cell*, was sourced from Pat's detailed correspondence with an American convict who wrote to tell her how much he'd enjoyed *Deep Water*. ('I don't think my books should be in prison libraries,' said Pat – and made the convict give her the particulars of prison life.) As always, she followed her unruly feelings in reversing her new novel's line of logic. Philip Carter is a classic Highsmith 'criminal-hero' – with his orphan background and professional training; his high culture and low behaviour; his sluggish libido and ambiguous affections. In *The Glass Cell*, his punishment has been enacted *before* he commits a crime. He is unjustly accused, wrongly imprisoned, physically tortured, and entirely innocent.

Philip Carter and his prison mate Max (a forger who dies in a prison riot) approach intimacy and practise French, and Max seems 'more real' to Carter than his own wife. Carter reads Swift, Voltaire and Robbe-Grillet (and keeps the complete Verlaine in his cell), murders his wife's lover when he's released (guiltlessly and with a piece of classical statuary), and weeps while listening to Bach. He lies to everyone, forces 'guilt' and 'innocence' to change places and exchange definitions, and knows the police will follow him for ever. Still, murder has made his life better: 'Everything was going to be all right now,' he thinks.

* Tom Ripley, the 'criminal-hero' of Pat's best-known work *The Talented Mr Ripley* (1955), is Highsmith Country's most prominent ambassador. A socially sinuous, fragilely gendered serial killer, forger, fraudster, and identity impersonator, he is also Highsmith's darker emissary to herself; her *semblable*. It was Ripley, Pat said disconcertingly, who wrote that novel; she was merely taking dictation. And she added Ripley's name to her Edgar Allan Poe award.

But in *The Glass Cell*, the push-broom of Pat's paragraphs sweeps the detritus of confinement steadily before it, trailing strings of objects or mundane actions or simple thoughts in a dogged accumulation of detail as dispassionate as that found in most prisons – or most pornographies. Her gut-punch prose – she's the court recorder here, not the judge but her style (as spare as a prison bunk) is convincingly mimetic – suggests that Carter has carried his private incarceration (his 'glass cell') into the world with him. The world is his prison now, nor is he out of it.

Nothing if not practical, Pat liked to furnish her houses of fiction with the large and small irritants of her daily life. In *A Suspension of Mercy*, the only novel she both wrote and set in Suffolk, she used her circumstances to make a work at war with itself – a comedy of terrors – and lent her 'criminal-hero' more of her own qualities than even she imagined.

Sydney Smith Bartleby, a young American novelist displaced to Suffolk by his upwardly mobile English marriage, is beginning to chafe. He's in a situation not unlike his author's – and he's burdened with most of her local irritations, too: a collaborator on a television script; a frustrated desire to see a body carried out in a carpet (a gambit Pat considered for other works and parodied in this one by leaving the body *out* of the carpet); a partner in absentia (Sydney's would-be painter wife is taking a holiday from their marriage and its meannesses); some difficult writing to get on with; and an imagination unable to refrain from replacing the dullish realities of his life with the homicidal narratives he wants for his work.

Sydney's names, yoked together by violence, are clipped directly from the baptismal rolls of Highsmith Country. 'Sydney Smith' was the wit, writer and clergyman on whom Jane Austen is said to have based the attractive protagonist of her Gothic satire *Northanger Abbey* – while 'Sir Sydney Smith' was Edinburgh's renowned forensic expert on methods of murder.

And 'Bartleby' is Herman Melville's inscrutably persistent Wall Street scrivener. The ways in which Pat uses *A Suspension of Mercy* to juggle these contradictions and toy with the conventions of crime and suspense are both experimental *and* satirical – though the smiles are properly constrained and the laughter suitably stifled.

As Sydney relaxes his ability to distinguish between the fantasies he's staging in his head and what he'd really like to do about his absent spouse, he begins to rehearse the actions, the feelings, and the false identity of a guilty wife-killer; falling under suspicion for his wife's murder after she disappears. In the course of his games, the principles of Highsmith Country, greatly exhilarated by his masquerades, come out to play: deeds before motives, effects before causes, punishments before crimes – and Sydney unintentionally frightens a suspicious neighbour to death, then languidly commits a murder which is both there and not there.

For this ostensible murder – and for his accidental one, too – Sydney feels no guilt. He looks forward to recording what he's just lived through in his writer's notebook. It's a brown notebook, we are told quietly; the same colour as the writer's notebooks Patricia Highsmith used all her life.

Strictly speaking, there is no homicide in Pat's third Suffolk novel, *Those Who Walk Away* (1967). Once again, a murder is there, and not there – and Pat began to imagine the novel's rapid reversals and deep disruptive shocks late in 1966 on a trip to Venice: a city whose end-stopped streets and serpentine canals might have been designed for the psychological volutes of a Highsmith novel.

Pat's first intention for *Those Who Walk Away* sounds like something out of *Sunset Boulevard*: 'A suspense novel from the point of view of the corpse'. But the suicide of the painter Peggy Garrett, wife and daughter, respectively, of the two male protagonists (one of whom, an artist, blames the other, a gallerist, for her death), predates the novel's first page, pervades the work, and tries to pass itself off as the trigger for the purest expression yet of Highsmith Country's 'infinite progression of the trapped and the hunted'.

The dead woman's husband, Ray Garrett, is pursued by Ed Coleman, the vengeful painter who is her father. Ray starts a game of hide and seek with his potential murderer, chasing his own death by following Ed to Venice after Ed tries to shoot him in Rome. Filled with the inspiration of art and artists, Ray seeks what all Highsmith males look for: total oblivion through the dissolution of his burdensome identity.

Just like wrestlers unable to leave the mat, Ray Garrett and his father-in-law try out different holds and postures on each other, different ways of winning and losing, different means of being brutal and being passive. But there is no death in Venice, and Ray and Ed are both caught in the mantrap Highsmith's imagination first sprang in *Strangers on a Train* – and then prised open again in *The Talented Mr Ripley* (1955).

In *Those Who Walk Away*, Pat Highsmith, always a little more frightening than any of her characters, imagines a 'reality' built around the *whole* of the hunt: the hunter, the hunted, their constant exchange of roles, and the terrible necessity of the pursuit itself. Someone as creatively caught up with hunting as Pat was could never choose the hunter over the hunted – or vice versa. Hence her constant shifting of roles and shuffling of identities: a compellingly forceful premise in her fictions – and a cruelly exhausting one in her life.

With her usual discipline, Pat continued to write in Suffolk as her London relationship slowly, then rapidly, declined. She began 'a religious television play' based on a Jesus-like character – and put it to perverse use as a frame for *Ripley Under Ground* (1970). She finished her second snail story, 'The Quest for Blank Claveringii', wrote a 'ghost' tale, 'The Yuma Baby', and in a single month completed a short, artistic autobiography disguised as a handbook for would-be writers: *Plotting and Writing Suspense Fiction* (1965). From Earl Soham she travelled to Hammamet in Tunisia for weeks of immersive research for *The Tremor of Forgery* (1969), another book about another American writer losing his sense of moral balance in expatriatism. Back at Bridge Cottage, she finished a film script for her novel *Deep Water* (1957). She never stopped working.

She went on drawing and sketching too, and jotted down little inventions and quirky ephemera in her notebooks: 'The Gallery of Bad Art', a 'sweating thermometer', some free-form 'lamp-shades'. Her 'strychnined lipstick' expressed her feelings for women just as much as her idea for a cookbook, 'Desperate Measures', represented her response to food. The best that can be said of her scheme for the global deployment of children (as tiny territorial ambassadors) is that it adds a new terror to child development.

The final breakdown of her English love affair – she described it as 'the worst time of my entire life' – swept her across the Channel to France and Switzerland, where she moved from region to region, relationship to relationship, and drink to drink. She went on writing as though her life depended on it (it did); monitoring her thoughts the way a searchlight sweeps a prison yard for escaping convicts. And she continued to curate her expatriate's museum of American maladies.

The pearl of a girl from mid-century Manhattan turned into an embittered old oyster in her last home, her Fortress of Solitude (a modernist citadel with jutting twin wings) in a sunny canton in Switzerland: the country, as Scott Fitzgerald wrote, where many things end and few begin.

Even the manner of her dying sustained that volatile attachment to duality which haloed her life and allowed all her contradictory emotions to meet and mate and ignite into art. For

Patricia Highsmith – she could have written this ending for herself and perhaps she did – expired of two competing diseases. Her doctors said they could not treat the one without exacerbating the other.

Welcome to Highsmith Country.

Joan Schenkar, 2014

THE GLASS CELL

I

It was 3.35 p.m., Tuesday afternoon, in the State Penitentiary, and the inmates were returning from the workshops. Men in unpressed, flesh-coloured uniforms, each with a number on the back, streamed through the long corridor of A-block, and a low hum of voices rose from them, though none of the men seemed to be talking to anyone near by. It was a strange, unmusical chorus, and it had frightened Carter on the first day – he had actually been green enough to think that a riot might be in the offing – but he accepted it now as a peculiarity of the State Penitentiary or perhaps of all prisons. Cell doors stood open, and into certain cells along the ground floor and along the four tiers above, certain men vanished, until the corridor was nearly empty. There would be twenty-five minutes now in which to wash up at the basin in the cell, change a shirt if one cared to or had a clean one, to write a letter or listen with the earphones to the disc-jockey programme that was always on at this time. The bell for supper rang at 4.

Philip Carter was walking slowly, dreading the sight and the company of his cellmate Hanky. Hanky was a short, chunky fellow, in for thirty years for armed robbery ('bargaining') and murder, and seemingly rather proud of it. Hanky didn't like Carter and called him a snob. There had been several minor tiffs in the ninety days Carter had spent with him. Hanky had noticed, for instance, that Carter disliked using the single seatless and exposed toilet in the cell in his presence, so Hanky made his own use of the toilet as noisy and vulgar as possible. Carter had taken this with good-natured indifference at first, but ten days ago, when the joke had become rather old, Carter had said, 'Oh, for God's sake, Hanky, cut it out,' and Hanky had become angry and called Carter a worse name than snob. They had stood up to each other with fists clenched for a moment, but a guard had seen them and broken it up. After that, Carter had kept a polite and cool distance between himself and Hanky, handing him the single pair of earphones, if he was nearer to them, handing Hanky his towel or whatever. The cell with its two bunks was too narrow for one man to pass another comfortably, and, by tacit agreement, if one man was up, the other took to his bunk. But this week Carter had had a piece of bad news from his lawyer Tutting. There was to be no re-trial, and, since ninety days had passed, a pardon was out of the question also. Carter faced the fact that he was going to be in the cell with Hanky for some time to come, and that he should perhaps not be so hostile and aloof. The atmosphere between them was not pleasant, and what did it accomplish? Hanky had sprained his ankle last Friday, jumping off the truck that took the inmates back and forth to farm work. He might at least ask Hanky how his ankle was.

Hanky was sitting on the edge of his lower bunk, fondling his incomplete deck of dirty playing cards.

Carter nodded to him and glanced at his bandaged ankle. 'How's your foot today?' He unbuttoned his shirt and headed straight for the basin.

'Oh, so-so. Still can't walk on it.'

Hanky lifted the bedding at the foot of his bunk, and produced two packs of Camels that he had been hiding there.

4

This Carter saw as he straightened up, drying himself with his small rough towel. Hanky didn't smoke. The ration was four packs a week, which the inmates bought with their own money. The inmate's salary was fourteen cents a day, the cigarettes twenty-two cents a pack. Hanky saved up his own ration and sold it at a profit to other inmates. The guards knew about Hanky's sideline and winked at it, because Hanky occasionally gave them a pack or even gave them a dollar.

'Do me a favour, Cart? Take these to number thirteen down here and number forty-eight third tier. One to each. I don't feel like walking that far. They're paid for.'

'Sure.' Carter took them in one hand and started out, buttoning his shirt with his other hand.

Number thirteen was only two cells away from his and Hanky's cell.

An old Negro with white hair sat on the lower bunk.

'Cigarettes?' Carter asked.

The Negro rolled sideways on one fleshless hip and pulled a small piece of paper out of his pocket. With stiff, black fingers, the Negro pushed Hanky's receipt into Carter's hand.

Carter stuffed it into his pocket, tossed a package of Camels on the bunk, and went out. He walked towards the end of the corridor, where the stairs were. The guard called Moony – a nickname for Moonan – quickened his slow walk and frowned as he came towards Carter. Carter had the other pack of cigarettes in his hand. He saw that Moony saw it.

'Deliverin' cigarettes?' Moony's long, thin face scowled harder. 'You gonna start deliverin' milk and newspapers, too?'

'I'm taking them for Hanky. He's got a sprained ankle.'

'Let's have y'hands.' Moony took his handcuffs off the clasp of his belt.

'I didn't steal the cigarettes. Ask Hanky.'

'Y'hands!'

Carter held out his hands.

Moony clicked the handcuffs on his wrists. At the same instant, two toilets near by flushed simultaneously, and simultaneously Carter saw over Moony's shoulder a pimply-faced, pudgy inmate smirking slightly with vague pleasure as he watched. A few seconds before, Carter had thought Moony might be joking. He had seen Moony and Hanky joking a few times, Moony even swinging his stick playfully at Hanky. Now he knew Moony was not joking. Moony didn't like him. Moony called him 'the professor'.

'Walk to the end of the block,' Moony said.

Moony's voice was loud. While Moony had been talking to Carter, a silence had fallen in the two or three cells in either side of the block which could observe them, and it was spreading over the whole ground floor. Carter walked, with Moony behind him. At the end of the corridor were two stairways going up to the second tier, the elevator's barred doors that Carter had only twice seen open for hospital cases on their way up, and two plain doors, their fronts flush with the stone wall, with large round locks in them. One led to the next cell block, B-block, the other to the Hole. Moony stepped in advance of Carter and swung off his big ring of keys from his belt.

Carter heard a soft, collective groan from the men watching, a hum as anonymous as a wind.

'What's the matter, Moony?' asked a voice, so self-assured Carter knew before he glanced behind him that it was a guard's.

'Got the great engineer here deliverin' cigarettes,' Moony said, and opened the door. 'Step down,' he said to Carter.

The stairs went down. This was the Hole.

Carter paused after a couple of steps. He had heard about the Hole. Even if the inmates exaggerated, and he was sure they did exaggerate, it was a torture chamber. 'Listen, an offence like this – doing a favour for Hanky – it's just a few demerits, isn't it?'

Moony and Cherniver, who was coming along too, chuckled superiorly, as if at the remark of a half-wit.

'Git goin',' Moony said. 'You already got more demerits than I can count or you either.' Moony shoved him.

Carter kept his balance, then descended the steps, watching his footing carefully; for if he fell, he could not easily save himself with manacled hands. He had taken a fall the day he was put into prison, and at that time his handcuffs had been shackled to a heavy leather belt. It was true that he had a lot of demerits, but they were mostly due to the fact he did not yet know everything he could and could not do. You got demerits for not keeping in step in a line marching to the mess hall, for saying 'Excuse me' or saying anything on the way to the workshops (but not on the way back), for flicking a comb through your hair at certain times, for looking too long at a visitor (a stranger, perhaps, man or woman) through the double-barred wall at the end of A-block; and four times, due to demerits, Carter had been unable to see his wife on Sunday afternoons. This was doubly infuriating, because on each occasion the two letters per week that he was permitted to write had been sent to Hazel too early to tell her that if she came that Sunday he could not see her. There was no list of regulations anywhere that an inmate could read and so avoid committing misdemeanours. Carter had asked some inmates for all the ways of incurring demerits, and he had listened to thirty or forty, and then one inmate had said with a reconciled smile, 'Ah, there must be about a thousand of 'em. Gives the screws somethin' to do.' Carter supposed now that he was due for twenty-four or forty-eight hours of solitary in the dark. He took a deep breath and tried to be philosophical about it: it wasn't going to last for ever, and what were three or six missed meals of the lousy food they served here? He regretted only missing his daily letter from Hazel, which would be brought to his cell around 5.30 p.m.

Carter's feet found level stone. There was an unfamiliar dampness in the air and a familiar smell of stale urine.

Moony had a flashlight, but he used it to guide his and Cherniver's steps behind him, while Carter went ahead into darkness. Now on right and left Carter could see the small doors of the cells he had heard about, tiny black holes that a man could not stand up in, big step-ups at the doors so one had to crawl into them. The prison had been built in 1869, Carter remembered, and these must have been part of the original prison, the part beyond improvement. The rest of the prison was said to have been improved at one time.

'. . . the hose?' Cherniver asked in a low voice.

'Somepin' stronger. Here we are. Stop! Go on in.'

They were beside a cell with no door at all, a cell with a very high open doorway. As Carter walked in, he heard from another cell a groan or a grunt and the snuffle of a nose. There was at least one other person down here. It was comforting. The cell was huge compared to the one Carter shared with Hanky, but there was no bunk or chair or toilet in it, only a small round drain in the centre of the floor. The walls were of metal, not stone, black-grey and red from rust. Then Carter noticed hanging from the ceiling a pair of chains that ended in black loops.

'Gimme y'hands,' said Moony.

Carter extended his hands.

Moony removed the handcuffs. 'Cherny, ol' pal, can you git me a stool from sommers?'

'Yes, *sir*,' said Cherniver and went out, drawing his own flashlight from a pocket.

Cherniver returned with a square wooden stool like a small table, which he set down below the chains.

'Step up,' said Moony.

Carter stepped up, and Moony after him. Carter raised his hands before he was ordered to. The straps were leather with a rubber lining, and they buckled.

'Thumbs,' said Moony.

Obediently Carter turned up his thumbs, then realized with a shock what Moony intended. Moony fixed the straps between the first and second joints of his thumbs, then buckled them tightly. The straps had holes every half inch and all along their length.

Moony stepped down. 'Kick the stool away.'

Carter was strung so high, he was on tiptoe and could not kick it away.

Moony gave the stool a kick that sent it a couple of yards in front of Carter and turned it over. Carter swung. The first stab of pain prolonged itself. Blood rushed to the tips of his thumbs. His back was to the guards, and he expected a blow.

Moony laughed, and then one of them kicked him in the thigh and he began to swing back and forth, twisting a little. Then a push in the small of his back. Carter suppressed a groan. He held his breath. Now sweat trickled in front of his ears, down his jaw. Carter's ears were ringing loudly. He smelt cigarette smoke. Carter wondered if they had a time limit, vaguely a time limit, such as an hour, two hours? How much time had passed already? Three minutes? Fifteen? Carter was afraid he would scream in another few seconds. Don't scream, he told himself. The screws would love that. Muscles down his back began to flutter. It was hard to breathe. He had a brief fantasy that he was drowning, that he was in water instead of air. Then the ringing in his ears drowned out the guards' voices.

Something struck him in the back. Water hissed over the stone floor in front of him, and a bucket bounced and clattered. Everything seemed in slow motion. He felt much heavier, and he imagined that the two guards were hanging on to his legs.

'Oh, Hazel,' Carter mumbled.

'Hazel?' a guard said.

'That's his wife. Gets letters from her every day.'

'Not today, he won't.'

Carter felt his eyes were bulging from their sockets. He tried to blink. His eyes felt dry and huge. He had a vision of Hazel walking nervously up and down in his cell, wringing her hands, glancing at him now and then, saying something that he could not hear.

The scene shifted to the trial. Wallace Palmer. Wallace Palmer was dead. *Then what do you think he did with the money? . . . Come now, Mr Carter, you're an intelligent man, a college graduate, an engineer, a sophisticated New Yorker.* (Your honour, that is irrelevant.) *You don't sign papers not knowing what you're signing!* I knew what I was signing. Receipts, invoices. It wasn't my job to know the exact price of things. Palmer was the contractor. The prices could've been raised on the receipts after I'd signed them, raised by Palmer . . . I did not know our material was second-rate and I told him so. *Where is the money, Mr Carter? Where is the two hundred and fifty thousand dollars?* And then Hazel was on the stand, saying in her clear voice, My husband and I have always had a joint bank account . . . We've never had any secrets about anything to do with money . . . with money . . . with money . . .

'Hazel!' Carter cried, and that was the end of it.

Several buckets of water sluiced over him.

Behind him, voices seemed to be chanting. There was chanting and laughter. They faded and he was alone again. He realized the chanting was the pulsing of his own blood in his ears. He imagined his thumbs two feet long now from the pulling. He was not dead. Wallace Palmer was dead. Palmer who could be made to talk, if he were not dead. Palmer had fallen from the third floor scaffolding down to the ground beside a cement mixer. Now the school building was finished. Carter saw it, dark red and four stories high. It was shaped like a wide U, like a boomerang. An American flag waved on top of it. It stood, but it was made of bad materials. The cement was no good, the plumbing didn't work, the plaster had started cracking before the building was completed. Carter had spoken to Gawill and to Palmer about the materials, but Palmer had said that was okay, that was what they wanted, the school board was cutting corners and it wasn't their concern if the building materials were bad. Then the word got around, and the safety board or whatever they called it said that children ought not to be allowed to set foot in it, that it all might fall on their heads, and the school board had not been cutting corners, they had paid for the best, and who, who was responsible? Wallace Palmer was responsible, and maybe a few others in Triumph had got a share of the $250,000 – Gawill could hardly have been blind to what was going on, for instance – but Philip Carter was the chief engineer, worked closest with the contractor Palmer, was an out-of-towner, a New Yorker, a wise guy, a man out to feather his nest at the expense of the South, a professional man who had betrayed the honour and trust of his calling, and the State was going to have his blood. 'Let the school stand empty, until the next hard wind blows it down,' said the prosecuting attorney, 'a disgrace and an expensive disgrace for all the State to look at!'

Two men came and took him down. Carter's head cracked against the stone floor. Clumsy attempts to carry him. Curses. They left him crumpled on the floor while they went away again. Carter retched, but nothing came up. The men returned with a stretcher. The journey was a long one, down corridors that Carter barely saw through partly opened eyes. Up stairs after stairs they went, Moony and somebody else – what was his name, the one of last night? Or when? Up they went, nearly sliding him backwards and head first off the stretcher. Then along corridors, narrowish ones, where inmates – Carter knew from their flesh-coloured clothes – and a few Negroes in blue overalls, also inmates, stared in silence as they passed by. Then the smell of iodine and disinfectant. They were going into the hospital ward. He lay on the stretcher on a hard table. A voice was murmuring angrily. It was a nice voice, Carter thought.

Moony's voice replied, 'He's out of order all the time . . . He's out of order. What're you gonna do with guys like him? . . . You should have my job, mister . . . All right, speak to the warden. I'll tell him a thing or two myself.'

The doctor spoke again, lifting Carter's wrist. 'Look at this!'

'Ah, I've seen worse,' said Moony.

'How long was he hung up?'

'I don't know. I didn't string him up.'

'You didn't? Who did?'

'I don't know.'

'Would you mind finding out? – Would you mind finding out?'

A man with round, horn-rimmed glasses and a white jacket washed Carter's face with a large wet cloth, and squeezed some drops from it on to his tongue.

'. . . Morphine, Pete,' said the doctor. 'A whole half grain.'

They rolled his sleeve higher and gave him a needle. Pain began to ebb quickly, like a flood receding, like an ocean drying up. Like heaven. A pleasant, sleepy tingling invaded his head, lightly dancing, like gentle music. They began to work on his hands, and he fell asleep during it.

2

When Carter awakened, he was lying in a firm white bed on his back, his head on a pillow. His arms lay outside the covers and his thumbs were huge lumps of gauze as big as the rest of his hands. He looked to right and left. The left bed was empty, the right held a sleeping Negro with a bandaged head. Pain seeped back into his thumbs, and he realized that it was the pain that had awakened him. It was growing worse, and it frightened him.

He looked at the approaching doctor, wide-eyed with fear, and, realizing that he looked afraid, Carter blinked his eyes. The doctor smiled. He was a small dark man of about forty.

'How are you feeling?' asked the doctor.

'My thumbs hurt.'

The doctor nodded, still faintly smiling. 'They took some punishment. You'll need another shot.' He looked at his wristwatch, frowned slightly, and went away.

When he came back with the needle, Carter asked, 'What time is it?'

'Six thirty. You had a good sleep.' The needle went in, stayed a few seconds. 'How about something to eat – before this puts you to sleep again?'

Carter did not answer. He knew from the light at the window that it was 6.30 in the evening. 'What day is it?'

'Thursday. Scrambled eggs? Milk toast? I think that's all you'd better try – Ice-cream? Does that appeal to you?'

Carter's brain turned tiredly over the fact that this was the kindest voice he had heard since entering the prison. 'Scrambled.'

Carter was in the ward for two days before they removed the bandages, and then his thumbs looked enormous to him and they were bright pink. They did not look as if they belonged to him or to his own hands. The thumbnail was tiny in the mass of flesh. And they still hurt. The morphine shots came every four hours, and Carter wished they were more often. The doctor tried to be reassuring, but Carter could see that he was worried because the pain did not diminish. His name was Dr Stephen Cassini.

On Sunday, Carter was allowed no visitors, whatever the state of his demerits, because he was in the ward.

At 1.30 p.m. on Sunday, when the visiting period began, Carter imagined Hazel in the big grey-green lobby downstairs protesting that she had come to see her husband and that she was not going to leave until she had seen him. Dr Cassini had written a letter to her which Carter had dictated, saying that he would not be able to see her, and the letter had been smuggled out some time on Friday, but Carter was not sure Hazel had received it by Saturday. Carter knew that, if she had, she would come anyway, because he had said his hands were 'slightly injured', but he also knew that the double gates of grey bars in the lobby, the officials in uniforms who examined identifications of visitors and checked on inmates' status would defeat Hazel at last, and he writhed in his bed and pressed his face into his hard pillow.

He got her last two letters from under his pillow and re-read them, holding them with two fingers.

... Darling, Timmie is bearing up pretty well, so don't worry about him. I lecture him daily, though I try not to make it sound like a lecture. The kids are picking on him at school, of course, and I suppose human nature wouldn't be human nature if they didn't ...

And in the last letter:

Darling Phil,

Have just spent over an hour with Mr Magran, the lawyer David has recommended all along over Tutting, you know, and I like him very much. He talks sense, is optimistic but not so optimistic (like Tutting) that you start to get suspicious. Anyway, Tutting has now said there is 'nothing more' he can do. As if there weren't the Supreme Court, but I wouldn't even want Tutting handling that. I have paid Tutting off, that is, the last $500 of his fee, so if you're quite agreed, Magran can take over. Magran said it will cost $3,000 to have a transcript of the trial typed up for the Supreme Court, but you know we can afford that. He wants to see you as soon as possible, of course. Oh, dammit darling, those idiotic regulations I'm greeted with every Sunday: 37765's demerits do not permit him to have visitors this week. And for being out of step in a cafeteria line, you said. For goodness sake, darling, do your best to conform to their stupid rules.

Magran is also writing to the Governor direct. He will send you a copy of the letter. You must not worry. Like you, I know this cannot go on for ever, or even very long. Six to twelve years! It won't even be six months ...

Magran's fee would be at least $3,000, Carter thought, and the $3,000 for the transcript besides would just about clean out their ready cash. Every figure seemed astronomical. $75,000 for his bail, for instance, which of course they hadn't been able to raise, and Carter had not wanted to ask his Aunt Edna for it. Their $15,000 house was mortgaged, their Olds was worth $1,800, but Hazel needed it for marketing and also for driving the twenty-seven miles on Sundays to see him, or try to.

And now his thumbs were out of joint. That was the final absurd fact. The doctor called it something else, but essentially that was what it was, and an operation, according to Dr Cassini, would be of very dubious value. The prison – in which Carter had thought a couple of weeks would not be unbearable, not even a serious episode in his life – had now branded him for ever. He would never have much articulation in the second joints, and a sort of hollow would remain below them. He would have funny-looking thumbs and he would not have much strength in them. Imaginative people, seeing them, might guess what had caused the deformation. He wouldn't be able to deal a hand of bridge so adroitly, or whittle a bow and arrow for Timmie, and, by the time he got out, Timmie might not be interested in bows and arrows, anyway. He had written to Hazel within a couple of hours after the removal of the bandages that day, Sunday, holding the pen in a wobbling fashion between his index and middle fingers, and he had had to tell her what had happened, ghoulish as the story was, to account for his strange writing, but he minimized it and said it had been for several hours instead of nearly forty-eight. His thumbs were permanently deformed because a man called Hanky for some strange reason had it in for him. Why? Because he hadn't shown Hanky the picture of Hazel? 'You got a wife? . . . You got her picture? . . . Let's see it,' Hanky had said the first afternoon of their acquaintance. Carter had said as amiably as he could, 'Oh, some other time.' 'You ain't got her picture.' That had been his opportunity, perhaps, to show it and appease Hanky, but he had muffed it. The picture he carried in his wallet of Hazel was cut out of an enlargement of a colour photograph in which she was standing in the snow in front of their New York apartment on East Fifty-seventh Street, hatless, her dark hair blowing, laughing, a wonderful, typical expression on her face, which was why Carter preferred the picture, and what possible pleasure could a pig like Hanky get from looking at a picture of a woman with the beaver collar of her coat pulled up to her chin?

Sunday afternoon around 4, Dr Cassini came in and made his rounds of the forty-odd patients in the ward. When he came to Carter, he said:

'Well, Carter, want to try taking a few steps?'

'Absolutely,' Carter said, sitting up. Pain streaked down his back, but he did not let it show in his face. He staggered at the foot of the bed and had to catch his balance on the doctor's extended hand.

Dr Cassini smiled and shook his head. 'You keep worrying about your thumbs. Do you know those knots in your legs were shutting off the circulation and you could have got gangrene? Do you know only yesterday morning you were running a temperature of a hundred and three and I thought you might be in for pneumonia?'

Carter was glad to sit. He felt faint. 'When is this going to go out of my legs?'

'The knots? With time. And massage. Walk around the foot of the bed, if you like, but don't try anything more,' Dr Cassini said, and moved on to the next patient.

Carter sat there breathing as if he had been running. He remembered what Dr Cassini had said yesterday, that he was after all thirty and couldn't recuperate from an experience such as his as quickly as a nineteen-year-old. Dr Cassini had a cheerful, matter-of-fact way of talking about the Hole, and victims of it whom he had treated, that gave Carter an eerie feeling that he was in a madhouse instead of a prison, a madhouse in which the caretakers were the madmen, as in the old cliché. Dr Cassini seemed to pass no judgement on what happened in the prison. Or was that quite true? Dr Cassini had asked him yesterday what he was in for, and Carter had told him. 'Most fellows, I don't bother asking why they're in,' Dr Cassini had said. 'I know already, breaking and entering, bargaining, car-stealings, but you're not like the most of them.' Dr Cassini had asked what school he had gone to – Carter had gone to Cornell – and then why he had come south. Carter wished he had asked himself that, eight months ago, when he and Hazel had decided to come. Carter had come because the offer from Triumph Builders had sounded very good, $15,000 a year plus various perquisites. 'What did Palmer do with the money, do you think?' Dr Cassini had asked, and Carter had said, 'Well, he had a girl friend in New York and one in Memphis. He saw one or other of them every weekend. He was always flying off somewhere on Fridays. He bought them cars and things.' And Dr Cassini had nodded and said, 'Oh, I see,' and he did, and he believed it, Carter thought. It was true. But it had not been believed by the Court of Quarter Sessions. Even when the girls were brought down and questioned, it hadn't been believed that Palmer could spend $250,000 in about a year on two women, and that the two women between them had nothing more to show for it than one mink coat worth about $5,000 and one diamond bracelet worth about $8,000. Nobody seemed to know or care that Palmer could eat and drink about $500 worth a month, and did, or that his airline tickets cost him anything, or that both girls had got rid of expensive automobiles just before they came down for the trial, or that Palmer might have salted some away in Brazil.

Carter crept back into bed. While he had been sitting on the edge of the bed, the Negro with the bandaged head had stared at him unblinking, as if he watched a boring movie. Carter had tried to talk to him a couple of times, but had got no response, and Dr

Cassini this morning had told him that the Negro had abscesses in both ears, had had a series of them, and that he did not expect to preserve much, if anything, of his hearing.

He re-read Hazel's last four letters, one that he had had in his pocket when they strung him up and the three that had been delivered since. Carter held them between his fingers while his fat thumbs throbbed in unison like silent drums between his eyes and the pages. Hazel had put a drop of her perfume on her last letter, which was the most cheerful of the four. The male nurse Pete came with the morphine needle and silently prepared it. Pete had only one eye, the other was a sunken hollow, whether the result of disease or injury, Carter could not guess. The needle slid into his arm. In silence, Pete went away, and Carter lifted his letters again. As the morphine stole through his blood, he began to hear Hazel's voice reading her own words, and he read all the letters as if they were brand-new. He heard also Timmie's voice interrupting her, and Hazel saying, 'Just a minute, sweetie, can't you see I'm writing to Daddy? – Oh, all right, your catcher's mitt. Why, it's right there in front of you. On the sofa. That's a fine place for it, anyway, can't you take it up to your room?' Timmie socked a small fist into the undersized mitt. 'When's Daddy coming home?' 'Just as soon as ...' 'When's Daddy coming *home*?' ...When's Daddy coming home? ...' Carter changed his position in bed and forced himself away from that vision, lay passive with his eyes on Hazel's writing until another vision swam into its place. He saw their bedroom. Hazel stood by her dressing-table, brushing her hair for the night. He was in his pyjamas. As he moved towards her, she smiled at him in the mirror. They kissed, a long kiss. With the morphine to enhance memory, it was almost as if Hazel lay beside him in the hard bed.

Carter could watch his visions as if they took place on a stage. No one was in the theatre but him. He was the sole spectator. No one had ever seen the show before. Nobody ever would, but him.

Here the voices of the inmates were shut out. At least for his ruined thumbs he had been granted a few days of quiet, more or less. A groan of pain from someone, the clatter of bedpans were like music compared to the excretory sounds of 6.30 a.m. in the cell block, or the insane titters in the night, like women's laughter, and the other no less deranging sounds of men who sought relief by themselves. Who was mad, Carter wondered. Which ones of them? Which jurors and which judges out of the thousands who had sent these six thousand men here?

3

It was Wednesday before Carter could walk. Dr Cassini got for him a new suit of prison clothes, which fitted him better than the ones he had been wearing. He was still weak. His weakness shocked him.

'It's not unusual,' said Dr Cassini.

Carter nodded, his mind baffled and blank as it always was when the doctor spoke in his matter-of-fact way about the Hole. 'But you said you'd seen other cases – like mine.'

'Oh, yes, a few. After all, I've been here four years – Look, I'm not saying what they do is right. I've sent letters to the warden. He promises to look into it. He fires a guard or has him trans-ferred.' Dr Cassini's hands flew out in a hopeless gesture, then he adjusted his rimmed glasses nervously and blinked at Carter. 'You try to fight city hall and you go crazy. I'm not going to be here much longer.' He nodded, as if to confirm himself, and Carter immediately became suspicious. 'It's time for another shot for you, isn't it?'

Carter wrote a letter to the warden, whose name was Joseph J. Pierson, with regard to Moonan and Cherniver. He had intended to make the letter brief, calm and to the point. The result was such a masterpiece of understatement, Carter was seized briefly by an attack of mirth. It read:

Dear Warden Pierson,

I should like to call to your attention that on the afternoon of March 1, I was strung up by the thumbs in one of the basement rooms of the institution for nearly forty-eight hours. I was repeatedly revived with buckets of cold water when I fainted. The result is that my thumbs are permanently damaged, the second joints having been pulled from their sockets. The guards who did this are Mr Moonan and Mr Cherniver. I respectfully request that you exercise your authority in regard to this incident.

Yours faithfully,

Philip E. Carter

(37765)

P.S. I would be grateful if I could have a full list of prison rules and regulations so that I may avoid an accumulation of demerits in future.

Carter had heard from one of the inmates that Warden Pierson was scrupulous about acknowledging letters of all sorts, but never answered any of them. At any rate, Carter dropped the letter in the slot marked 'Intramural', and that was that. Patience and fortitude, he thought. It was going to be a long, slow fight, whatever Hazel thought. He was going to see Hazel on Sunday. Dr Cassini had put in a special request that he might see his wife. In just seventy-two more hours, he would see her for twenty minutes. A cheerful fatalism buoyed him up: they couldn't very well kill him before Sunday afternoon, so nothing seemed to stand in the way of his seeing Hazel. In the hospital ward it was impossible to acquire demerits, because he was not actually doing anything, walking anywhere, or using any prison tools or facilities other than the toilet.

He re-read *Wuthering Heights*, and wrote to Hazel:

My darling,

Imagine sitting in prison and reading Emily Brontë? Things are not so bad, are they? Please do not worry, above all don't get angry if you can help it. I was angry the first weeks here and it got me nothing but a lot of demerits and ill will from the guards. Best not even to feel the anger if you can help it. Make like the yogis or the passive resistance boys. We are up against something a lot bigger than we are.

Am glad Timmie is doing better with his reading, glad also he is not getting any heckling lately at school. Or are you sure? He would tell you, wouldn't he? But I'm not so sure. He might frown and be silent. Is he frowning and silent? Tell me. I am writing him a letter next, so you will miss one from me, but meanwhile tell Timmie I think he is great for doing such a good job as man of the house while I am not there. I mean snow shovelling. After all a half-inch of snow is a rough job!

Am helping out in the ward as much as I can – bedpans and other charming chores. Don't worry about my hands. Am not writing too badly as you see. I love you, darling.

Phil

The effort of writing tired him like hard labour, and the writing was pretty bad – wobbly and nearly every letter separate from the next.

'Mistuh Carter,' said the Negro urgently. 'Mistuh Carter –'

Carter went to the foot of the Negro's bed, lifted between his two palms the bedpan from the low table there, and slipped it under the covers.

'Thank y', sir.'

'You're welcome,' Carter murmured, although the Negro could not hear him.

On Sunday, Carter took extra care with his shaving. It was another great advantage of the hospital ward that he could shower and shave daily, instead of twice a week being herded with the others to the showers and the barbers. He had a second shower at noon, and he also shined his heavy shoes. He took as much trouble with himself as he had for his wedding, and he considered telling Hazel that and decided not to, because she might not think it very funny. Carter pressed his baggy trousers in a room down the hall from the ward which had an iron and an ironing-board and a sink in it. Then he put on the white shirt that inmates were allowed to wear on Sundays, if they had a visitor. It was a short-sleeved shirt with over-long collar tabs – inmates were not allowed ties because they might hang themselves, Carter supposed – but at least the shirt was white, and a change from flesh-colour was a treat.

He looked at himself in the mirror by the ward door, and tried to see himself as Hazel would. There were depressions under his eyes, though they were not dark. Certainly his face was thinner. And he looked at least thirty-five, he thought, not thirty. Even his lips seemed thinner and more taut, even his head narrower, but that was due to the prison haircut, of course. His blue eyes looked out at him like the eyes of another person, tired, hard and vaguely suspicious.

Dr Cassini walked up and slapped him on the shoulder. 'All dolled up, eh, Philip?'

Carter nodded, smiling, and suddenly his heart began to beat faster with excitement. He had a feeling of giddy anticipation, as if time had turned back and he were about to call for Hazel on a date, rushing back down to Gramercy Park in a taxi with a box of flowers across his lap, running up her front steps two at a time – and Hazel opening the brown door with the brass knob before he touched the knocker.

24

'Want another shot?'

'No, I'm okay, thanks.' His thumbs were starting to hurt a little, but he didn't want another shot now, at 12.30. He had had a shot at 10, and he thought it should last until 1.50, when Hazel's visit would be over. By ten past 1, the jabs from the pulses in his thumbs were growing more acute, and Carter was tempted to get a quick shot from Pete, which he could have had just for the asking, but he decided to stick by his little vow to himself that he wouldn't, just before he saw Hazel. He had Pete bandage his thumbs so they would not shock her.

He went down in the elevator with his pass signed by Dr Cassini and the guard named Clark in the hospital corridor. Carter had to show the pass three times, each time acquiring a new signature or initials, before he reached his old A-block, at the front end of which was the entrance to the visiting-room. By then he was beginning to feel weak in the knees.

Carter saw Hanky's blobby figure walking ahead of him and along the left side of the corridor, heading for their old cell, probably. Carter slowed his walk so that he would not overtake Hanky or be seen by him. Carter peered through the bars as he walked towards them, but he could not identify Hazel among the figures in the waiting area. The lobby or waiting-room had benches like church pews with an aisle down the middle. At the back near the outside door was a coffee-vending machine and a candy and gum machine. Between the cell block and the waiting-room was an area of some twenty feet square enclosed on two sides by walls and on the other two sides by bars that went from floor to ceiling. This enclosure was called the cage. There were always two guards in the cage, and the two doors were never opened at the same time, nor was a visitor ever allowed in the cage while an inmate was in it, even if the inmate was only handing the outgoing mail-bag to a guard. In the cage, to the right as one faced the waiting-room, was a locked door through which visitors were admitted to the visiting-room one floor below the block. Inmates who had visitors were admitted by a door near the cage in the corridor.

Carter saw Hazel when he was about twenty feet from the cage. She was standing at the tall desk on the right in the waiting-room, showing her identification card to the officer there. Carter's heart floated up in his chest, and he slowly turned around, so that the guard who leaned against the wall on his right would not assume he had come to stare.

'Santoz!' called the guard by the prisoners' entrance door.

'Here!' A man trotted forward.

'Colligan!'

Sullen, indifferent, vaguely envious faces watched as men in white shirts detached themselves from the sluggish mass in the corridor and came alive, hurrying to the visiting-room door with their passes.

'Carter!'

The guard took his pass, scribbled on it, and motioned him through. Carter went down the dimly lighted stairway. It led to a long room divided by a glass wall with a shallow, table-high shelf and straight chairs on either side of it. Nearly all the chairs were taken. The visitors had their entrance at the other end of the room and on the other side of the barrier. There were four armed guards, one in each corner of the room. Carter kept his eyes on the visitors' door as he walked, looking for Hazel.

Then she came in, and he moved forward, still looking at her, towards a free chair which was on the other side of the barrier, pointed to it, and managed to find an empty chair for himself. Hazel wore her blue tweed coat with a bright scarf tucked in at her neck. To Carter, the colours she wore seemed spectacularly brilliant and beautiful, like flowers or birds' plumage. Her red lips smiled, though her eyes were tense. She looked at his hands.

26

Carter pushed his underlip out, smiled and shrugged. 'They don't hurt – You're looking wonderful.' He tried to speak loudly and distinctly, because of the glass.

'What do they say is the matter with them? Did they say anything else?' Hazel asked.

'Nothing else.' Carter swallowed and glanced at the clock. He sat on the edge of the hard chair. Before he knew it, the twenty minutes would be gone, and he was already wasting precious seconds in silence – except that he was seeing her. 'How is Timmie?'

'Timmie's all right. He's fine.' Hazel moistened her lips. 'You've lost some weight.'

'Not much.'

'Mr Magran said he would come today to see you.'

Her voice reminded him of clear, cool water. He had not heard a woman's voice in six weeks. 'It's wonderful to see you.' Carter was annoyed by the voice of the man on his left, who was talking to a man in a dark suit on Hazel's right, perhaps the inmate's lawyer. The inmate was saying in a loud, annoyed voice: 'I dunno, I just dunno. Why d'y' keep askin' me that?' The inmate's voice was louder to Carter than Hazel's.

'Did you get a statement yet from the doctor?' she asked.

His thumbs pulsed more quickly. His forehead was cool with sweat. 'He – he has to take more X-rays. He can't say what's the matter yet. Not entirely.'

'Then it's worse than you told me, isn't it?'

'I just don't know, honey. It's the joints –' *Tell me the names of the guards who did it*, Hazel had written in one of her letters. *It's absolutely illegal in this day and age.* The word illegal was strange, in view of some of the things he had seen in the prison. What about the old man in A-block whose false teeth had broken in half and who couldn't get them fixed and couldn't eat anything now but soup? Was that a legal way to treat a man in jail? Carter felt he was choking, as if he might burst into tears. *I only want to* put my head in her lap, he thought, and he sat up straighter. 'I'll get the statement from Cassini as soon as I can.'

'David can use it, you know,' Hazel said earnestly.

'David? I thought Magran wanted it.'

'David said he'd take it to the Governor in person. David's a lawyer, too, you know. He'd take it sooner than Magran. Right away.'

'Who's handling my case, Sullivan or Magran?' Carter said quickly. His hands rested on the table like a boxer's. The thumbs pulsed as if blood were going to come shooting out the tips of the bandage at any moment. 'I hear you're seeing Sullivan a lot,' he said, and saw in her face that he had hurt her.

'I see him as often as I tell you I see him. I'd really be down in the dumps without him, Phil. All the neighbours calling and dropping in – What can they do? David at least knows something about the law.'

'That might be – might be something we'd all better forget about.'

'What?'

'The law. Where is it? What good is it?'

Hazel sighed. 'Oh, darling. You're tired and you're in pain.' She reached nervously into her bag for a cigarette, started to extend the pack to Carter before she remembered the barrier that went all the way to the ceiling. 'Haven't you got a cigarette?'

'I forgot 'em. I don't want one. It doesn't matter.' He did want one, and he watched her closely as she lighted it. Her hands shook slightly. A frown put a line between her brows. Her forehead was very smooth, quite without lines. Her complexion was very clear, and to Carter it seemed now so beautiful it was unreal, like something painted on canvas or on glass. There was a natural pinkness in her cheeks and in her lips. She had a small mouth and the softest lips Carter had ever seen, or kissed. He wondered if Sullivan had kissed them, or if Sullivan ever would.

'What are the guards' names?' Hazel asked. 'Were you afraid to write them in a letter to me?'

Carter glanced to right and left automatically. 'I wasn't afraid, I just thought it might get censored. It's Moonan and Cherniver.'

'Moonan and what?' Her dark blue eyes looked directly at him.

'Cherniver. C-h-e-r-n-i-v-e-r.'

'I'll remember. But I want you to get that statement immediately from the doctor. The X-rays can wait. We'll get another statement about those.'

'Okay, honey.' He racked his brain for something cheerful to say to her, some incident to make her smile. There had been laughter in the ward over a few things, but now he could not think of one. Carter smiled. 'Sullivan taking you out to dinner tonight? As usual?'

'As usual?' Her frown was back.

'I meant, it's Sunday. You usually see him Sunday evenings, don't you?'

'I wouldn't say usually. Phil, I tell you every time I see him and what we talk about and even what we eat.'

That was true, and Carter clamped his teeth together. It was only Gawill who had made a couple of cracks in his last letter, and Gawill was no doubt exaggerating or making things up.

'You never mention what you eat,' Hazel said.

Carter could suddenly laugh a little. 'I don't think you'd care for it. Hog jowl –' And other things unidentifiable that had their prison names.

'You can complain to me. I only wish I could share it with you.'

The pain in his thumbs made his mind swim. He spoke to keep alert. 'I don't like to think of you here. I don't want you to know all about it, because it's too disgusting. Sometimes I don't even want to look at the picture I have of you here.'

She looked surprised and also frightened. 'Darling –'

'I don't mean I don't want you to visit me here. My God, I don't mean that.' The sweat rolled down in front of his ears.

'Two more minutes,' said the guard, strolling behind Carter.

Carter looked wildly at the clock. It was true.

'Mr Magran said he'd already written to the warden about your thumbs,' Hazel said.

'Well, the warden won't reply to it,' Carter said quickly.

'What do you mean? It's a letter from your lawyer.'

'I mean,' he said, trying to sound calmer, 'he'll acknowledge the letter, but he probably won't refer to the stringing up. I know he won't.'

Hazel wrung her fingers together. The cigarette trembled. 'Well, we'll see. – Oh, darling, how I wish I could cook a few meals for you!'

Carter laughed, a laugh as if someone had crushed his chest. 'There's an old fellow here named Mac, nearly seventy. All he talks about is his wife's cooking – apple pies, venison *Sauerbraten*, popovers. Popovers, imagine!' Carter burst out in another laugh, his shoulders shaking, and he saw Hazel laugh, too, almost in her old way, and it transformed her face. 'It's funny because' – Carter wiped tears from his eyes – 'because all the other guys talk about how they miss their wives or their girls in bed or something, and he talks about food. He spends all his spare time making ship models or making *one* ship he's been on since I got here. It's four feet long and his cellmate complains because it takes up too much room. He's just up here.' Carter waved a hand sideways and up to the right, as if Mac's cell were visible.

'Time's up,' said the guard.

Carter half stood up, his lips apart, staring at Hazel.

Hazel was already standing up, to leave him. 'That's the first person you've told me about here. Tell me more. Write me. See you next Sunday, darling.' She blew him a kiss, turned and went.

He began the long walk back down the cell block. He had to

have another shot before he could sit through twenty minutes with Magran. Near the end of the cell block, he looked left, and at last he came to Mac's cell. The door was open and Mac sat there on his straight chair, so absorbed in the delicate sanding of his ship's hull that he did not notice Carter looking at him. The ship was not yet painted, but Mac had made great progress since Carter had last seen it. The rigging looked finished.

'Hello, Mac,' Carter said. 'My name's Carter.'

'Oh, hello, hello,' Mac said, cordially but not recognizing him, and turned back to his work. 'Got time for a visit?'

'No. Sorry, I haven't. Some other time.' Carter walked on. Mac had made some kind of peace with himself, and for that Carter envied him. Mac hadn't even noticed his bandaged hands, and that was somehow comforting to Carter, too. Mac hadn't even *seen* him, Carter thought, only heard his voice.

4

Carter got his shot from Pete, then sat on one of the wicker chairs at the end of the ward. He was so tense, he could not keep his heels from jittering on the grey linoleum floor. The visit from Hazel had made him realize something terrible, that he had been enduring the past three months in a deliberate fog, in a kind of mental armour that was not after all strong enough. Among the inmates and with Dr Cassini, he could keep it up. With Hazel, he had been himself for a few minutes. The pain in his thumbs had been the *coup de grâce* to his morale. He had whined to her, he had shown bitterness and ingratitude. He had been everything a man should not be with his wife.

He sat back and let the morphine work its miracle. The morphine was attacking the pain, and as usual the morphine was winning the battle – would win for nearly two hours. Then the pain would rally its forces and counter-attack the morphine, and it would be the pain's turn to win. It was another game, futile and unreal, like the prison game. Carter saw it as a series of shocks and a series of efforts at adjusting. The first shock had been stripping naked with a dozen other men who were being admitted to the prison the same day, one with red sores on his back, another with

32

a head wound, still drunk and belligerent, one a scared-faced kid of nineteen or twenty with a shapely, small mouth like a girl's, a face Carter had puzzled over for an instant, wondering if that was the kind of innocent face that could mask the worst criminal of the lot of them. Then the first meals, the first dreary lights-out and the broken sleep until it was time to get up before dawn, the first nights of cold in December, the night he had stripped off his clothing and pyjamas, wet them in the basin and, while Hanky held a match so he could see, stuffed the clothes into the cracks between the stones at the back of the cell. Hanky had thought it very clever of him to wet the clothes so they would freeze tight, but there had been more cracks than clothing. He remembered Christmas with bronchitis in bed in his cell, and the first approach of a homosexual in the shoe factory. All this Carter had more or less got used to or at least learned to tolerate without fury. Even the stringing up he had tolerated, he thought, with some fortitude, but what if that fortitude were to collapse? What if it collapsed very soon because of the nagging pain in his thumbs? Would he run screaming through the corridors, tackling guards, hurling his fists in anybody's face – until they shot him down or he banged his brains out against some stone wall?

Clark came and told him that he had a visitor downstairs. Carter made some lumpy instant coffee with water out of the tap, put three teaspoons of sugar into it for energy, and gulped it. Then he took a pass from Clark and went down in the elevator.

Once more the long walk to the visiting-room. If this was Magran, Carter thought, he had no idea what he looked like, but Magran could recognize him by the bandages on his thumbs. Carter pulled his shoulders back. He had to make the best impression he could on Magran, not as to innocence, but as to confidence: Magran would report to Hazel on the interview.

In the visiting-room, a man stood up and beckoned to him with a slight smile.

'Lawrence Magran. How do you do?' said Magran.

'How do you do?' Carter sat down as Magran did.

Magran was a short, round man with thinning black hair, rimless glasses and hunched shoulders, and he looked as if he spent most of his time at a desk. He asked Carter how he was feeling, if his hands gave him much pain, if his wife had come earlier to see him. Magran's voice was surprisingly gentle and soft. Carter had to lean forward to hear him.

'I think your wife's talked to you about the Supreme Court appeal. It's a slow business, but it's our only hope now.'

'Yes, she has. I'm glad to hear you use the word hope at all. I can use some,' Carter said.

'I'm sure you can. And I don't want to hold out too much. But people have appealed successfully to the Supreme Court, and that's what we're going to try, if you're willing.'

'Certainly I'm willing.'

'And face the fact that it may be a good seven months before we have an answer, and the answer may be no.'

Carter nodded. Seven or six months, as Tutting had said, what was the difference?

Magran questioned him from some notes he had brought.

Carter replied, 'As I said at the trial, I signed the invoices and the receipts when Palmer was somewhere out on the construction grounds. Lots of times he was away from the shed. I mean, where the truckers came in.'

'Your wife said you had the idea Palmer was often deliberately away so you'd have to sign them. Is that true?'

'Yes, that's true. That's the way I remember it.'

Magran scribbled a few notes, then he stood up. He said he would write to Carter in a few days. Then, with a cheerful wave of his hand, he was gone.

Carter felt cheered. Magran hadn't mentioned the cost of anything, hadn't extended a single false hope or even hope, really.

'Get the doctor's statement on your thumbs,' Magran had said, and that was all on the subject. Carter was walking past the visiting-room door guard, when the guard touched his arm and said:

'You got another visitor.'

'Thanks.' Carter looked towards the cage. Sullivan, he supposed. He turned and went down the steps to the visiting-room.

It was Gregory Gawill. Carter spotted him at once. He was heavy, dark-haired, about five feet nine, and he was wearing his oversized polo coat with white buttons. Gawill gestured with a forefinger to an empty chair, then sat down in it. Carter pulled up a chair opposite him. Gawill was a vice-president of Triumph, Inc. It was the second time Gawill had visited him in prison. The first time, he had been breezy and cheerful, saying like everyone else that it was only a matter of reaching 'the right people' and Carter would be out in no time. Today he was serious and commiserative. He had heard about the denial of a re-trial and about Carter's thumbs.

'I happened to call your wife the same day she heard herself, about the denial. She sounded pretty blue and I'd have gone over to see her, but she said she had a date with David Sullivan that night.'

'Oh.' Carter was on guard. Gawill's speech sounded rehearsed.

'Sullivan's got a lot of influence over Hazel. He's got her thinking he's the next thing to God.'

Carter laughed a little. 'Hazel's no fool. I doubt if she thinks anybody's the next thing to God.'

'Don't be too sure. Sullivan plays it close to his chest. He's pretty much in control of her now, don't you realize that?'

Carter felt rattled and angry. His left hand moved towards his cigarettes. 'No, I didn't realize that.'

'For one thing, Sullivan's investigating me. Surely you've been told about that.'

Carter had a twinge of guilt, but he shrugged. He had suggested

35

to Sullivan that Gawill might be as guilty as Wallace Palmer. 'Sullivan carries on his own affairs. He's a lawyer, I'm not. And he's not my lawyer.'

Gawill smiled, without amusement. 'You don't get what I mean. Sullivan's trying to ingratiate himself with Hazel, and he's doing damned well at it, by saying he'll come up with something against me. In regard to the Wally Palmer business, of course. Lots of luck, Mr Sullivan, is all I can say.'

'How do you know this?'

'People tell me. My friends are loyal. Why shouldn't they be? I'm not a crook. I could punch Sullivan right in the mouth. It's bad enough that he's playing up to your wife. How low can a man sink, playing up to another man's wife while her husband's stuck in prison and can't do anything about it?'

Don't believe half of it, Carter told himself, even a tenth of it. 'What do you mean by playing up?'

Gawill's dark eyes narrowed. 'I think you know. Do I have to go into details? Your wife's a very attractive woman. Very.'

Carter remembered the evening Gawill had made a pass at Hazel, at a party at Sullivan's house. Gawill had had several too many that evening and made a lunge at Hazel, upsetting somebody's plate (it had been during a buffet supper), grabbing her around the waist so roughly that a snap had come open at the back of her white dress. Carter felt again the impulse he had had to pull Gawill away from her and hit him with his fist. Hazel had been furious, too, but she had given Carter a glance that said, 'Don't do anything,' so he hadn't. Carter was bending and unbending a matchbook cover.

'Well – why don't you go into details? If you have any,' Carter said.

'Sullivan's there all the time. Do I have to be any plainer? The neighbours're talking about it. Hasn't any of them dropped you a hint in a letter or something?'

The Edgertons hadn't. He'd had two letters from them. The Edgertons lived next door. Their house was within sight of the Edgertons' house. 'Frankly no.'

'Well –' Gawill shifted, as if the subject were too distasteful to go on with.

Carter pressed the matchbook cover harder. 'Of course, when you say all this, you're making quite a judgement on my wife, too.'

'Aw, no-o.' Gawill drawled the word in his New Orleans accent. 'I'm making a judgement on Sullivan. I think he's a slimy bastard and I don't mind saying so. He's got a nice exterior, that's all. Well brought up, dresses well. Subtle.' He gestured. 'And I say he's working on your wife. In fact, I know it.'

'Thanks for telling me. I happen to trust my wife.' Carter meant to smile a little, but he couldn't.

'Hm-hm-hm,' Gawill said in a manner that made Carter want to sock him through the glass wall. 'Well – to get on to a pleasanter subject, Drexel's going to pay you a hundred dollars a week of your salary while you're in this clink. Retroactive and continuing as long as your contract would have gone on. I had a long talk with Drexel on Friday night. About *you*.'

Carter was surprised. Alphonse Drexel was the president of Triumph. He had stood by in cold neutrality during Carter's trial, and when pressed had put in the barest of good words for him: *As far as I know, he's done a good job for me with what he had to work with. If you ask me if I think he took the money or part of it, I just don't know.* Carter said, 'Very nice of Mr Drexel. What happened?'

'Well, I did a lot of talking,' Gawill said, smiling. 'I've practically convinced Drexel that Wally Palmer was the crook and the only crook in this thing, so – I made him feel he didn't say enough at the trial to help an innocent man out of the jam you were in, so he feels guilty about it, naturally. Paying you some salary's one way of making him feel better. Anyway, I suggested it to him, and I thought you could use it.'

Had it been that simple and direct, Carter wondered. Obviously, Gawill wanted all the credit for it. Why? Because Gawill was as guilty as Palmer? Carter simply didn't know. Palmer and Gawill had never been particularly chummy as far as Carter knew, or anybody at the trial had known, but that proved nothing at all. Nothing proved anything except little pieces of paper, cheques or banknotes, that might have passed between Palmer and Gawill.

'Thanks a lot,' Carter said. 'Hazel'll be very pleased, too.'

'Wasn't the first time I'd talked to him about it,' Gawill murmured. He looked at Carter's bandaged thumbs and shook his head. 'Your wife said your thumbs still hurt.'

'Yep,' Carter said.

'That's a hell of a thing. They give you pain-killers for it?'

'Morphine.'

'Oh. It's easy to get hooked on that stuff.'

'I know. The doctor here's going to give me something else. Demerol or something.'

Gawill nodded. 'Well, there's always a fall guy, I guess, and you sure were it this time.'

Carter frowned at the dirty metal ashtray in front of him. What did it all mean? Did Drexel now think he was absolutely innocent or what? Half innocent? Why didn't Drexel write him a letter about it, or was he afraid of putting anything down on paper? Carter suddenly realized who Drexel reminded him of: Jefferson Davis. A wizened, grey old man with an unpredictable temper.

'It's good Hazel's going to get away for a few days. She must have had a pretty rough time these last months.'

'Away?'

'Up to Virginia with Sullivan for Easter. Didn't she mention it? You saw her today, didn't you?'

A painful emotion exploded in him – composed of jealousy,

38

anger, a childlike feeling of having been left out. 'Yes, I saw her. We had so many other things to talk about, she didn't mention it.'

Gawill watched him carefully. 'Yeah. Sullivan has some friends up there with a big house. An estate, horses and a swimming-pool and stuff. The Fennors.'

Carter had never heard of the Fennors. Had Hazel not mentioned it, Carter wondered, because she thought such a pleasant prospect might make him feel worse, sitting in prison?

'Sullivan's very thoughtful about her,' Gawill went on. 'I don't think he'll have much luck, but I think he's really in love with her. Well, she's pretty easy to fall in love with.' Gawill grinned. 'I remember the night I was loaded and made a pass at her. Hope you weren't too sore about that, Phil. You know it never happened again.'

'No, no, I know.'

'I'm sure Sullivan has a subtler approach,' Gawill said, and chuckled.

Carter tried to show no concern at all, but he squirmed in his chair and inwardly he writhed. Sullivan was very smooth, he was very civilized, his passes would be civilized. He was quite a lot of things that Hazel liked. If nobody else was around, mightn't Hazel have a very discreet affair with him? Hazel could be very discreet. She might never tell him, because she knew it would kill him. And they were getting started early, Carter thought, after he'd been only three months in prison. That was the way such things had to start, early or not at all.

Their time was up. Carter jumped to his feet at the sight of the approaching guard. Gawill got up, too, made a bad joke about bringing him a file the next time he came to see him, waved a hand and was gone. Carter walked stiffly out of the visiting-room.

When he arrived at the ward, supper was being served. Pete was collecting the trays as they came up on the dumb waiter beside the elevator. The food came from a long way and was always cold.

Carter ate his dinner sitting sideways on his bed, because there was no table at the end of the ward big enough for the tray plus a book. He put the open book on the bed, and propped himself up on his left elbow. It was a large mediocre historical novel which at first he had not liked, but which he later found passed the time very well, because of its complete difference of scene from his own. Now he stared at the book between bites without seeing a word of it. The meal on his tray consisted in hamburger that gave off a smell of putridity, and some lima beans and mashed potatoes that had swum together in pale grey gravy, now stiffened with cold grease. There was no plate. The food was held in depressions in the tray. The only really edible part of the food was the bread, and there were always two slices and a thin pat of butter. He ate with a spoon. The inmates were not permitted knives or forks. He gulped the weak coffee from the plastic cup, and took the tray to the hall and set it on the floor near the dumb waiter. Later Pete would chuck trays and cups and spoons down a chute.

Carter went back to his bed and from his night-table got his pen and the letter he had begun to Hazel yesterday. He added below what he had written:

Sunday 4.25 p.m.

My darling Hazel,

Was very impressed by Magran as you said I would be. I am so sorry I was gloomy today. Can you forgive me? You were right my thumbs were hurting (I hadn't taken any shot for them before I saw you) and it is sort of like a toothache that keeps on and on at you till it gets on your nerves. Things are much better now.

G. Gawill came bringing good news: Drexel has decided

to pay me $100 of weekly salary retroactive and for the duration of contract. G. also said you were going away Easter with David S. A good idea no doubt.

Bless you, my darling. I love you and miss you. No more room here. P.

There was so little room, his initial was tiny. He twisted around on the bed and lay down with his face buried in the pillow, exhausted with the effort of writing, exhausted, too, by what he recognized as self-pity. He felt heroic in having said he was glad she was going away with Sullivan, and yet quite obviously he was not heroic. He was quite the opposite of heroic. What was heroic about doing a favour for Hanky, and for the purpose for which he had done it, to be on a slightly more friendly footing with a slob? Mightn't he have suspected that Hanky had some trick up his sleeve? It was simply stupid of him that he hadn't suspected. And to go a little farther back, didn't any idiot know enough not to sign something that he hadn't read or checked on, such as the receipts for the Triumph Corporation? The prices could as well have been upped when he signed them. He wouldn't have known the difference. And to go still farther back, to sheer carelessness, he had answered only two questions out of three on his final examination at Cornell, because he had not read the instructions thoroughly, or had not turned the page. He had graduated with quite a good rating, though not what he would have had if he had answered all three questions. One of his professors had written a complimentary statement about him which he said Carter might find of use in getting a job, but Carter had had a job arranged before he graduated. It had all been so easy for him. All his life he had simply fallen into lucky, comfortable spots – until now. His parents had died, first his mother shortly after his birth and then his father when Carter was five, but there had been his affectionate, childless and well-to-do

Uncle John to take him in in New York. John's wife Edna had been even more indulgent than a mother, Carter felt, because she had no children of her own and because he was a handsome, bright little boy related to her husband. The money of his parents had been put into a fund for him, and had been more than enough to see him through school, to provide him with plenty of clothes, a car when he was eighteen, money for dates. He had never had to work during summers. There had been many girls, once he was out of school and had his own apartment in Manhattan, affairs which now seemed very juvenile to him and which he realized had done nothing to him but feed his vanity. Then he had met Hazel Olcott, who had been engaged then to someone called Dan, an exporter with a plantation in Brazil. Carter had met her at a party given by a friend in New York, he had immediately noticed her and asked his host about her and learned about the exporter named Dan, who in fact was at the party, a very self-confident fellow of about thirty. Then Hazel the same evening had asked him if he would like to come to a surprise birthday party that she was giving for her mother, and Carter with his usual good cheer had accepted, thinking the fiancé was going to be there, too, the mother, too, and that it was the most unpromising of invitations. But the fiancé had not been there, and Carter had got along very well with Hazel and her mother and her mother's middle-aged friends. One meeting had led to another, because her fiancé always seemed to have business engagements, though they were supposed to be married in August and it was then July. And though Carter felt that Hazel was giving him some encouragement, he had been afraid to tell her that he was in love with her, because for the first time in his life he felt he was going to be unlucky. And Hazel, he thought, would have considered such a declaration in poor taste, since he knew she was engaged. Then as July came to an end, and Carter thought he had nothing to lose, he had stammered out that he

42

was in love with her, and Hazel, not at all surprised, had said, 'Yes, I know, but don't worry, because I broke it off with Dan three weeks ago.' The incredible ease of it, the miracle! Carter had begun to be really happy for the first time in his life. His happiness had lasted exactly seven years and two months, until the month Wallace Palmer had fallen off the scaffold.

Carter and his Aunt Edna wrote to each other only about twice a year now. Since Uncle John died, Aunt Edna had lived with a sister in California. He had not written to her since before the trial had begun. For one thing, he had thought the nightmare would pass, would be straightened out somehow, and he had not wanted to burden and confuse Edna with it. She was now in her seventies. But the nightmare was not blowing over. Carter supposed he ought to write to her. There were several New York friends who had seen small items in the paper and written him friendly notes that he should have answered, but hadn't. The prospect of writing them now was dreary indeed. And yet not to write, he felt, was like an admission of guilt.

Carter awakened from a dream, tense with anxiety. He half raised himself in bed and looked at the clock over the door. 10.20. He lay down again. A light sweat covered his face, and he was breathing rapidly. He swallowed, twisted to reach his water glass and found it empty.

A movement in the corner of the room caught his eye. Dr Cassini stood up from a straight chair and came towards him, smiling, his dark eyes distorted and enlarged by his glasses.

'No, I don't need another shot,' Carter said.

'Oh, I didn't say you did,' said Dr Cassini. 'Had a bad dream?'

'Um-m.' Carter got out of bed to get a glass of water. He carried it back in a cat's cradle of his two little fingers and his forefingers. His method of carrying glasses had ceased to be amusing to him or to anyone else. The most difficult task for him was fastening the buttons of his shirt and trousers.

Dr Cassini was still standing by his bed. 'I was thinking you could go back to the cell block tomorrow, if you'd prefer it.'

Carter sensed a challenge in his words. Dr Cassini evidently thought he was well enough. Carter's head was ringing from morphine.

'Or you could stay on here, if you'd like to help out. You can see we need people, even if they haven't got their thumbs.' Dr Cassini looked at him with his dark head cocked, as if he were saying something of importance about which Carter might have to make an earth-shaking decision. 'In the cell block – well, I don't know what kind of work they could give you, farm work, shoemaking, carpentry, everything I can think of is out because of those thumbs. Then in about a week, we could make some more X-rays. The inflammation should be going down. It might be just as well that you're up here.'

What *was* he saying? Carter had a moment of nausea. The smell of disinfectant, the memory of bedpans, pile cases, bed sores, hernias, came all at once – plus a fear of becoming dependent on the morphine, just because it was easy to get here.

'You can't get your morphine so easily, you know,' said Dr Cassini crisply.

'I know. You said you could give me something else.'

'It won't be as good.' Dr Cassini folded his arms and smiled.

Carter thought that Dr Cassini might be a morphine addict himself. It had crossed his mind before, but he wasn't sure and he really didn't care, but it seemed that Dr Cassini was urging him to stay on it, to get himself hooked as Dr Cassini was hooked – maybe. 'I can still try them,' Carter said, and sat down on his bed.

'All right. I'll give you the pills tomorrow morning and you can go down to the zoo, if you like.' He turned away, then looked back. 'If you run into trouble with the work they give you, just let me know. I can do something about it.'

5

The next morning, with a dozen pills in his pocket, his possessions tied up in a shirt, and a pass, Carter went down to A-block. Dr Cassini had bandaged his thumbs for protection. It was around 9 o'clock. The inmates were at their jobs. The guard looked at his pass, glanced at his thumbs, then took Carter to his old cell, number nine, and unlocked it for him. The guard was a new one to Carter. The cell was occupied by two men now, Carter saw from the two shingles with numbers hanging over the door, and from the two towels and washcloths on the rod on the rear wall. Hanky was still here: he remembered Hanky's colour photograph of a blonde propped up on the table.

'Maybe have to put a cot in here,' said the guard.

Carter knew that many cells had three men in them, though the cells were originally built to hold only one man. He dreaded being back with Hanky plus still another man, each bumping into the others if he moved at all. 'Isn't there any other cell –'

'If it says number nine, it's number nine,' said the guard, waving Carter's pass. 'Wait here.' He went off towards the cage.

Carter knew it would be a long wait. He crossed the corridor

45

and sank down on a wooden bench. He waited nearly forty-five minutes, and then the guard came back. Carter stood up.

'They'll bring a cot up in a couple of minutes, so go on in,' he said.

Carter went back into number nine. Without even a cot as an object of his own, he did not know where to put his things. He dropped the shirt bundle on the floor in a front corner, then lay down gently on the lower bunk and let his feet hang over the side.

The cot arrived, carried by an inmate Carter had never seen before. Carter tried to help him put the cot up, but it was hopeless, with bandaged thumbs.

'S'okay, never mind.' The inmate got the cot up quickly, as if he had done it many times before. He was a young, dark-haired fellow who might have been an Italian. 'They string you up by the thumbs?' he asked in a low voice.

'Yes.'

The young man glanced quickly at the half-open cell door. 'Nice of the shits to bandage it. Well, I hope you got one nice guy in here who'll help you with the cot.'

'Thanks. Thanks a lot.'

'My name's Joe. C-zoo.'

'Mine's Carter.'

The boy left.

Carter put a pill in his mouth and bent down to the water tap in the basin, sucking the water up from his cupped fingers. He lay back on the cot and waited for the pill to take effect. After ten minutes, Carter noticed no change at all in the pain. He suspected that Dr Cassini had tricked him, given him some other kind of pills, or placebos. Carter cursed him in silence. It was 11.05 by his wristwatch. In another ten minutes, the men would come pouring back from the workshops for the fifteen-minute interval before lunch. Dr Cassini had said, 'If you think you need a shot, just tell a screw to give you a pass up to the ward.' But Carter hadn't that on paper. He took another pill, for whatever it might be worth, then went out of the cell.

The guard on duty now – there was nobody else in the corridor – was Cherniver, and he looked at Carter in wide-eyed surprise, perhaps at seeing someone come out of a cell he had thought empty, perhaps because Carter was to him like a figure emerging from a tomb.

'I'd like to get a pass to the hospital ward,' Carter said.

'What's the matter?'

'I'm in pain. Dr Cassini said I could have shots when I needed them.'

Cherniver's lean face wrinkled up in a grimace of distaste or disbelief. 'So you're back in the zoo again.'

'Yes, sir, but I'm allowed to go to the ward if I have to.'

Cherniver bared his teeth impatiently, and walked off to the cage. He strolled through the cage, was passed by the second cage guard, and disappeared behind the blur of the double bars.

Carter waited. He was standing about midway in the cell block. He might have gone to the end of the block and rung for the elevator, but he had no guarantee that the operator would take him to the ward without a pass, even if he appeared to be in distress. Carter waited until the men started streaming back from the workshops, until there were so many in the corridor, he could not have seen if Cherniver was on his way back or not, or if Hanky and the other man had gone into number nine. Carter feared for his possessions there. Hanky wouldn't bother finding out whose they were, and, seeing the cot and resenting a newcomer, might just toss his bundle out in the corridor, where his books and letters and Hazel's photograph might become anybody's property. With his pain and his faintness, Carter lost all hope of a pass. Cherniver was probably drinking coffee by the slot machine in the waiting-room now.

'Hi, Cart!' somebody said in a cheerful tone, but by the time Carter looked in that direction, he saw only the backs of bobbing heads. Carter looked around for another guard. He grabbed at the bars of a cell door that was standing open, had a glimpse of the surprised face of a Negro in the cell saying something to him that he couldn't hear, and then he passed out.

He came to on the cot. Hanky was looking down at him, his fat fists on his round waist. A slender Negro inmate, his eyes so wide the whites showed brightly, stood at the foot of the cot, also staring at him. Carter's forehead and hair were wet, either with sweat or from water they had thrown at him.

'You back here?' Hanky asked him.

Carter heard the words Hanky said, but was unable to attach a meaning to them. He managed to stand up. 'I've got to go to the hospital ward!' He managed a couple of steps towards the door, and the Negro stepped back and so did another inmate who was standing and watching just beyond. Carter walked on, staggering, into the corridor. He turned in the direction of the elevator. There was a general flow now towards him, because the men were on their way to the mess hall, and the passage to it was to the left of the cage. Men bumped into him, or he into them. Hard shoulders sent him reeling backwards, and caromed him into other people. There were angry shouts at him.

'Hey, are you drunk?'

'Where'd he get it?'

Laughter.

'You're goin' the wrong way!'

It was only another few yards, he thought, to the elevators. He would demand that Dr Cassini come down, if he couldn't go up.

'Hey, Carter!'

'It's Carter!'

'*Hey*, there!' That was a louder voice, a guard's.

Then a nightstick cracked against Carter's head and his head rang like a bell. As he sank down, something slammed into his stomach. Then he saw black. He heard a vast roaring, like a huge sea round him. A siren sounded. They were stepping on his thumbs. They were stepping all over him, though nothing really hurt except his thumbs. Now he was being dragged backward by the arms. They dropped him against bars, and he sagged to the floor.

A whistle blew three times. Guards shouted in the sudden silence. Through half opened eyes, in a sidewise vision, Carter saw the flesh-coloured inmates slow down and separate, then there was only the hiss of shoe soles on the stone floor. A guard lay in the corridor only about twenty feet from Carter. He was bleeding from the face. His cap lay not far from his head. Two guards with drawn pistols approached the guard on the floor, looking all around them at the inmates who were still falling back. One of the guards stood up on his toes and yelled:

'Who did this? Who touched this guy?'

The hundreds of inmates stood where they were, so silent they seemed not to breathe.

'Back to your cells, all of you! All of you, you hear?'

There was a moan, grumbling in the background, unidentifiable, invisible, and then a laugh, high and loud, almost feminine. The flesh-coloured masses slowly stirred to life and dragged their feet in a sibilant crescendo as they started back to the cells. One of the guards looked with a wild face at Carter, then stooped with the other guard who was on his knees by the fallen man. Now Carter saw that the guard on the floor was Cherniver.

The cage door clanged and four new guards came in, trotting past a few of the inmates who were still straggling back to their cells. The four guards had pistols in their hands. Their shoes rang on the stone.

'Cherny?' one said.

'He's dead.'

'Who did it?'

'Ah, the lot of 'em! All of 'em. The block was full of 'em.'

'Yeah, and it shoulda been *you!*' roared a voice from somewhere down the row of cells, and the cry was bolstered by laughter, cheers. 'Throw him where you throw the rest of your shit!'

The four new guards ran up and down the block, brandishing their pistols, shouting at the men in the cells.

'Shut up! – Shut up, you wise guys, or you'll get bullets right through the bars!'

A guard with a deeper voice said, 'Close your doors! All doors closed! Close those *doors!*'

Clang! Clang-clang! Clang! from above and below.

Now they were all closed, but the closing did not lock them. They had to be locked by brakes at the front of the block by the cage.

The guards strode up and down, scowling defiance at the cells. There was a humming sound now, like the approach of a horde of bees, or like a wind. Looking at the row of cells opposite him, Carter could see that each man standing behind the barred doors was close-mouthed and calm-faced, yet a steady and quite loud hum came from the entire cell block.

'Cut out the humming!' one of the guards yelled. 'Cut out that humming or you'll all go to the Hole one by one!'

The humming only grew louder. A couple of brakes closed with a long groan and a jolt.

'Cut the *humming!*' But the voice had no effect whatsoever.

Two guards were now carrying Cherniver's limp body away, towards the cage. One guard stumbled and nearly fell. Somebody laughed insanely at this.

A few cell doors rattled. Other doors took it up. Suddenly it was a din, a metallic clatter like a tremendous machine gone awry. More guards burst into the block and ran up and down, shouting with their mouths wide open, though their voices could not be heard at all. A gun went off. Carter did not know which guard had fired, but suddenly they all fired, up at the ceiling, any-where. Their pistols smoked. A silence fell, such a silence that Carter could now hear the guards' gasping breaths. Their mouths were open, their eyes wide as they glanced around everywhere to see if any inmate dared make a move. More brakes closed above.

Two guards, Moonan and somebody else, walked slowly on opposite sides of the block, their guns still drawn, and, seeing that all was quiet now, they trotted towards the cage at the end of the block. There was another hum, a collective groan of complaint. The men behind the bars knew that they were going to miss lunch.

'Who's this guy?' asked one of the guards as he approached Carter. 'Who're you?'

'Carter. Three seven seven six five.'

'What's the matter with you?'

The guard's restless feet seemed about to kick him, so Carter made an effort to get up. He held to the door of the cell nearest him, and felt the helping hand of an inmate who reached through the bars to lift him by the forearm. It was a black hand. 'I'm sup-posed to get to the hospital ward.'

'Where's your pass?' asked the guard.

Carter wiped a trickle from his cheek and was surprised to see that it was blood. 'I was on my way to get a pass. I got knocked down.'

'Where you belong?' asked the guard.

'A-block, number nine,' Carter answered automatically. 'The doctor told me I could have a shot when I needed it.' He raised one hand slightly.

'Come on,' said the guard, and walked off in the direction of the cage.

Carter made it, supporting himself now and then, pushing

himself on by the bars of the cells he passed. He heard words of encouragement whispered from several cells, curses at the screws. The guard went into the cage, and Carter clung to the bars of the first cell and waited. The guard came out with a pass and beckoned to him. Carter started towards him and fell to the floor. The guard shouted:

'Eddie! Frank! Gimme a hand here!'

They took him by the arms and hustled him towards the other end of the block, which now looked ten miles long. By the time they got to the elevator, the guards mumbled to each other about Cherny getting killed because of *this*, because of this guy's thumbs. 'What a life, and look what they pay us . . . ' 'Sons of bitches . . . ' 'And if we accidentally killed one of *them* – Ha!' The elevator door slid open.

Pete came up with a surprised look on his face, his one eye open wide.

'He got a little beat up,' one of the guards said to Pete.

Helped by Pete, Carter reached his old bed, protecting his thumbs to the last until he was lying on his back and could let his hands drop to his sides. Pete was busy with the needle.

'What happened?' Pete asked. 'Jesus, you got a knot over your eye like a baseball. Wait a second.' He went away.

The morphine had not yet begun to fight. He imagined it coursing vigorously through his veins, looking to right and left for pain, finding it and then – attack! Quick as a pouncing tiger. Pete was swabbing his forehead with alcohol.

What happened? I heard there was nearly a riot. We could hear it way up here. One of the guards got hurt? The doc got called down – They beat you up again? The screws beat you up?' There was no sympathy in his voice, only curiosity.

'Cherny got killed,' Carter said.

'Wasted,' Pete was saying. 'Well, well, well. Who did it? Could you see?'

'All of 'em,' Carter answered drowsily. 'Pete, I've got to get my stuff from number nine.'

'Okay, I'll go down now.' Pete went.

Then Carter was alone with the dreams in his head. He saw Hazel in a blue and white bathing suit with a white cap on, as she had looked one summer in – Where? What summer? He saw a long, sunny beach, and they were going to take a run in a moment with Timmie along the sand at the water's edge. The sky stretched endlessly blue above them. Afterwards, they went to a restaurant on the shore and had broiled bass and especially good French fried potatoes, then they drove back to the cottage they had rented. Hazel took her bandana off and let the wind blow her hair. Carter remembered: that was in New Hampshire, two sum-mers ago.

Later, still not quite waking up, Carter began to toss and turn as the pain seeped back. He saw Pete bending over him, his face and head very large, and though Carter always avoided looking at Pete's pink, empty socket, he now stared straight into it as if it magnetized his own eyes. Pete smiled with pleasure and a strange amusement at Carter's inability to take his eyes from his empty socket.

Then Carter woke up and looked straight into Pete's face, into his empty eye, smaller now but real, and he screamed. Carter screamed a second time and twisted to get away from Pete's restraining hands. Then Dr Cassini rushed up, and Carter stopped his screaming, though his mouth stayed open. He was on his side now, propped on one elbow, one big bandaged thumb almost in his own face.

They gave him another needle.

'That's not all morphine,' Dr Cassini said cheerfully. 'That's mostly sedative. Boy, what a morning, eh, Philip? Ha! Mis-ter Cher-ni-ver got it.' He spat the words out with satisfaction.

The killing of Cherniver, the humming and the door rattling

were discussed a great deal in the hospital ward in the following days by Pete, Dr Cassini and Alex, the sweep-up for A-block. It was agreed that the disturbance bore no resemblance to a riot. Riots generally had no causes, or the causes were pretty small, like a particularly bad meal in the mess hall. The killing of Cherniver was a little incident, and as the men talked, it seemed to Carter to become smaller and smaller.

Attendance at the 10 a.m. church service on Sunday was compulsory for every inmate who could walk, so Carter went. He was greeted, quietly, by more men than he had ever been greeted by before in the prison, but after all they were only twenty or thirty out of hundreds present. The chaplain, after the routine prayers and hymn singing, spoke about the guard Thomas J. Cherniver who lost his life on Monday in the course of his duty, and called upon the men to cleanse their hearts of guilt, to forgive those momentarily benighted and misguided men who had contributed to the deed, and to pray for the repose of Thomas J. Cherniver's soul. Carter bowed his head with the rest of them. He was sitting near the back, and heard a few muttered remarks and some not at all repressed giggles.

6

In the month that followed Cherniver's death, Carter had two more interviews with Magran, who was now going over the ground that Tutting had, but in a more thorough manner. Magran had found one more witness, a certain Joseph Dowdy, a postal employee, who remembered assigning a post box to Wallace Palmer last July at a town called Pointed Hill, some sixty miles away from Fremont. Dowdy remembered Palmer from his photographs, though Palmer had taken the box out in another name. During the trial, there had been much talk of a Box 42 in Ogilvy and a Box 195 in Sweetbriar. Palmer had them noted on a card in his wallet. But no letters had come for him at those boxes after his death. Some of the supply companies that Triumph paid (with school board funds) did not exist. Palmer had invented the companies and the supplies from scratch, and received money for them at the various boxes that he took out under other names. Carter asked Magran outright if he thought Gawill might have been taking money from Palmer, and Magran had answered in his solemn, conservative way, 'There is a possibility. That money went somewhere.'

David Sullivan on the other hand – he visited Carter once

during that month, his third or fourth visit to the prison – seemed over-confident of Gawill's complicity and also over-confident that he could pin it on him. Sullivan said he was talking often with Magran, that they were working 'together' on the material they were gathering to present to the Supreme Court. But Sullivan was a corporation lawyer, not a criminal lawyer, and not in Carter's pay. Carter had a faint but disquietening suspicion that Gawill was right, and Sullivan was trying to make a good impression on him and counteract any resentment Carter might feel because he was seeing so much of Hazel.

Easter came and went in that month. Carter had seen Magran on Easter Sunday. He had had a good shot of morphine just before the interview (Carter now gave the shots to himself, holding the needle between his fingers and pushing it with his palm), and the morphine and the business-like tone of the interview had helped to lift Carter's vague gloom because Hazel was not coming that day. Later, lying on his bed in the ward, he had been able to smile as he thought of what Hazel might be doing at that moment, sunning herself with a tall drink by her host's swimming-pool, laughing and talking with Sullivan and the Fennors, and perhaps in the background good music would be playing on a stereo hi-fi. Then they would sit down at a long table with a crisp white linen cloth on it and thick napkins, and every item of food would be superb. And perhaps Sullivan would be paying Hazel compliments and giving her affectionate, even amorous looks across the table? Well, Carter didn't mind that. Hazel liked flattery.

The night of Easter Sunday he could not sleep, despite all the morphine. Time after time, he staggered up in answer to some moan or a mumbled call for Pete. He felt very humble that night. He felt in fact like nothing at all, and somehow like no one, as if something, some mysterious Parcaean scissors, had cut his tie even to Hazel. He could conjure her up as distinctly as ever in his memory, but he felt nothing when he did. It was as if they were no longer married and had never been married, as if she did not love him and had never loved him, and it seemed unbelievable, like a fantasy, that he had thought, only the day before, Nothing can really hurt me, because Hazel belongs to me and she loves me.

Back in his bed, Carter had visions of Sullivan and Hazel lying in bed together, perhaps sleeping now after having made love. No, Sullivan would have tiptoed back to his room, of course, in the Fennors' house. Carter turned in his bed. He didn't really believe that. Or did he? If he didn't believe it, why did he think of it? Or if he didn't really fear it, why did he think of it? Of course he feared it. He had admitted that long ago, hadn't he? Yes.

Carter turned over in bed and forced the ugly thoughts away. He had to arrive at a 'right attitude' or else. One had to have hope, and at the same time not take things too seriously. His thumbs – Well, some people got their hands taken off in prison machinery. It was difficult to arrive at a right attitude, when the letters Hazel had written and made him write also to congressmen and civil rights organizations had resulted in nothing but brief acknowledgements or politely sympathetic replies. He thought of Magran's new witness, Joseph Dowdy, and wondered what kind of man he was. Then Carter remembered the prosecution's' witness, and he suddenly grew tense. Louise McVay. She was a bank teller, and she remembered Carter coming into the First National Bank of Fremont with a $1,200 cheque on Triumph made out to Wallace Palmer and signed over by Palmer to Carter. Palmer had needed some cash in a hurry that day, and had asked Carter to pick it up for him, as Carter had to go to the bank anyway for himself. And the prosecution, the school board with its unlimited funds for tracker-downers and its unlimited wrath for having been exploited by crooked contractors and engineers, had managed to find Miss McVay who remembered what Carter had done that day with the cheque from Wallace Palmer. Carter had cashed it and pocketed the money. The cheque had been a perfectly

57

legitimate pay cheque, but it looked as if Carter were being paid off. It had made a strong impression on the judge and jury.

There was a clatter at the elevator, cries for Dr Cassini, and, sitting up in bed, Carter saw two guards with a bleeding, half-conscious inmate standing in the hall outside.

The wounded man was young, with curly blond hair. He had been stabbed in the throat and there was also a cut on his head from which most of the blood was coming. Dr Cassini, in the little room off the end of the ward called the 'operating room', stitched up the boy's head. The doctor said the throat cut had not hit the artery, but blood came out of the boy's mouth every few seconds, and it looked bright red to Carter. The neck wound was a jagged shiv cut, the second Carter had seen. The shivs were made from mess-hall spoons, and Dr Cassini said there were plenty of shivs in the cell blocks, despite the efforts the guards made to see that every man tossed a spoon back with his tray. Dr Cassini stitched the neck wound, too, and Carter clipped the sutures for him.

They got the boy into a bed and gave him a needle, but Carter had hardly got back into his own bed when the boy sat up and screamed, fighting his invisible assailants.

'Dr Cassini!' Carter yelled.

Dr Cassini came back, disgruntled, tying the belt of his robe. 'Ah, these queens. Where's the needle?'

Carter and the guard held the boy down, the guard at his head and Carter sitting on his feet.

'Jesus, nothin' like peace and quiet,' somebody said from one of the beds.

'If you don't like it, go back to your zoo and get a shiv in your neck like this fellow!' Dr Cassini yelled back.

The boy began to quieten down, and finally he was only gasping, relaxing. Carter stood up. The guard dismissed himself with a wave.

Carter walked to his own bed and stood beside it, squeezing his eyes shut. The dim, yellowish-purple light from the hall door was a perfect light for his state of mind, he thought, like a sick, false dawn.

Dr Cassini slapped him on the shoulder, laughing softly, and Carter recoiled. Emergencies, suffering, blood seemed to put Dr Cassini in a crazily chipper mood.

'I've seen this guy many a time,' Dr Cassini said. 'His name is Mickey Castle. Older than he looks. The queens know how to hang on to their youth. Ha! He gets cut up every few months. C-zoo, a nasty zoo.'

A man down the line of beds groaned aggressively, annoyed by Dr Cassini's chatter.

Carter sank down on his bed, and the doctor went back to his room down the hall. It was twenty past three. The night seemed endless.

A wild scream roused Carter from his pillow. Mickey was up again, stumbling from his bed, punching with sleepy fists at the air.

Carter walked towards him. 'Take it easy, Mickey! You're in the hospital ward!'

Carter hurried to the hall to call Dr Cassini and the guard –who must have gone to the toilet, because he wasn't there – and Mickey came at him. Carter heard him and side-stepped, and Mickey crashed against the door jamb and sank to the floor. By now the ward was in an uproar, and Dr Cassini came down the hall at a run.

The guard and Dr Cassini got Mickey on to his bed again. This time the boy had knocked himself out.

'He's bleeding at the throat again,' Carter said.

'Oh, that's not too serious. I'll take care of that in the morning,' said the doctor.

The morning was only forty-five minutes off, so Carter said

nothing else. Carter lay down on his bed again, and thought for a few seconds of Mickey's stitches having possibly opened under the bandage on his throat, thought that if he had not been protecting his own thumbs, he might have blocked the boy's charge against the door jamb. But if Mickey did not get it this way, he would get it another, and was it up to everybody else in the world to be his keeper, his protector?

Mickey was dead in the morning. Carter noticed him before anyone else. Under the sheet and blanket the bed was soaking with blood, caught by the rubber sheet below the bottom sheet. Carter was unnerved by the sight. Pulling the sheet and blanket back was like unveiling a crime – which of course was what it was.

Dr Cassini blew his stack. He cursed the screws and he cursed the animals. He addressed the entire ward, and many of the men propped themselves up on their elbows to listen, impressed by the fact that one of them had been murdered. 'So it's another pop goes the weasel. And what are the damned screws for, if not to prevent things like this? But how can anybody prevent things like this, if you all behave like a bunch of mad dogs?'

Carter listened, like the rest, standing motionless. Breakfast trays went uncollected from the dumb waiter. Carter and Pete could not have done anything about removing the blood-soaked sheets, anyway, as Dr Cassini was using the bed and the corpse as props for his harangue. Some of what he said sounded quite noble and sincere, reminding Carter of the first words he had heard from Dr Cassini when he had been brought into the ward almost unconscious. But Dr Cassini's righteous indignation had not lasted long. There were two people in Dr Cassini, at least two. The morphine might create still more personalities in time. Carter was now sure he took it, because he had seen a supply the doctor kept in the room in which he slept.

That day, Carter could not write anything to Hazel. He was too shaken, not entirely by Mickery, but by everything. Was Dr

Cassini reliable enough to make a judgement on the X-rays of his hands? Carter doubted it. Reliable enough to perform an operation? That was a grim, nightmarish prospect. Carter gave himself a seventh shot of morphine before he went to bed at 9 o'clock. There had been no letter from Hazel that day. Of course, on Saturday, taking off with Sullivan, she had probably been too busy for a letter, but she might have dashed a card.

An unhappy idea came to him in the middle of the night. He felt he should suggest to Hazel that she move to a bigger town as long as he was in prison. She would probably protest that she didn't want to go to New York or anywhere else that would keep her from seeing him frequently, but Carter thought he ought to insist. If she went to New York, it would also take her away from David Sullivan, he realized. Carter sighed. That wasn't his main objective, it really wasn't his main one.

On the following Sunday, Carter mentioned it to her.

'New *York*,' Hazel said, and was silent for a few seconds, but Carter saw in her face that she had considered it before. 'No, Phil, don't be silly. What would I do in New York?'

'What're you doing here? I know how boring that town is. I can't see that we've met any fascinating people in the year we've –'

'I told you in a letter just last week I might go in with Elsie on her shop idea. She doesn't need any capital from us, you know, just a little hard work.'

'She's over fifty. You'd be doing all the hard work.'

'The town needs a good dress shop.'

'Is there anybody with taste enough to patronize it? – Are you getting interested in that lousy town?'

'As long as I'm there –'

'Honey, I don't want you to be there. Not another month, not another week! I want you –'

'Quiet!' said a guard, coming towards Carter. 'You think you're the only guy in here?'

Carter said a four-letter word under his breath, looked at Hazel, and saw that she had heard it, or seen it. 'Sorry. What I was going to say – the fact that you're twenty miles or so from where I am isn't doing anything about getting me out of here any faster, honey.' He glanced at the clock. Six minutes to go.

'I don't want to talk about it any more, Phil. I want to see you just as much as you want to see me. That's all we've got – just now.'

Carter drummed with his fingertips on the table, desperate for something to say. 'So you – you had a good time Easter, you said.'

'I didn't say a good time. I said it was all right.'

What was she angry with him about, he wondered, the four-letter word? His proposition that she move to New York? The time was so short to straighten things out! 'Darling, don't be annoyed with me. I can't stand it!'

'I'm not annoyed with you. You don't understand,' she said, and looked at the clock also, as if she were eager to be off when the time was up.

Carter went to the movie that night. He was going to the prison movies more frequently, though the bill of fare was always, or had been so far, stuff that he would never have wasted time on outside of prison. He realized that he listened with enjoyment now, too, to the mediocre and usually filthy jokes for which Alex, the sweep-up, often buttonholed him. Without some compromise, without the movies, and maybe even without the wild stories that passed for jokes, he'd go mad. Men who tried to buck prison life, rejected the movies, counted off their time, became stir-crazy, like animals pacing cages in a zoo. Carter had heard Dr Cassini talk about such cases, men brought up to the ward with nothing physically wrong with them, yet completely insane or intractable, so that they had to be sent to the next station on the line, the State mental institution, if there was any room for them there. Carter could see that the men who got along best of all were those in good health with nobody in their lives, not even a sister or a mother or a brother who took any interest in them, the men who could laugh at the whole business of prison with a loud and cynical guffaw. These men never missed a movie or a ball-game. Even the guards seemed to like them. And if they were asked, they said they'd do it again, whatever it was that got them to jail. 'Like they say in the sociology books, I'm just here improving my style. Ha! Ha!'

Do a good deed, find God, learn a trade, pray to be a better man, realize that your time in prison can be a blessing, because it can provide time for meditation on your mistakes, and so forth and so forth, said the prison newspaper. It was a four-page newspaper called *The Outlook*, written entirely by the inmates, except for the warden's column, which had just as many grammatical mistakes as the rest. Lots of times Carter flung the rag, with its lousy cartoons, its Bible lesson, its corny jokes, its line-up of base-ball or basketball players that looked like teams recruited from Skid Row – flung it to the foot of his bed or the floor and indulged in a quiet, 'Oh, Jesus.'

7

Hazel went into partnership with Elsie Martell in the dress shop venture, and in May her letters were full of descriptions of the shop's decor, the colours of this and that, even the details of certain dresses and suits they had stocked, though she knew Carter was not very interested in women's clothes. 'You only like dresses once I'm *in* them,' he remembered Hazel saying once.

The Dress Box was on Main Street, 'next to the big drugstore almost,' Hazel said in a letter. Hazel a partner in a dress shop called the Dress Box on Main Street in a town called Fremont. It seemed fantastic and ludicrous. But it seemed quite real when Hazel wrote that David Sullivan came by in his car at 8 in the evening, had come by a couple of times when they were still working on the wallpapering and staining the new dress racks, to take Hazel out to dinner. Once he'd taken both Hazel and Elsie out (that was nice of him), but on at least three evenings, he'd taken Hazel out, ' . . . a real treat since I didn't feel like going home and fixing anything. I'm afraid I was pooped and not very good company. Absolutely too tired to dance, so you can imagine.' She had gone home at 6 to give Timmie his dinner on those evenings. Millie, a teen-ager who lived in their neighbourhood, was now baby-sitting quite often. Timmie was all right in the afternoons, dropped by the school bus, letting himself in the house with his own key which was on a string around his neck, and getting the snack from the refrigerator that Hazel always left for him.

Carter was brushing up his French in his spare time. Hazel had sent him his French dictionary and his complete Verlaine, and from New York she had ordered the last Prix Goncourt novel. He had had five or six years of French in high school and college. Now, in his reading ability, he was certainly better than he had been in college, but the speaking of it was another matter. Unfortunately, there was no one with whom Carter could practise.

He had also begun to learn *judo-karate* from Alex. Alex had said out of the blue one day, 'Do you want to learn judo? You ought to, because you're not going to be able to sock anybody very hard with those thumbs.' Carter thought Alex had a point. One never knew when it might be necessary to sock someone. So, partly to pass the time, Carter began to take lessons from Alex. Alex was shorter than Carter, but close to him in weight. He was careful not to grab Carter's thumbs in their mock battles. They used the hall for their practice, to the amusement of the bored guard on duty there, usually Clark. Alex had got from somewhere a couple of filthy, lumpy mats that they put down on the floor. Carter wrote to Hazel after three practice sessions: 'I'm learning judo from Alex. He learned it in the army and seems to know a lot, but can you get me a book on it? You'll probably have to order it from the bookshop in Fremont.' He wanted to add that he was still not very good at wrist-grabbing and pulling, because of his thumbs, but the slicing blows with the side of his hand he could execute quite well. Then he decided not to write that, because Hazel was squeamish about violence. One of the blows Alex taught him, to the front of the neck, was what Alex called 'a blow to kill'. Hazel got the book, but it was not passed by the censor and Carter never saw it. It was returned to Hazel. Yet the judo practice went on under the eyes of the guard. Carter practised banging the sides of his hands against wood to harden them, but it jarred his thumbs badly, and he did not get very far with this.

The Southern summer was long and hot. Despite the fact that the prison was on rather a height, there was almost never a breeze. When a breeze came, it was hot also, but men in the fields straightened to receive it, took their caps off in defiance of the hellish sun, and let the moving air touch their sweating foreheads. The bricks and stones of the old prison absorbed the sun's rays week after week, and retained the heat as they had retained the winter's cold, and by August the cell blocks were like vast ovens, breezeless and suffocating even by night, stinking of urine and the sweat of blacks and whites.

In August, when, Hazel said, the town of Fremont was nearly empty and what people there were were so dazed by the heat that they never left their houses, she went to New York with David Sullivan. Sullivan had some friends there called the Knowltons who had an apartment on West Fifty-third Street, just opposite the Museum of Modern Art, and they offered their apartment, which was air-conditioned, to Sullivan for the month of August while they were in Europe. Carter had at first been aghast at the idea of her going, then angry, then simply stunned, or possibly defeated. He went through these emotions within three days of getting her letter about it. It was true that the Knowltons' twenty-year-old daughter would spend a couple of weekends at the apartment (it seemed to be a huge apartment with a penthouse), since she had a summer job at some resort outside of New York and she had weekends off. It was true that Timmie would be with Hazel. But a big apartment to Carter seemed just as private, just as suspect, in plain words, as a single room in a hotel where they registered as man and wife. Carter wrote, 'Haven't we got money enough for a hotel?'

And Hazel wrote back, 'Do you know what it costs to stay a *month* in New York at a hotel? And eating every meal out with Timmie also? I'll see you Sunday and can talk better then . . .'

On Sunday, Hazel said, 'I am very fond of Dave, darling, it's true, but I swear to you he's become an old shoe – like an old shoe.' And she laughed, in sudden good spirits such as Carter had not seen since the days they had been together in the house in Fremont – the house where Sullivan was now such a familiar figure, he was like an old shoe.

'I don't think he thinks of himself as an old shoe to you,' Carter said, not smiling at all.

Hazel looked at him and lifted her eyebrows. 'Are you saying you don't want me to go to New York? With David? Go ahead. You have the right.'

Carter hesitated. Sullivan could escort her, of course, to places she couldn't go to very well on her own. She'd have more fun with Sullivan. Carter couldn't deprive her of that. 'No. No, I'm not.'

Hazel looked a bit relieved. She smiled at him. 'Are you saying you don't think there's such a thing as a platonic friendship between a man and a woman?'

Carter smiled. 'I suppose that's what I'm saying.'

'I can assure you from a woman's point of view there is.'

'A woman's point of view – is never the same as a man's.'

'Oh, bosh. Male chauvinism.'

'Older women, not so attractive women, maybe. But you're too pretty. It gets in the way.'

Anyway, she went, and August for Carter was not an easy month to get through, despite the stream of postcards and letters from Hazel. Timmie adored the Museum of Natural History. Sullivan had taken him one day to the Planetarium, while Hazel went shopping for shoes: she bought three pairs at a sale. 'The black patents I'll save. We'll go dancing one night and I'll put them on for the first time ... What did Dr Cassini say about the last X-rays?'

Dr Cassini said a lot of mumbo-jumbo, but the essential thing was that the posterior end of the second phalanx was abnormally large now and could not be put back into its socket. The paring down of the bone, which Carter suggested, was an operation evidently beyond Dr Cassini's abilities. He did not advise trying it. Carter wanted to see another doctor, a hand specialist, but he thought he might be out by the autumn, or by December, after the Supreme Court hearing, so he did not press to get a specialist's examination in August. It would involve permission from the warden, armed escort in case he had to leave the prison to see the specialist, a snarl of red tape that dismayed Carter even to imagine. The swelling was much less in his thumbs, and he did not wear bandages now, but the skin was pink, as if it glowed with the faint and ever-present pain beneath. There was no strength in his thumbs to mention. They were as useless as appendices, almost, yet not quite, otherwise Carter would have considered having them amputated. He still took at least four big shots, or about six grains, of morphine per day. That amount was a necessity. He had started out with one or two grains per day. So his addiction had increased.

Hazel and Timmie were away three weeks and two days. She flew back on a Saturday so that she could see him the next day. On that Saturday, a day so hot there were seven cases of heat prostration brought up to the ward, Carter received a letter from Lawrence Magran saying with great regret that the Supreme Court of the State had denied the request for a new trial.

Carter had a strange reaction. He sat down with the letter on his bed. He felt no shock at all, no surprise or disappointment, even though in the last month or so he had been feeling more and more confident that he would get a new trial. Magran had found three more witnesses of Palmer's cheque-cashing and two more banks had been uncovered to add to the three others where Palmer had been tucking money away like a squirrel. It had certainly seemed 'new and significant evidence' to Carter, and that was what was needed to warrant a new trial. Magran himself had thought so, too, even though Palmer's total deposits amounted to less than $50,000. Magran said he was surprised and profoundly sorry, and that he would come to see Carter, if not this Sunday then the next. Carter got up and walked to the window at the end of the ward. Half a mile away, shimmering in the heat of the sunset, he saw the great arched sign, like signs he had seen at the entrances to amusement parks or cemeteries, that spanned the road to the prison: STATE PENITENTIARY it said, backwards, and on clear days without heat waves the letters were quite legible from the window. A black car moved towards it, raising a trail of dust, passed under the sign and out, into the world. Hazel doesn't know yet, he thought suddenly. At that very minute she was in the air. Her plane was due to land at 7.10 p.m. She was flying home at several hundred miles an hour – for this piece of rotten news.

The prison has absolutely knocked out my feelings, Carter said to himself, and it was this that made him angry.

By 7.30 p.m., his thoughts had entirely changed, and he was sitting at Dr Cassini's typewriter in a room down the hall, laboriously (as far as the typing went) writing a letter to Lawrence Magran. After acknowledging Magran's letter and its news, he wrote:

I see no hope anywhere now except in what David Sullivan may be able to discover in the way of new facts and in particular facts as to Gregory Gawill's connections, if any, with Palmer's activities. Or – if any – Gawill's deposits in various banks. I realize this would only spread the guilt a little more thinly, but Sullivan may yet come up with more witnesses. According to my wife, he is still keenly interested in the case. Would eight or ten witnesses, if we had them, count for more than the few we've got?

Carter went to bed, though it was not much after 8 o'clock. He felt too discouraged and paralysed even to take a morphine shot as he usually did before trying to sleep. His thumbs were throbbing gently, just enough to be annoying, just enough possibly to keep him awake – for how long? Until 1, perhaps, when the pain would get so bad he'd have to take a shot? The morphine he saw as another enemy. Was that going to get him, too, like the prison? A curious enemy, the morphine, both a friend and an enemy, just like a living person. Like David Sullivan, for instance. Like the law, which in some cases protected people – there was no doubt of that – and in some cases persecuted them, there was no doubt of that, either.

Hazel had heard the news when she came to see him on Sunday. Carter knew she had as soon as she came into the visiting-room. Her smile was a little forced, there was none of the sparkle that usually radiated from her, attracting the eyes of guards and inmates, too. She said that Sullivan had telephoned Magran that morning, and Magran had told him. Then Sullivan had called her.

'I'm sorry, Haze,' Carter said. He thought of the many letters she had written, angry letters, naïve letters and – with such patience and second drafts – formal letters to the local newspaper, to the *New York Times*, to the Governor. Hazel had always sent him the carbons to read.

'David's here,' Hazel said. 'He wants to see you.'

She sounded so low, Carter made a great effort to appear strong. 'Well, Magran once said there's no law against appealing twice to the Supreme Court. Magran didn't say anything about coming today, did he?'

'No. I don't know. He might've said something to David.'

They made an effort to talk about New York, about pleasant things she and Timmie had done there.

Carter said, 'Timmie's not too bored, back in Fremont?'

'Oh, Phil!' Hazel suddenly plunged forward, her face in her hands.

The top of her head, her glossy hair was very near Carter's hands, separated from his hands by the glass. 'Darling, don't cry,' Carter said, trying to laugh. 'We've got eight minutes yet.'

Hazel looked up and sat back. 'I'm not,' she said calmly, though her eyes were wet.

And then, somehow, they managed to talk about New York until the time was up.

'I'll write you tonight,' Hazel said as she left. 'Stay for David, darling.'

Sullivan was just then walking into the room.

'I have a visitor,' Carter said, indicating Sullivan.

The guard verified on Sullivan's pass that he was to see Carter, and then Carter and Sullivan took chairs opposite each other.

David Sullivan was about thirty-five, a couple of inches taller than Carter and more slender ordinarily, though Carter had lost about fifteen pounds since going to prison. Sullivan had blue eyes, rather like Carter's but the blue in Sullivan's was stronger. His eyes were smallish, and their expression was nearly always the same: calm, poised, thoughtful, like Sullivan himself. Sullivan did not waste words in commiserating with him over the Supreme Court rejection.

'Of course, you can appeal a second time,' Sullivan said. 'I'm sure Magran has that in mind. Don't take this as a defeat, Phil. We'll just come at them again with more facts and we'll have more time to gather them.'

Carter's feelings were ambiguous, his thoughts also. Carter felt his case had become a sort of hobby with Sullivan. Years from now, if Sullivan ever wrote his memoirs, there would be a few pages devoted to the baffling and maddening Carter case. 'Carter's wife became my wife, the partner of my ...' Carter checked his wandering mind and tried to listen.

'I'm doing the same with Gawill, in other words, as Tutting tried to do with Palmer. I'm checking even with his liquor dealers, and believe me there's plenty of them, as to how much and when he spent it. Unfortunately, a lot of the dealers haven't kept their old bills.' Sullivan's tanned forehead wrinkled, his sun-whitened eyebrows jutted forward as he ground out his cigarette in the ashtray. 'Gawill was with Palmer in New York on at least two occasions. They were careful enough not to stay in the same hotel or even to fly from here in the same plane. That's part of what I was doing in New York, inquiring at ten or twenty hotels there.'

Part of what he was doing.

'All this takes time. I know it's not fun for you spending the time in this superannuated –' Sullivan looked around him, at the ceiling. 'They should've torn this place down about the turn of the century. If not before.'

'Or never built it.'

'That's more like it,' Sullivan said with a laugh. He had good teeth, a trifle small for his long face, like his mouth.

Carter knew he should comment on Gawill's having been to New York when Palmer was there. Gawill had probably been sharing Palmer's girl friends. Gawill was a party-loving bachelor, too, like Palmer. But Carter couldn't comment. 'So you had a good time in New York – Hazel said.'

'Oh, I hope she did. She was off on her own a lot, except in the evenings. I was introducing my old friends to Hazel and she was introducing hers to me, so the evenings were usually pretty social. Timmie went with us most of the time, because we were at people's houses a lot and we could just put him in a back room when he got sleepy.'

72

'How do you think Hazel's bearing up – really? You can spend so much more time with her than I can.'

Sullivan's face grew more serious.

Carter waited, wishing his question hadn't sounded so plaintive, so dependent on what Sullivan thought.

'I think it's a good thing she went into this dress shop venture. It gives her something to do. Not that she hasn't enough to do, but to take her mind off – You know. She's got a lot of strength. Strength of will, I guess you'd call it,' Sullivan said.

'She's very fond of you – she says.'

'Oh, yes. Well, I hope so,' Sullivan said in a frank tone.

'And – I'm sure you like her, too, or you wouldn't spend so much time with her.'

Sullivan blinked, on guard, but he smiled slightly and his face was quite unworried. 'Phil, if I had any dishonourable intentions with your wife, do you think I'd come visiting you in prison? Do you think I or anyone else could be that hypocritical?'

Gawill had simply said Sullivan was that hypocritical. 'I didn't say you had any dishonourable intentions,' Carter said, feeling uncomfortable now.

'Hazel's probably the most loyal woman I've ever met.'

Because he'd tried her and found out?

'It shows in everything,' Sullivan went on. 'All she talks about is you, writing you, seeing you. And around Fremont, when we take drives, she points out spots where you walked or had a picnic.' Sullivan shrugged, looking pensively down at the table-top now. 'She talks about the things you'll do when you get out. She wants to go to Europe. You two were there once, weren't you?'

'Yes.' They had had their honeymoon in Europe, a present from Uncle John and Aunt Edna. 'Are you in love with her?' Carter asked.

A flush came in Sullivan's cheeks, and a blank, solemn expression came over his face. 'There's really no reason for you to ask that.'

73

Carter smiled a little. 'No, maybe there isn't. But I'm asking.'

'I don't think it's of the slightest importance.'

'Oh, come on. I think it's of great importance,' Carter said quickly.

'All right, since you're asking,' Sullivan said, his voice steady and professional again, 'I am in love with her. And nothing can be done about it. I'm not trying to do anything about it.'

'Oh. Did you tell her?'

'Yes. She said – it was impossible. She said maybe I'd better not see her any more. And she was sorry, that I could see,' Sullivan said with a glance at Carter. 'Consequently, I was sorry, too, that I told her.'

Carter's eyes were fixed on his face.

'So I said, all right, I didn't ever have to mention it again, but I'd still like to see her.'

'I see,' Carter said, not seeing at all, really. All he saw was a dangerous situation in which something would have to explode at some time.

'I suppose it was six months ago that I told her. Since then I've never mentioned it.' He looked levelly at Carter, serious and self-possessed, and rather as if he thought himself pretty noble.

'Do you enjoy this kind of self-torture?'

'I don't consider it self-torture. I like it better than not seeing her at all,' Sullivan said, without a trace of humour or a smile.

Carter nodded. 'If I hadn't been in prison, would you have told her? Would you even have been in love with her?'

Sullivan took a moment. 'I don't know.'

'Yes, you know,' Carter said in a nasty way, and saw it jog Sullivan as if he had poked him in the face.

Sullivan pushed his chair back from the table and re-crossed his legs. 'Well, you're right. Of course it had something to do with it. I didn't know how long you were going to be in prison, neither did Hazel. Neither do we now. A man can ask, can't he, if he's in love? That's all I did.'

Carter pressed his thumbs against the matchbook he was holding on the table. 'I thought you said you told her, not asked her anything.'

'I didn't ask her anything. I told her I loved her. It didn't go on from there.'

Carter did not believe that. But if Hazel was still willing to see Sullivan, what he had said could not have been too annoying, or importunate. Carter knew Hazel: she wouldn't spend time with any man who annoyed her. That, in fact, was the most important thing in the picture. 'It's – sort of like working at cross purposes, isn't it, being in love with Hazel and trying to get me out of this place?'

Sullivan gave a laugh. 'Don't be silly. As far as Hazel goes, I think I'd have the same chance with her whether you were in or out. The point is, I have no chance.'

What kind of sense did that make, Carter thought, when Sullivan had just said he wouldn't have said anything to Hazel, if he hadn't been off the scene – in prison?

'You might say,' Sullivan went on, 'if I really care about Hazel, I'll help her to get what she wants and that's you.'

Carter spread his elbows on the table and smiled. A couple of colourful prison expressions for that kind of talk came to his mind. 'I don't believe in the age of chivalry. Any more,' he added.

'Oh. I'm sure you do. From what Hazel tells me here and there. Don't let prison make you callous, Phil.'

Carter said nothing.

'Do you think I'm dragging my feet on this Gawill investigation?' Sullivan asked, leaning forward. 'I'm inquiring about his behaviour on his former jobs, too, from New Orleans to … to Pittsburgh. Back to here. Gawill knows it. Even if he's innocent – I mean in the Triumph affair – he hasn't a clean past and the word is spreading and Gawill's squirming. Drexel knows about it. Drexel might fire him, just on the suspicions I've raised about him. Drexel ought to fire him, but it'd look too much as if Drexel weren't very bright about his own staff when your trial was on.'

Sullivan looked at him expectantly, then in a baffled, angry way as Carter said nothing: 'If I go too far – if I'm a little too successful, Gawill, I'm sure, wouldn't mind putting me out of commission.'

'How could he?'

'I mean killing me. Having me killed, of course.'

'Do you really mean that?'

'He was with a very tough company in New Orleans, and there was a mysterious killing there. Gawill kept clear of it, of course, so did the whole company he was with. But a fellow named Beauchamp who was in the State Legislature and very noisy about upholding parish laws, was found strangled in a bayou. Then the company Gawill was with pushed their building plans through. Oh, it's a detail from your point of view, maybe, but my point is, Gawill is that kind of man. He'll have somebody eliminated who's –'

A guard touched Carter's shoulder, and Carter rose. 'Sorry,' Carter said.

Sullivan stood up, and his frown of intensity left his face. He was once more upright and calm. 'I'll see you soon again, Phil. Keep your chin up.' Then he turned and walked quickly away.

8

From time to time, Carter took medicines and pills to inmates in the various cell blocks. There were six cell blocks, and C was the worst, as Dr Cassini had said. The grey stone walls of C-block looked dirtier, it was darker (due to several electric lights not functioning), and the men seemed older and quieter, yet the atmosphere was more sullenly hostile than in the other blocks. The memory of Cherniver's murder was still fresh in Carter's mind and perhaps in the minds of all the others. The inmates could pass over a man like a flood. For a few seconds, a score, any score of them could get their whacks in, and then the flood could move on, innocent of face, calm in manner, the guilty ones nameless, unidentifiable, because they were all equally guilty. And if he had been in good health with a strong pair of hands, Carter thought, and if he had been walking close enough to Cherniver that day? Yes, he might have got his whack in, too, even without the added inspiration of having been bullied by Cherniver personally.

The cell blocks of the State Penitentiary were connected, all six of them, though only four, A to D, were of the original structure. These did not connect at right angles and did not form a square. Blocks E and F were simply hitched to each other, E-block to one end of D-block. From a distance, and Carter remembered it from his approach by car in November, the prison looked like an ancient wreck of a six-carriage train in which the carriages had piled up due to a sudden stopping of the first. Double doors with a guard at each door divided blocks A to D, and individual men with passes were let through in the same manner in which guards let men through the cage at the front of A-block. The mess hall and workshops and laundry were below some of the blocks, and men marched in double file to these places. The pairing off and marching began as each batch from its own block entered a new block. The L that E- and F-blocks made had been turned into an enclosure by a high fence of heavy wire topped by barbed wire. This was the recreation yard, where, between 4 and 5 o'clock, shifts of men pranced and trotted under the eyes of a dozen guards who stood around the edges armed with machine-guns. The prison was now so over-crowded that not all the inmates could eat at once, and there were two shifts for meals.

In E-block, there was a bull of a man about fifty years old with a sore behind his left ear. Dr Cassini had seen him up in the ward and dismissed him with instructions to use a certain ointment. Now Carter was delivering a second tin of it. The man was alone in his cell. Carter asked him where his cellmate was.

'Lucky bastard went home. Mother died.'

'Home?'

'Yeah, he'll be gone for two nights. Chicago. See his wife.' The bullethead lifted and looked at Carter with a sly wink.

The man rambled on. A couple of furlough screws went with Sweepey, and he'd had to go handcuffed, even on the train up, but he'd get to spend two nights with his wife. Carter was lost in a kind of incredulity, as if the man had told him a fantastic story of physical disappearance, metamorphosis, of slipping through keyholes.

Carter shook his head suddenly, shocked by the intensity of his own thoughts. 'Lucky guy,' he said automatically.

The bullethead scowled at him, angry at the interruption. Then, to Carter's complete surprise, he stood up and drew his right fist back.

Carter stepped back, over the raised threshold of the cell and into the corridor.

The man yelled a two-word curse and threw the little tin of ointment as hard as he could. It hit the wall of the cell beside the door, came open and the lid spun, sounding like a silly giggle, before it came to rest on the floor.

Four days later, Carter faked a request, got a pass from Clark, and went back to cell twenty-seven in E-block just to see Sweepey. He carried another tin of the ointment. It was just after 4, when the inmates of E-block were in their cells awaiting the bell for late supper. This time the bullethead was not in the cell, but Sweepey was, sitting with the earphones on, whistling and jigging in his chair and snapping his fingers.

'Hello, pill-pusher, and what can I do for you?' He seemed so elated, he might have been drunk.

'I brought some more stuff for your chum.'

'Okay, okay, I'll tell him.'

Carter's eyes moved from the man's dark hair down his body to his prison shoes and up again. 'Heard you just went home.'

'Yeah, not much fun, but still it was home. My mother died.' He was still in the mood of the music, obviously wanting to put the earphones on again.

'Well – at least you saw your wife,' Carter said with a blunt naïveté. He was ready to leave, he had not even entered the cell, only tossed the ointment on to the lower bunk, but he could not tear himself away. He stared at Sweepey, trying to see some magical sign of it all.

'Yeah, it's gotta last me a long time.' Sweepey guffawed. 'My old man's dead, nobody left except my sister and she's the pitcher of health!' He put on the earphones and turned back to the little table. 'Thanks for Jeff,' he said.

Carter went away.

It was two or three months after that, around Thanksgiving, that Carter met Max Sampson. Max was in B-block, where Carter was delivering some cough medicine. The delivery was not to Max's cell. Carter noticed him because he was reading a French book – paperbound with the title *Le Promis* in red – sitting at the little table in his cell. He was alone. Carter paused by the half open cell door.

'Pardon me,' Carter said.

The man looked up.

'You're French?'

The man smiled. His face was friendly, calm and very pale. His large strong forehead looked almost white below his black and slightly wavy hair. 'Naw. I just read it sometimes.'

'Can you speak it?'

'I used to. Yeah, I can speak it. Why?' Again he smiled.

The smile by itself was a pleasure for Carter, a smile being such a rare thing in the prison. Sneers, yes, and guffaws, but not simply a natural, happy-looking smile. 'I only asked because I'm studying it – on my own. Vouz pouvez parler – vraiment?'

'Oui.' Now the wider smile showed strong white teeth, whiter than his face.

Carter talked with him for ten minutes, until the bell rang for lunch and Max had to leave. They talked both in French and in English, and Carter became strangely excited and happy. When Carter hesitated for a word, Max supplied it, if he could guess it. Max had about twenty books lined up in a row at the back of his cell, and half of them were French books. Very generously he pressed two of them on Carter, one a book of eighteenth-century French poetry, the other selections from Pascal's *Pensées*. They were a loan, of course, but Max said he did not care when he got them back. Carter returned to the ward feeling completely changed. Max was the first person he had met in the prison whom he felt glad to know, with whom he felt a friendship could grow. It was a wonderful thing. In that ten minutes, he had learned that Max was from Wisconsin; his father had been an American but his mother was French; and from the age of five to eleven he had lived in France with his mother and gone to school there. He had been in prison five years, he had said airily in answer to Carter's question. He had not said why he was in prison, and Carter was really not interested in knowing.

Max had said that he was competing with another inmate in B-block to achieve the whitest prison pallor by Christmas Eve. The bet was six cans of instant coffee, and Max thought he was going to win, even though his competitor was a blond. Because of the bet, Max shielded his face carefully in the twice-a-week airings in the recreation yard. A panel of six inmate judges had already been chosen to pick the winner. 'I've always been pale,' Max had said in his slow, distinct French, with a smile. 'Very early it was plain I was marked for a life in prison.'

They had an appointment to meet again at 3.35 in Max's cell the following day.

In the golden light of his new acquaintance, Hazel's last letter sounded melancholic, even lugubrious. She had written:

Darling, do you think that fate (or God) put this awful trial in our path to test us? Please forgive me if I sound mystical. That's the way I feel tonight – and many nights. One way of looking at this – our awful lives now, each awful in its own way – is that it is a test given to very few people. We have come through it so well up to now, I mean as far as fortitude goes. So let us continue and see it through. My thoughts are no doubt influenced by the talk I had (over the phone) with Mr Magran this afternoon ...

Magran had told her that they couldn't appeal again until mid-January to the State Supreme Court, owing to the holidays. That seemed now no blow at all to Carter. He wrote:

You are always asking me why I haven't met anybody decent in this place, and I'm always saying there isn't anybody decent, but as of today I take that back. By accident I met a nice fellow who knows French (reads and speaks it) so now I have someone to practise with. His name is Max Sampson, he is about my age, tall, dark-haired and very pale. More about the pallor when I see you. He is in B-block, but I think I can visit him when I like.

Then Carter realized he had nothing more to say about Max, because he didn't know anything more, except the bit about his French mother.

In the next days, Carter still did not learn much more about Max, but their twenty- or twenty-five minute meetings in Max's cell were the high-spots of Carter's day. Max's cellmate was a large, good-natured Negro, who couldn't understand more than 'oui' of their French, but he kept out of their way in the upper bunk while Carter was with Max, and read his old worn-out comic books or listened to the earphones. Carter's letters were now full of Max, and he talked about Max to Hazel when he saw her on Sundays. To Carter's surprise, Hazel seemed almost resentful of his new friend.

'I thought you wanted me to find someone I liked in this hell-hole,' Carter said.

'Do you realize that out of nearly twenty minutes you've spent more than ten talking about him?' Hazel smiled, but her annoyance was plain.

'I'm sorry. It's a dull life I lead here, darling. Had you rather I talked about – oh, say, the couple of dimwits in the ward now who nearly blinded themselves drinking alcohol from the typewriter repair shop?' Carter laughed. He laughed more easily since meeting Max. 'I'd like you to meet Max. He's – Well, I think from a woman's point of view, he's not even bad-looking.'

But Hazel was never to meet Max. She might have met him by asking to see him one Sunday, by stating that she was a friend, and Carter thought of this, but Max declined it. 'Oh, I think it's better if I don't. Bad luck,' he said in English, so Carter never proposed it again. He had not proposed it to Hazel either, sensing that she would say no also. Hazel could never see Max even in the visiting-room, because Max never had any visitors. He had no family, he said, and the only person who had ever visited him was his former landlord, a man who had rented a room in his house to him just before Max went to prison. He had come twice to the prison, but that had been in Max's first year. Still, Carter thought it spoke well for Max that his last landlord had visited him twice. But Carter asked no questions about Max's past. Max had asked none about his, but he had noticed Carter's thumbs, knew what had caused their deformity, and had said only, 'This is a cruel place,' in a tone of resignation, in French.

Max and Carter went to the movie together on Saturday and Sunday nights. It was good to have someone beside him who thought the films just as mediocre as he did. Their friendship was noticed, of course, by some of the guards as well as many inmates. Some of the inmates assumed they were homosexual, and made comments to Carter's face and behind his back, within his hearing. Carter was not bothered by the comments, but he was a little concerned about what they might lead to. Some inmates took a pleasure in beating up men who engaged in homosexual practices. Carter was careful to look behind him as he walked to Max's cell block in the afternoons, lest anybody jump on him. The door of Max's cell was always open when he was there – not that one could not have seen through its bars, anyway – and the Negro was there, too. Carter realized he had never even touched Max, even to shake hands.

'Studying forgery?' the guard in Max's cell block asked one afternoon as he let Carter by.

'Forgery?'

'I seen you writing sometimes in there.' He nodded towards Max's cell. 'He's a good forger, Max. One of the best.' The guard smiled.

Carter waved a hand, tried to smile, and went on. He thought of Max's slow, clear writing which Carter had seen in his notebooks. Max kept a diary sporadically, and occasionally he wrote a poem in French. His handwriting had a curiously innocent look. Forgery. It was an unpleasant shock to Carter, as if someone had snatched off Max's clothes and Carter saw him in the nude. Well, Carter thought, at least he wasn't in for murder.

It had occurred to Carter that, because of knowing Max, a second rejection from the Supreme Court, if it came, would be easier to bear. Thus Carter tried to prepare himself in advance for the worst. The second rejection came in the 5.30 p.m. post one day in April. This time, it shocked him more than the first rejection. His impulse was to run at once to Max's cell, but it was not possible to see Max at that hour. Carter went into the toilet and lost the supper he had eaten an hour before. He did not want to see anyone or talk to anyone, but he could not achieve that condition either. In the prison, there was no privacy.

That night he slept very little, and finally out of sheer boredom with his own thoughts, took a Nembutal. The next morning he did his work with a stony face and mind, ate no lunch, and at 3 o'clock fixed himself a cup of coffee on the burner in the washroom. The coffee was from one of the three cans of Nescafé that Max had given him for Christmas. Max had won the bet for prison pallor, and had shared the spoils with Carter.

When he got to Max's cell, he sat down on the lower bunk

with his hands over his face. He wept shamelessly, not caring that the Negro was standing there beside Max, bewildered, that a screw, an inmate, whoever looked in and saw an inmate sobbing, would stop and stare for a moment.

'I know,' Max said. 'It's the Supreme Court thing, isn't it?' he asked in French.

Carter nodded.

The Negro heard 'Supreme' and understood. 'Holy, holy Jesus,' he said mournfully, then lumbered out of the cell so they could be alone.

Max lighted one of his cigarettes and gave it to Carter.

Carter told Max about his job with Triumph, about Wallace Palmer, about the trial, about being sent to prison over last September and how unbelievable it had been to him. He told Max about Gawill and about Sullivan, and about Sullivan and his wife.

'I've got to make Hazel go away now, back to New York,' Carter said, banging his fist down on his thigh, heedless of his thumb.

'Don't decide anything today,' Max said in a calm, deep voice, like the voice of God himself.

Carter sat in silence for a while.

Max began to speak in French, about going to France when he was five, and of his childhood there. When his father died and the alimony stopped, his mother brought him back to Wisconsin, where he had been born. They had a few relatives there on his father's side. His mother had remarried, but his new stepfather had no intention of putting him through college, so after high school, Max had got a job in a printer's shop and learned the trade. He had met Annette when he was twenty-one and she nineteen, and they had wanted to marry, but her father had made them wait two years because he did not want his daughter to marry before she was twenty-one. 'I waited, but still I was happy because I was in love,' Max said. Then Annette, when they had been married not quite a year, had died. Max's mother had been visiting them, and Annette had driven a car over a cliff with his mother in the car also. Annette had swerved the car to avoid a deer that suddenly ran across the road, according to a man in another car who had seen the accident. Annette had been pregnant. Then Max had started drinking and had lost his job. He had come south and in Nashville had met a lot of 'bad characters', including ex-jailbirds and forgers. Max had learned how to forge, and the robbers and pickpockets of the gang used to bring him their travellers' cheques and anything else that needed a signature. 'Certainly I knew I was a crook,' Max said, 'but I was alone in the world, nobody cared, and I didn't care.' It was a profitable business for all concerned, and he had thought he was in a particularly safe position in the outfit, but their headquarters were raided one night by two plain-clothes men. Max killed one of them in a fight, so he was in for both forgery and manslaughter and had been sentenced to seventeen years.

'And now I'm thirty. It's a funny life, is it not, my friend? Life is funny.'

Carter sighed. He felt very weary.

Max stood up and pushed Carter back on the bunk. 'Lie down.'

Carter collapsed sideways on the lower bunk, and dragged his feet up on the blanket. It was Max's bunk. Then he suddenly sat up.

'What's the matter?'

'It's about time for the supper bell. I don't want to fall asleep.'

Max paced slowly in the cell, swinging his hands in front of him, touching his palms together. His face was calm, his dark eyes alert and almost twinkling. Max looked today exactly the same as he always did. The news he had brought had not affected him at all. Carter took a curious comfort in this.

'Life is funny,' Max said again. 'It is necessary both to see

86

oneself in perspective and not to see oneself in perspective, yet either one can lead to madness. The two things must be done at the same time. It is difficult. You are suffering a day of seeing yourself in perspective.' Max stooped and rose up with a book. 'Read some of this tonight,' he said, and the supper bell went off on his last words, jangling, nerve-shattering, ten times louder than it needed to be, painfully familiar. Max smiled at Carter with amusement until it was over. 'Well, I'm off for this evening's *pièce de résistance, canardeau à l'orange*, no doubt.' He poked the book at Carter.

Carter took it without even looking to see what it was. He smiled with Max, at what Max had just said. It felt good to smile.

9

Once again, Hazel had heard the news before Carter had to tell her. Magran had called her up the day he wrote to Carter. Carter had had one letter from her in which she sounded depressed but quite in control of herself. But he was shocked when he saw her on Sunday. There was a despair in her eyes that made her look almost wild, as if she were drugged.

'You've got to get away. You ought to go to New York now.' His mind had not at all changed.

She didn't answer for a moment. 'You say it so coldly. You've changed so much, Phil.'

'No, I haven't.' But he knew he had. 'Months ago I said the same thing. Now there's all the more reason for you to go to New York and less reason to stay here.'

'You don't talk at all about what's the next thing to do.'

We can keep on with special pleas, Magran had written. What did that mean? 'Magran was pretty vague about it himself in his letter to me.'

'No, he wasn't. He talked about letters to people and – there's a committee in New York – I can't remember the name, but it's about civil liberties. Mr Magran mentioned it on the telephone.'

88

Carter sighed. 'You know, Haze, I'm not the only fellow in this kind of a spot. Do you think they're doing so much to get the other guys out? They write, too. Who's got the time to help? Who's got the power, first of all?'

'But there are committees for this very thing,' Hazel said firmly. Her hands were clenched on the table. 'Mr Magran said you were supposed to write them, too.'

'Well, tell me who they are. I'll write, of course.'

Hazel looked at the clock. 'I don't think Max is doing you any good, Phil.'

'Why?' Carter frowned.

'You've changed – since you met him.'

'Really? Well – he makes life here a lot easier to take, Haze.'

'Just because *he* takes it easier – He's been here five years, you said. He's a real criminal, Phil. You said he was a forger, an "expert" forger. He's used to prison. Maybe he wouldn't know what to do if he got out. I've read about people like him. They're incapable of leading an ordinary life with responsibilities and a job and all that. He seems to be making you that way, too – enough to tolerate people like him. And once you start tolerating them, you're going to end up being like them yourself. You really give me the feeling you're beginning to think this place isn't so bad, and if you feel that way, it's the end.' Her words were like an ultimatum between them.

Carter had listened patiently but with resentment. An attack on Max was like an attack on himself. 'I wanted you to meet Max, but you don't seem to want to. I wrote you about what happened to him, his wife dying when they'd only been married a couple of months.'

'Lots of things happen to a lot of people. It doesn't make them criminals.'

'He's in for one mistake. It's not as if he had a trail of crime behind him. Max is civilized, at least compared to the morons and

89

the animals that the rest of the guys are here. I'm glad I found him. Maybe there're a few others, there're six thousand men here, but I'll only meet a few hundred, if that.' It was not fair to Hazel to say that she alone hadn't wanted to meet Max, because Max hadn't wanted to meet her either. There was also the fact that Max about three months ago had asked Carter to bring some morphine down to his cell. Carter had told Max it was locked up, which was true, but Carter now had the key to the cabinet. Twice a screw had searched Carter when he was on the way to see Max, and if he were found with dope on him, it could go badly for him. Carter had not been surprised at Max's request, but he was certainly never going to mention it to Hazel. 'Darling, I wish you'd understand about Max. I see him only twenty minutes a day, after all, and not even every day.' Twice a week, the inmates went to the showers at that time in the afternoon. 'I know what the books say about prisons. And criminals. We've got a few books on it in the library here. I've read them.'

'Then you know what I mean. Don't let it happen to you.'

Carter sat rather straightly in his hard chair. He stared down at his hands and was conscious suddenly of the picture he presented through the glass and wire. He wore the Sunday-visiting, short-sleeved white shirt that he no longer felt silly in, but positively elegant, compared to the workshirts of every day. His short hair didn't bother him, though the cut – compulsory once a week – was never even. There was a little grey at his temples now, hardly visible in the hair that was cut so short, but Carter knew that Hazel would have noticed it, because she noticed everything. Lines in his forehead and between his eyebrows were deeper. And he was, of course, pale. It would not be a pretty picture that he presented to Hazel. 'I'm – fooling around some in the carpentry shop these days.'

'Oh, good. *That's* nice. What are you making?'

'Just now I'm doing certain jobs on things the whole shop is building. Shelves for the laundry, for instance. I couldn't do every step of making anything. I can do pretty well on the rotary saw.'

In the last ten minutes, they talked about Timmie as usual. Carter asked about the dress shop, though he knew: it was just pulling its weight, and neither she nor Elsie were making any money. For her part-time work, Hazel got $57 per week take-home pay, plus a commission on what she sold. It was simply something for her to do.

That afternoon, Carter did not go down to see Max. Hazel's words had disturbed him profoundly. He awaited with a strange anxiety Hazel's letter which would arrive on Tuesday. She no longer wrote to him on Sundays, as she used to do as soon as she got home after seeing him. But on Tuesday he would get her letter after she had spoken to Magran on Monday.

The letter, when it came, had a calmer tone than Carter had expected. She gave him the names and addresses of four com-mittees and organizations and of two men in Washington to whom he was supposed to write. Two of the committees' names Carter recognized: he had written to them months ago, and one had not even acknowledged his letter.

He continued to visit Max four or five times a week. Now Carter was writing compositions in French and taking them to Max, who, like a schoolmaster, corrected them overnight and dis-cussed them with Carter in the following session. 'My Day' was the title of one, a rather funny account of his day in the hospital ward from the time of rising until lights-out. 'A Day I Should Like to Spend If I Could' was another, quite an exercise in subjunctives and a fantasy about home and Hazel and Timmie and eating and driving in the car, fishing in the afternoon, cooking out over a wood fire, and sleeping under a tent; and in that rustic scene a hi-fi machine was also thrown in, with music by Schoenberg and Mozart. Then there was 'What I Think of Prisons' and 'On the

Passage of Time: A Personal Attitude'. Carter took his corrected essays back with him to the ward, and in his spare moments copied them over again, making the corrections that Max had made, so that he had finally a batch of fifteen or twenty 'perfect' if rather simple essays of his own in French. It gave him a tremendous sense of pride.

Hazel wrote:

Darling, what is the morphine situation now? You have not mentioned it in ages. The last you said was that it was still necessary and would be for some time. Isn't there something else you could take? I've been reading about morphine – the principal alkaloid of opium (if you don't think I know what an alkaloid is, I now do!) Please watch it ...

Her words struck a small pang of guilt in him. He tried cutting down. He could do on three shots a day, and he had been taking four. But he noticed the difference in his spirits: they weren't quite as good, or as cheerful. He asked Dr Cassini for some Demerol or anything that deadened pain, and the doctor gave him something – something real this time. It worked, but it did not work as well as morphine, which, Carter very well realized, had a most pleasant way of changing reality into a form much easier to bear. For two weeks, Carter took no morphine, and then he began mixing his anodynes, depending half on morphine and half on the pills.

In July, a letter came from Hazel in which she said she had decided to move to New York with Timmie. She said she had a prospective buyer for the house, someone Sullivan had found.

'It's easier writing this to you than trying to tell you through that awful glass,' she wrote, 'which gives me the feeling I have to shout everything even when I don't. You know I do not want to leave you, and I won't be really, but as you have said a hundred times the awful summers here plus the boredom are enough to drive one batty, and here we are in another of them. I thought even two weeks ago I could stick it out in Fremont another summer, but even the shop is about to close for a month . . .'

She said that she and Timmie could stay at Phyllis Millen's in New York until she found an apartment. Phyllis Millen – the name, her face, were like something dredged up out of the murk of ancient time to Carter – was an advertising copywriter, about thirty-eight and unmarried, whom he and Hazel had known casually since Timmie was a baby.

Well, now it was done, Carter thought. Soon there would be no more Sunday visits from Hazel. She must have been planning it for several days, because it was clear that she had got an answer from Phyllis about staying there. She had known last Sunday that she was going, and hadn't mentioned it. What was the difficulty of telling him through the glass? Was it that she couldn't face him when she told him?

Carter added to his letter in progress to her: 'So glad to get your letter today saying you are going to New York. I only wish you'd gone months ago. You'll be happier really and therefore I will be too.'

Lawrence Magran, having been paid his fee for the two efforts with the Supreme Court, was now going to work on a freelance basis, Hazel wrote to Carter. It was slightly annoying to Carter that Magran had made this arrangement with Hazel instead of writing to him about it. It was as if Magran now thought Carter was a dead duck, but he was still going to make certain gestures over the corpse.

Hazel wrote to him every day during the week before she left. It was as if she felt guilty about leaving. His own feelings were utterly mixed: he felt resentful for moments at a time (usually when he was tired or in pain) and he felt glad and happy for her sake at other times. He was careful to write her only when he felt glad.

> ... The fact is, I am in this prison, may have to stay about four more years, at worst. But at least I am better off than 99 per cent of the men who are here in cells half the time. At least think of this when you think of me.

She was looking her prettiest on the last Sunday that he saw her. A new pale-pink linen dress, sleeveless, an apple-green scarf of thin silk around her neck, fastened with an antique gold pin he had given her on one of their wedding anniversaries – the third, fourth? – of a coiled dragon with a ruby eye. Her hair looked as if she had just washed it, shiny and soft. But she did not smile as much as usual. For the first time, Carter noticed a line in her face, a fine horizontal line across her forehead. It was, somehow, horribly ominous.

Hazel said, 'I've just had a big Scotch.'

Carter smiled. 'I wish you could have piped some over to me.'

He didn't notice any effect of the Scotch. Not a tear, not any sentimentality. They both tried very hard to be brisk and cheerful, but they went over things they had already said in letters, they both reassured each other that Magran had not abandoned him by any means, and that he was still one of the best criminal lawyers in the country.

'Maybe the trouble is I'm not a criminal,' Carter said, and they both laughed, a little.

She had received a down payment of $8,000 on the house they were selling for $15,000. This Carter already knew. Someone named Abrahol, a man with a wife and two teen-aged children and a collie, were moving in on the first of August.

Their efforts at cheerfulness were rather successful, Carter thought. Both of them were smiling as Hazel got up to leave. She would manage a trip to see him 'at least before Thanksgiving'. She looked back before she went out of the door, paused for an instant, and blew him a kiss. Carter was staring at her. Then she was gone – the column of pink topped with the dark brown hair which was Hazel.

He looked down at the stone floor as he walked. There was no threat of tears in his eyes. Was he turning to stone like the prison floor, like the prison? Was Hazel crying now? He stopped and looked back, as if he could have seen her, anyway, if she had been beyond the double bars of the cage. As if she would have lingered. No, Sullivan was probably waiting for her in his car outside.

Hazel's next letters were very lively, full of descriptions of new buildings that had gone up even since she had been to New York last summer. Finally, there came what Carter had been expecting: David Sullivan was coming the last week in August, on business, and would stay about a month in the apartment of the Knowltons where he had been before. Hazel now had an apartment on East 28th Street, a walk-up with three rooms, kitchen and bath. Carter had suspected Sullivan was going to go to New York. He was actually relieved and reassured by Hazel's telling him outright.

10

Hazel did not visit him before Thanksgiving. She was taking courses in sociology at the New School on 13th Street, and her schedule did not permit a break of any length before Christmas. Hazel had majored in sociology in college. She was taking these courses at the New School as refreshers, she said, and 'just to be doing something'. She visited him at Christmas, when she and Timmie came down as guests of the Edgertons for two weeks in Fremont. She looked a bit thinner, though she said she was not. She saw him twice over Christmas. Carter gave her a shelf that he had made in the carpentry shop. It was a shelf to hang on a wall, made of cherry wood. This was handed out to Hazel through the cage unwrapped because he had nothing to wrap it in, and if he had, the guard would have unwrapped it anyway. Along with it was a good-sized chest of oak with Timmie's initials carved in its lid, which Carter had also made. Carter wrote on the card to Timmie: 'I know you are getting too old for toys now, but from what Mummy says you could be a little neater around the house, so throw your sporting goods here.'

Then once more Hazel was gone, promising to return at Easter.

The Edgertons visited Carter once, and wrote him a couple of notes, meant to be cheerful, about their plants and their cat that had had kittens. Sullivan also wrote. He said that Gawill, after being 'fired' from Triumph, had gone back to New Orleans and was with a firm there that made metal awnings. It simply didn't matter now to Carter. It had been almost a year, he thought, since he had heard about Gawill leaving or being fired by Triumph. Sullivan attributed it to his investigations of Gawill and to his exposure of Gawill's spending during the time of the school fund embezzlement. Suppose that were true? Why wasn't Gawill charged with anything? Gawill might be guilty, but he was a free man. Wrong was right and right was wrong, and everything was made of paper: sentences, pardons, pleas, bad records, demerits, proof of guilt, but never, it seemed, proof of innocence. If there were no paper, Carter felt, the entire judicial system would collapse and disappear.

All over the prison and even in the hospital ward, men sat around writing letters with the aid of law books, lawyers' form letters and dictionaries. They wrote about *habeas corpus, coram nobis* and a thousand personal grievances. Carter was often asked to look over their letters for spelling and grammar. These mistakes he could correct, but not the pitiful organization of some of the letters, which at first so disturbed him, he had written some letters over for the men. Then finally, seeing not one result from their efforts, he had let the poorly organized letters stand. Some were disorganized as a cry from the depths might be disorganized. Other letters were from habitual whiners, and the disorganization came from stupidity. Some whiners were skilful and even literary, and these showed their letters to Carter not for corrections but because they wanted compliments. Their letters were a creative outlet, as well as an outlet for resentment and hatred. Especially in Max's cell block men came with letters, because they saw Max and him writing. Max wrote many letters for illiterate men. The prison permitted each inmate to write two such 'business letters' per month.

David Sullivan wrote to Carter:

Perhaps the situation doesn't sound very promising to you now, but all we need is a little more proof. Statements from people who were involved with Gawill, i.e. recipients of some of the money he was spending so lavishly during the time the money was disappearing from Triumph. Gawill and Palmer were reasonably cautious, but the men who could talk exist, and I've talked to two of them personally. Hazel knows their names, too, but it is best not to write them. Unfortunately they are afraid of Gawill's retaliation and would like to see him behind bars before they talk, but the law doesn't operate this way. However, the threat of this is breaking Gawill down slowly. He is back in N.O. on his old grounds and as usual the men around him are the dregs. I intend to go down there, even if it has to be in disguise ...

Max and his Negro cellmate acquired a third man who slept on a cot, and from then on the French lessons were less pleasant. He wanted to wash his hair at 3.30, or he needed the table to write a letter on, and even if Max and Carter sat on Max's lower bunk with their feet up on it, he complained about their 'mumbling', which was much lower than the voices from the corridor at that time of the afternoon. The new man was called Squiff. He was under thirty, blond, thin, with a scar on one cheekbone that went up into his temple. He had been in prison several times before, Max told Carter, though Max did not know why he was in now. He was probably in for the third time at least, and had received a heavy sentence. At any rate, he hated the world, and he certainly hated Max. Max was polite to him, considerate about space, generous with his cigarettes, but Carter saw that this only added fuel to Squiff's resentment. Carter said to Max in French that he ought to try acting a little tougher for his own good. Max only shrugged.

'I have a feeling he's going to start a fight with you.'

'Oh, I'm bigger than he is,' Max said.

'I mean a nasty fight,' Carter said, and he knew Max knew what he meant – a shiv wound, a blow on the head with a chair when Max's back was turned.

'Ronnie will help me,' Max said.

Ronnie was the big Negro. Carter knew Ronnie detested Squiff also, but very few Negroes – there were a few in the prison whose terrible hatred of whites showed – dared to touch a white man, no matter what happened. Negroes were usually bunked with Negroes, and if this wasn't possible, the white man was a Northerner of apparently easy-going nature, like Max. Carter said nothing more about how Max ought to behave with Squiff, but Squiff's presence irritated him more and more. He dared not look at Squiff, lest Squiff see his dislike in his face and start something.

'Are you wise guys talking about me?' Squiff said one day, whirling around from the basin, where he had been washing out a shirt, flinging drops of water on to Max and Carter and their papers.

'No, we're –' Max hesitated. 'We make up things to talk about. What's there ever to talk about in this clink?'

Carter forced himself to look down at his French dictionary. He did not even wipe away a droplet that stood on the page.

Slowly, Squiff turned back to the basin, wrung his shirt out, shook it and hung it so violently on a hook there was a sound of ripping. 'It's a pity you intellectuals can't take yourselves to the library or something.'

Max was talking about Keyhole, the little dog in the laundry. The dog had been in the laundry nearly a month now, carefully concealed, of course, as pets were not permitted. The laundry workers had got him from the driver of a delivery truck that came inside the prison walls. He was a small black and white mongrel with some fox terrier in him, and he was about a year old, Max thought. Seventy or seventy-five men who worked in the laundry knew about the dog, but no guard did and no other inmates. The laundry workers brought him bits of meat from their meals, and one man had braided a collar for him out of dental floss. If anybody saw a guard enter the laundry, the word was, 'Who's got the time?' yelled in a loud voice, then the inmates nearest Keyhole would whisk him into a clothes locker until the guard left. Keyhole slept in a large locker at night, where he had food and water and shredded paper as his bathroom. He seemed to be happy, and he had gained weight.

'You guys planning a break?' Squiff asked in a contemptuous, amused tone.

Max laughed. 'No, are you? Let me in on it.'

'Ain't there no French word for keyholes?' Squiff chuckled. 'Ought to be.'

Max said, 'It's the name of a little town. In Arkansas.'

'Oh,' Squiff said.

Carter had written to his Aunt Edna, answering a letter she had written to him and that Hazel had forwarded to the prison. He had explained why he was in prison as best he could, and had not mentioned the injury to his thumbs. One shock at a time was enough. He wrote the letter on the typewriter, so Edna would not see the change in his handwriting. When he sent the letter off, he felt very depressed and lost at the thought that Edna, who had always read a lot of newspapers and now that she was in California probably subscribed to the *New York Herald-Tribune*, her favourite, had not heard anything about his being in prison. He felt even worse when he received her next letter. She wrote:

I was just floored by your news. It is a terrible thing for Hazel and the boy, but knowing your Hazel I think she will bear up well even through this. But have you thoroughly examined your conscience *and* your actions? No one is totally innocent. I cannot believe that American courts of justice would sentence a man who is absolutely without guilt. You have always been forgetful, Philip, absent-minded when you should pay attention. If you realized how in some measure, however small, you behaved wrongly, it would take away some of your bitterness – and help you to make your peace with God . . .

Carter realized then that Edna was growing old. She was in her mid-seventies, not ancient for some people but evidently for Edna. He let weeks go by before he answered her, and then he wrote a shorter, more careful letter in which he explained more clearly the means Palmer had used to appropriate the funds assigned by the school board to Triumph. Edna never answered the letter. Her sister Martha with whom she lived wrote to Carter in July that Edna was bedridden with dropsy and a weak heart, and that her doctor was not very hopeful that she would pull through. And in August, Martha wrote that she had died. Carter was to inherit half her estate, which would amount to about one hundred and twenty-five thousand dollars. Carter knew where the other half had gone, to Martha, which he supposed was fitting, as Edna had lived with her for more than ten years now, and Martha had not much money of her own. But all his life, Carter had been told he would be the sole heir of his uncle's and presumably of his aunt's money when they died. Carter was neither resentful of the half nor happy about it. It simply did not seem to matter. He did not mention the money to Max. Carter wanted Hazel to enjoy it, to invest most of it, and to give up any idea she had of working. She now was thinking of taking a two-year course that would give her a master's degree in psychology and sociology, without which she couldn't take a job of any importance anywhere.

He had seen Hazel in July, when she again flew down with Timmie and this time she had stayed at Sullivan's house in Clayton, several miles from Fremont. Carter was now much more reconciled to Hazel seeing Sullivan. He did not think they were having an affair or had ever had one. And if they had not up until now, they would not, Carter felt. His love for Hazel had undergone a strange and profound change in the prison. It was now a sexless, fleshless love, as if that part of their love which had been so intense before had withdrawn in abeyance. Yet his love for her had grown. He felt that her loyalty to him was and would be the greatest thing he would ever experience. When she said to him in her summer visit, 'After all, the time here's half over even if we figure it's going to be six years,' then Carter felt quite calm and strong. Two years before, such words would have made him bitter and angry.

The promise of the hundred and twenty-five thousand dollars after the will was probated did not change Hazel's plans about the sociology degree, and she was going to start at Adelphi College in Long Island in September.

August was a vaguely troubling month for Carter. The heat seemed worse than in other summers. Sullivan was again in New York, in the Knowltons' apartment. Thus the years rolled on. In the last week in August, Keyhole was discovered. An inmate, rushing to hide him when a guard came in, had stepped on his foot and the dog had yelped. The guard – he had had to draw his gun to make himself obeyed, and then had failed – demanded that the animal be produced. By this time, Keyhole was in the locker, and nobody moved to get him out. Max said the laundry had been perfectly silent, all the machines turned off, and in the unusual stillness, Keyhole had barked. The guard had discovered the locker and pulled the dog out.

'The screw looked mad enough to have shot the dog,' Max said, 'but I swear if he had, the guys down there would have torn him to pieces.' Max spoke in French. Squiff was as usual present that day.

The dog had been taken to the pound in Bowman, a near-by town. Max said some of the men were going to write a letter to the Bowman *Eagle* and try to find a home for him. The inmates were also sending the three dollars that were needed to get a licence at the pound. The letter to the newspaper was to be signed by all the men in the laundry, so the prison authorities would not be able to pick on any one inmate or a few as the ones to blame.

By the next morning, the whole prison seemed to know about Keyhole. It was strange that for three months the dog's presence had been kept such a secret, and that within twenty-four hours of the dog's removal, six thousand men seemed to know about it. They were resentful. Max said there had been whispering in the mess hall at supper the day the dog was found, and the screws had to blast out a warning over the loud-speaker that any man caught talking would lose his movie privileges over the weekend.

'So you knew about Keyhole, but you wouldn't let me in on it,' Squiff said to Max. He was sitting on the straight chair, scraping his nails with what looked like a toothpick. 'You work in the laundry, don't you?'

Max said easily, 'Oh, come on, Squiff, if we'd told everybody, that dog wouldn't have been there two days. Some bastard would have told a screw.'

'But you told your friend here.' He nodded at Carter. 'He don't work in the laundry, he's a pill-pusher. Why'd you tell him?'

Two days later, Max said the letter signed by all the fellows in the laundry had been stopped. The censor had evidently shown the letter to the warden, because the warden had piped up now, and every man in the laundry was getting two months' extra time on his sentence and movie privileges taken away for the next month.

Carter had left Max and was standing at the end of A-block, waiting for the elevator, when he heard the first roar of voices. It was from the direction of B-block. At first it sounded like cheering – but who ever cheered? The elevator door slid open, the operator heard it, and a stiff, surprised expression came on his face. All the inmates in the corridor of A-block stood silent, facing the growing sound. Others came out of their cells to listen.

'It's *on*!' somebody shrieked in a voice that cracked.

'Come on in,' the elevator operator said quickly to Carter, but just then an inmate jumped on the operator, pinned his arms to his sides, and they both fell to the elevator floor.

Suddenly everybody was running. Carter was knocked aside by three or four men who rushed into the elevator, yelping and laughing. A shot was fired within the cell block, but it sounded faint in the roar of voices. The elevator door shut. Carter turned and saw that the door into B-block was wide open and that men from A-block were pouring through it. He didn't know where to go, had an impulse to duck into one of the cells near by for safety, but he had hardly started towards the cells when he collided violently with a big man who was running. Carter gasped painfully, geting back the breath that had been knocked out of him. He was suddenly furious. He headed for B-block. The crush of bodies at the bottleneck of the door was terrifying. Carter was aware of a man's body under his shoes. A few men punched at the heads of the men in front of them. Then Carter was through the door. Men were streaming down from the tiers of B-block, all yelling. Water cascaded from one of the tiers, and the men under it, who were getting wet, shouted and pushed at the human sea around them. Max's cell was perhaps two hundred yards away, but it might as well have been two hundred miles. He gave up the idea of reaching him, and aimed for the cells on his left. An old man was trailing behind him, clinging to Carter's shirt like a drowning man, and saying, 'I want to get to my cell! My cell!'

'Get away, bud!' a mad-faced inmate said when Carter finally reached a cell. There were four others in there with him, and they were holding the door shut.

Carter pushed towards the next cell, going in the direction of Max. The whole mob was pushing towards C-block, and Carter supposed the doors were open. The next two cells had their doors open, but they were being raided, bedding torn up, mattresses flung on the floor. A toilet had been pulled out and water flowed. It crossed Carter's mind that a lot of toilets pulled out could flood the downstairs and drown them all. In another cell, a man was screaming in pain: six or eight men were in the cell, beating and kicking at the screaming man, who was not visible. Carter gave up the cell idea. What chance had he if hundreds had the same idea? He saw a single man desperately trying to hold a barred door shut on himself, and failing. A toilet was flung in a heavy arc over Carter's head, and at least two men dropped beneath it.

'Here we go! Pass him on!' someone sang out, and a man was passed feet first and horizontal, laughing and out of his mind, over the heads of all, touched by many, hit in resentment and fear, helped on by other laughing men, and soon he was far on the way to the door of C-block and out of sight.

'Hang the warden ! Hang the warden!' The chant grew.

Carter looked for Max. He saw Hanky, grinning and yelling, waving a homemade knife in triumph. Water slammed down on Carter and the men around him, and in the press to escape it, Carter was swept out into the centre of the corridor. But there the stream moved faster, and within seconds he was abreast of Max's cell, and he fought his way towards it.

Max's cell was occupied by about eight men, wide-eyed with fear, all standing rigid, holding the door shut.

'Where's Max?' Carter yelled at them.

'Who?'

'Max! That's his cell!'

The men looked blank. Maybe they hadn't heard him. He was shouting across a dozen men. Carter did not know any of the men in Max's cell.

The crowd was suddenly much thinner around Carter. They were finally pushing through into C-block.

'Shove on, buddy,' one of the men in Max's cell said to Carter.

'I'm not trying to get in. Don't any of you know where Max is?'

A few cell doors were opening now. Some men came out yelping and screaming with laughter. They had taken refuge only during the worst, and they were ready to join in again.

'Let's get out of here,' said one of the men in Max's cell.

Suddenly the cell door opened and they all slipped out in a fast stream, eight, perhaps ten men.

Max lay on the floor at the back of the cell.

When he turned Max over and saw his face, he knew he was dead. Max's face was full of blood and absolutely smashed. Carter gasped, took a few short, crazy breaths, then charged out the door. He ran towards C-block, after the ten men. One of them had done it, or more than one, fighting for Max's cell. A large man half jokingly reached out and stopped Carter with a thick arm. Carter raised a foot and shoved it into the man's stomach. The man reeled back and hit the wall. He went down. Carter jumped on him. He jumped on his face, his body, he kicked him. Loud voices near by cheered him on. Carter seized the man's shirt collar in both hands and banged his head against the stone floor.

Then a Negro inmate pulled Carter by his shirtfront, grinned into his face and said, 'Hey, man, you goin' crazy!'

Carter threw his fist at the Negro and missed.

The Negro hit back, and Carter was knocked unconscious.

When he came to, the cell block was silent, except for two voices at the far end. Two inmates stood there with guns in their hands. A third man stood by himself, also with a gun, at the other end of the block, much nearer to Carter.

'Thought you were daid, Joe,' said the nearest man with the gun, a Negro. He danced slowly from foot to foot.

Carter tried to push himself up, and his arm gave way, bending strangely, and he realized it was broken. He got up with the aid of his other arm and staggered towards the support of an open cell door. The cell was empty. He collapsed on the lower bunk, on the bare springs, because the bedding was all over the floor.

There he passed, by his watch, twenty-four hours. The lights were kept on all the time. The inmate guards were changed, there were several of them now at either end of the corridor. A couple of them brought Carter water from somewhere, twice, because the basin in the cell where he was had been broken: water trickled from the broken pipes down the wall, but the pipes had been broken off inches within the wall, and the water was running away somewhere inside. Carter's arm was swelling. He asked a couple of times to be taken to the hospital, but the guards said they couldn't leave their posts, they were under orders. They said it with pride, as if they now served in an army they loved and respected. One said he would try to get permission to have a couple of men take him away. Carter's arm throbbed like his thumbs. He longed for his morphine. He began to throw up the water a few minutes after he had drunk it. The men who took him away were in good spirits. They were also a bit drunk. Carter could smell the liquor on their breaths. One was coloured, one was white.

'Yes, suh,' said the Negro. 'We got a real efficient prison now. Stretchers 'n hot-water bottles, bamboo and moonshine!' He laughed like a soprano.

They staggered and jolted him. The elevator, they said, was broken. They took the stairs.

'You the fellow what killed Whitey?' the Negro asked in a pleasant tone, smiling.

Carter said nothing. He vaguely remembered one hard fight, remembered kicking a man. He had not the faintest recollection of the man's face, whether he was short or tall, fat or thin, white or coloured.

The hospital had been wrecked. Dr Cassini looked like a scared rabbit. He mumbled a hello to Carter as if he barely recognized him. Smashed bed tables were piled in a heap in a corner. There were no more straight chairs. Two inmate guards lounged at the window end of the ward with guns in their pockets, handles sticking out.

'Every time somebody comes in that door, I think it's another raid,' Dr Cassini said. 'Jesus! How much dope do they think we keep here? I been raided four times!' He was fumbling with Carter's arm, feeling it.

'Is there any morphine?' Carter asked, automatically whispering it.

Dr Cassini grinned, and looked around him. He bent low and said, 'I keep a private hoard. Just for emergencies like this. Penicillin, too. We'll be okay, Philip, me boy.'

Dr Cassini pulled his arm straight in a traction device, and for this he got an extra shot of morphine. Even so it was painful, the sharp-edged bone nipping away at the tender flesh around it. Carter pretended that he had promised Max to take it without a murmur, which was the way he took it. There were other minor matters, a cut on the forehead to be washed, cuts on his knuckles, a gash in his shin about two inches long that needed stitches and had so filled his shoe with blood, now dried like glue, that the shoe had to be soaked off. Forty-five minutes after the traction, Carter was strong enough to curse. He cursed to himself at first, then he began to mumble his curses. Sons of bitches, he called the men who had killed Max – Squiff or whoever they were. He cursed the lot of them in prison curses.

Pete told him that six men had been killed, possibly more. All the ward beds were full, and Carter's would have gone, too, if they hadn't saved it. Men were lying in the ward corridor. The inmates were holding six guards in C-block as hostages, and they were asking for steak twice a week instead of once, the transfers of about two hundred fellows, no three men in a cell any more and stronger coffee in the mess hall.

'Ah, they're nuts, they're nuts,' said Dr Cassini, listening to Pete. 'I thought they were rioting because of that dog they had in the laundry. Half the guys who come in here to get patched up don't know about the dog. I haven't slept since it started. I'm afraid to sleep. The militia ought to get here soon. They're bound to have called the militia. Then there'll really be some shooting.'

Carter didn't care. He didn't give a damn if the militia came right into the ward and shot him, too. Everything seemed remote and unimportant. He listened as if in a dream to Pete's rambling monologue. Some of the injured in the ward talked about the letters that the prison censor had stopped, but nobody really knew what had happened, except that it had started in C-block. A couple of fellows had jumped a guard and got his gun.

'Funny thing is,' Pete said, 'I heard the warden was going to make a statement in the mess hall yesterday about letting the dog letters go through. Only he was just a little late. Just about ten minutes late. Funny, isn't it?'

A couple of the inmates' leaders were talking by telephone with the warden, Pete said. Pete got wild reports of what the inmates were asking for, and even he knew some of them were not true: movies every night, furlough for everybody every three months, hot-water showers in the cells – this last sent Pete into paroxysms of laughter.

There was the sound of gunfire that evening around 8, and soon afterwards the ward heard that A-block was in the hands of the militia and the guards again. It was not yet dark, but there would be no more fighting until tomorrow morning, Dr Cassini predicted.

'The objective of the militia should be the kitchen,' Dr Cassini said with disgust. 'Starve those bastards for a few hours and they'll knuckle down. All they think about is their stomachs. That and sex, of course.'

They wrangled long into the night. Carter had thought he was so full of morphine, he could sleep, but his pains kept him awake. Somehow he did not mind. He thought of Max in a calm but bitter way. He thought of Max nearly all night. At least he had killed a man in return, not the man who had killed Max, probably, but one of the lot, and they were all alike. Carter was sure he had killed that man. And that seemed quite right and proper.

11

Within a month, the riot of the State Penitentiary, which had lasted three days and got nationwide coverage, was for Carter a thing of the past. It might have become a thing of the past for him sooner, but it took a month and more for the inmates to clean up the mess they had made, to re-install the toilets and basins, to repair the smashed locks (locksmiths had to be called in, as locksmithery was not a trade taught in the prison), to repair the broken machinery in the laundry, the carpentry shop and all the shops, and for the inmates to repair their own wounds and broken bones. These last Carter saw all around him. One of the saddest of the casualties was old Mac, who had no wound at all but was in the ward because his brain had snapped, as Dr Cassini put it. Mac had seen his ship model smashed to bits and trampled under prison shoes and his cell torn up. He had even managed to get his cell door locked by a guard, Carter had heard, but the inmates had broken the lock with a sledgehammer, just to get in and destroy his ship model. Carter wrote to Hazel about Mac. Since the riot had called attention to the conditions in the prison, there was a chance that Mac would soon be admitted to a mental hospital, which would be a good thing for him, because nobody knew how to handle him in the ward. He was not violent, but he did not much know where he was, and even had to have his food spooned into his mouth.

The riot was simply an 'incident' to Carter in an existence, a stream of time, that seemed to him one continuous riot, rebellion and hatred. He tried to explain this to Hazel. He thought he explained it very well and clearly, but she wrote back that his train of thought was so negative, not admitting of any good in human character or in the intentions of any of the officials of the penal system, that he was heading for a terrible depression and misanthropy unless he made an effort to see things differently, 'the way things *are*. Nothing in life is black and white. So sorry to be trite, darling, but as David once said, all true things are trite. They have been said very often, because human experience has shown them to be true ... ' There was some truth in it, Carter admitted to himself and to Hazel, but he commented on the results of the prison riot: people like Max Sampson murdered, Mac driven berserk – and the poor fellow couldn't even see his wife now, because he could not go down or be taken down to the visiting-room and visitors were not allowed up in the ward – and the toughest of the rioters, a man called Swede (although he was short and dark) had got what he demanded, a cell all to himself. Ostensibly this was because Swede was a 'riot-suspect', and as such had his number on a red shingle outside his cell; but that made no sense, because he associated every day with other inmates in the shop where he worked, and in the corridor of his cell block. He had got the private cell because he had demanded it, and the prison authorities were afraid of more trouble from him if they didn't give it to him.

David Sullivan moved to New York in the fourth year of Carter's sentence, and joined a firm of lawyers with offices in a new building on First Avenue. Hazel had taken her degree at Adelphi, had considered a job overseas and sending Timmie to school in Switzerland, but had given this up in favour of a job at a child welfare agency in Manhattan on the West Side. Carter had no doubt at all that her decision to stay in the United States was based on the fact that Sullivan had moved to New York.

She came down to see him three or four times a year, and stayed at the only hotel in Bowman, The Southerner. Money was no problem now, but Hazel's time was, because of her job. Some of her visits were for no more than a weekend. She wrote him two or three times a week. There were often pictures of Timmie in the envelopes, and Carter had a scrapbook of photographs, mostly of Timmie, several of Hazel, and a few of the friends Hazel had met in New York and talked about in her letters: the Elliotts who lived in Locust Valley, Long Island; Jeremy Sutter; a man Hazel had met at Adelphi who had married a girl called Susan; people whom Carter was not interested in but whose pictures he pasted in his book nevertheless. Their old friends, Blanche and Eddie Langauer, for instance, Hazel never mentioned. Eddie and Blanche had written to him twice in the first year of Carter's imprisonment, and Carter had answered. Later, the Langauers had moved to Dallas, because of Eddie's work. They had not written for a long while. And so it had gone with other New York friends, a startled, sympathetic letter or two, and then silence.

Timmie was now eleven. Carter got two letters a month from him on the average, but he felt they were rather squeezed out. Things would be better when he finally saw Timmie, Carter thought. Things would be difficult, of course, but he intended to play it cool, not expect his son to fling his arms around him or expect them to become buddies in a week or a month.

Carter now had a glass front on his bookcase with a door that locked: too many men had been borrowing his books without his permission. But he lent his books to ward patients, if they asked for them. Among his books Carter now had Swift, Voltaire, Stanley Kunitz, Robbe-Grillet, Balzac, a volume of the

Encyclopaedia Britannica that had part of the E's and part of the F's that had been mysteriously left by a departing ward patient, an American dictionary, a manual on plumbing. All these books he had read through. He kept a locked, flat wooden kit of draftsmen's pens and compasses under the mattress of his bed (the springs sagged, and the box filled out the hollow somewhat). His drawings of remembered machinery and machinery that he invented he kept in a cardboard letter-holder on top of his books in his bookcase. He had overcome the handicap of weak thumbs, so far as drawing went. He mentioned this to Hazel – it was important in regard to a future job – but Hazel still talked about an operation. She had discussed his thumbs with a hand specialist in New York. Carter knew he had let the matter slide through the years and knew that Hazel knew this, too. He was used to his thumbs now, but he did not say this to Hazel in so many words.

In the fifth year of his sentence, he tried to stop the morphine entirely. He backslid innumerable times, mainly because he did not think the situation very serious. His withdrawal symptoms were no more than sweats and jitteriness on the second or third day, for about twelve hours, which Carter considered a mild form of suffering. He proved he could go two months or more without morphine, if he took a milder pain-killer like Demerol. The pain in his thumbs was less. In the sixth year, he did without morphine for eleven months. He had an important objective in this, because once he got out of prison, morphine would not be so easily obtained. He also wanted to be able to tell Hazel that he could do without it completely.

The hundred-dollar-a-week payment of Mr Drexel had stopped when the time that Carter would have been working for Triumph, ten more months, had run out. There had been two more building jobs scheduled after the Fremont school. Mr Drexel promised to write for Carter a letter of the highest recommendation, but said he would wait until Carter was out of prison so that the letter would be 'up to date' when Carter looked for his next job. Carter was rather amused. 'Up to date' meant up to date of end of prison stretch. This man can be 'highly recommended' as an endurer of prison stretches. Carter was going to be out by December. A 'good conduct' grading for his service in the hospital ward had removed three years and several months from the ten years he might have served.

Dr Cassini praised Carter effusively in his report, which he showed to Carter. David Sullivan had also written for him. So did Mr Drexel, at Carter's request. Carter would be home for Christmas that year, and, unlike so many men who had to start from the bottom up again, he would have a wife, a child, a home, and money. He would be able to give them presents with his own hands, wrapped presents that no one else had opened, whose contents nobody but himself knew. By 1 December, in fact, he would be in the apartment in New York with Hazel, a free man with a good conduct record, though he had killed a man in prison. In the months after the riot, Carter had often thought some inmate with an unpleasant face might approach him in the carpentry shop, in a cell block when he was delivering medicine, anywhere, and say, 'I hear you're the guy who killed Whitey,' and then 'pop goes the weasel', as Dr Cassini would say. But things had not turned out that way.

12

On 1 December, a Friday, at 8 in the morning, Carter was driven down the unpaved road to the gates of the State Penitentiary and passed through them. Carter wore the brown suit of discharged or furloughed prisoners, and he had in his pocket the ten-dollar bill with which the prison sent its released men into the world.

Carter was let down at the bus-stop in Gurney, a tiny town about two miles from the prison.

'Don't forget the parole officer,' the guard said.

'I won't.' Carter was to report tomorrow at the parole officer's in New York.

The bus came almost immediately. The day was sunny and chill. Carter rode in the bus with his eyes wide open, as he had ridden in the car with the driver. He blinked frequently, and tried to stop staring at everything by looking down at his hands, but after a few seconds he would be gawking out the window again, or staring at a black straw hat with small, red-feathered birds on it just inches in front of him, or at the two boys who were standing, hanging on to the luggage rack, laughing and talking in Southern accents. They looked about fifteen. In only three years,

Timmie would be as nearly a man as these boys were, his voice changing, interested in girls.

In Fremont, there was a three-hour wait. He sent a telegram to Hazel telling her his time of arrival. Hazel had wanted to come down to the prison to meet him when he got out, but he had begged her not to. Carter spent the three hours wandering in the streets around the air terminal.

Hazel had sent him a money order for one hundred dollars, and the prison had cashed it for him that morning. He spent fifty-seven dollars and ninety cents for his ticket. They served lunch on the plane, a small, regal tray of brown beef roast so thick it was a chunk, delicately browned potatoes, tomato slices that were perfect circles lying on lettuce, and for this there was a tiny paper cup of cream-coloured dressing. Carter opened the cup by pulling the paper tab with his teeth. He was awkward with the knife and fork, would have preferred to eat everything with the spoon, but he felt that the man beside him was watching him, that he might look to the man like what he was, an ex-convict, just sprung.

They touched down at Wilkes-Barre and Pittsburgh, and then they were at La Guardia, exactly on time. Carter saw Hazel and Timmie and also Sullivan, standing at the rail of a balcony above him as he walked across a hall with the other passengers. He waved, he smiled. Hazel was waving excitedly. Sullivan waved once, quietly, smiling, and Timmie shyly. All this Carter saw at a glance.

Hazel kissed him on the cheeks, then on the lips. She was crying. She was also laughing. Carter blinked awkwardly at the lights that seemed so bright, at the dazzling colour everywhere.

'How are you, Timmie?' Carter extended a hand to him.

Timmie glanced at the hand, then took it firmly. 'All right.'

Timmie's voice was sweet to Carter. It was strong, a little shrill, a boy's voice. When he had last heard it, it had been a baby's voice.

'I've got the car,' Hazel said. 'Are you hungry? I've got dinner for us at home.'

'Take my coat,' Sullivan said, unbuttoning his. He pressed it on Carter.

Carter was trembling from the cold, so he took it. His arms slid easily into the silk-lined sleeves.

Hazel drove out of the maze of La Guardia, over the Triboro Bridge. The car was a Morris that Hazel had had for a year. The lights of Manhattan were coming on in the dusk, and the city looked as big as an entire world, quite big enough for Carter.

'I'm not staying for dinner, by the way,' Sullivan said. 'I just came along to see you in.'

'You won't come up just for a drink, David?' Hazel said. They were approaching Thirty-eighth Street and Lexington.

'No, thanks. I'll see you soon, Phil,' Sullivan said as he got out. 'It's great to have you back.' His overcoat was over one arm. Carter had insisted that he take it back.

Then they were alone, the three of them. Hazel parked under a tree on East Twenty-eighth Street, saying she was in luck again about the parking space, that she often got this very spot. Carter touched the tree trunk with his palm. Then he realized that Timmie was struggling to get his suitcase from the car.

'I'll take that, Timmie.'

'No, I'm okay.' Timmie had to prove he could do it.

The suitcase was not heavy. It contained only his toilet articles, his photograph album, his French compositions and a mirror whose frame he had made in the carpentry shop. His books he had had sent days ago. He asked Hazel if they had arrived. They hadn't. Timmie would not let Carter take the suitcase even up the last flight of stairs. It was a handsome, once-private house, the banister and stairway were polished, the carpet on it new and clean. Hazel unlocked a door, pushed it open and said:

'Voilà. This is ours, darling.'

The lights were on. Carter went in first, as she wished him to do. Theirs. Gladioli in two large vases caught his eyes first. There was also a large rubber plant. A whole wall of books. Some of the furniture he recognized from Fremont, but most of it was new to him. Then he saw some ancient dark blue house-slippers of his in front of an easy chair, and he laughed.

'Those old antiques!'

Hazel laughed also.

Only Timmie was silent.

Hazel took him over the rest of the apartment, Timmie's room, their room, the bedroom, kitchen, bath. He could not say anything except, 'It's great.' He caught a glimpse of his foolishly smiling face in a mirror and looked away. He looked wrinkled and old and vaguely dirty. 'Can I have a bath before dinner?'

'You can have anything you want,' Hazel said, and gave him a long kiss.

The kiss made Carter a bit dizzy. He was afraid even to contemplate her. Or rather, he couldn't begin to. He was unbuttoning his prison suit jacket. He suddenly could not wait to get out of his clothes.

'Want me to hang something up for you?' Hazel asked.

Carter smiled and handed her his jacket. 'I want you to take these damned clothes and burn them.'

Five minutes later, when Carter was in the tub, she knocked on the door and brought him a scotch and soda with ice.

He dressed in the bedroom in the new white shirt she had laid out on the bed. The trousers on the bed were an old favourite pair of Daks. His shoes were old but unworn, and they still fitted, unlike the trousers. On the chest of drawers stood a photograph in a silver frame of himself and Hazel at a costume party given by the Langauers years ago. How many years? Seven or eight at least, Carter thought. In the photograph he was barefoot and dressed as an Hawaiian in a grass skirt, a lei and a straw hat, and was swinging Hazel out in a dance. Carter looked about twenty to himself and Hazel sixteen in her sari and with flowing hair much longer.

Hazel was in the kitchen, putting the finishing touches on the dinner. There was nothing he could do, Hazel said in answer to his question. Timmie could do anything she needed. She was basting a duck. He could smell the orange sauce for it. He thought suddenly of Max's remark, '... the *pièce de résistance* for tonight ... *canardeau à l'orange*, probably ...' He started to tell Hazel that, then thought better of it.

Timmie kept staring at him. His eyes were like his own, but his nose was like Hazel's, narrow, straight and not too long.

'Timmie, how about showing me some of your constructions?' Carter said.

Timmie squirmed, but he smiled with pleasure. 'All right.'

'Now?' Carter had noticed some mysterious forms under plastic covers in Timmie's room.

'After dinner,' Hazel said. 'We're almost ready. Want to open the wine, darling? Or – can you?' she asked, suddenly anxious.

'Oh, sure. This kind of thing,' Carter said, smiling. The cork came out straight. Carter took the bottle into the living-room. The table had been set near the fireplace while he was having his bath, and the fire had also been lit. Two red candles stood in wrought-iron sticks that were new to him.

He ate more of Hazel's mashed potatoes than of the duck, but she did not press him to eat.

'Terribly rich, I know, but I had to have something nice for tonight,' she said.

'Did you play baseball in that place?' Timmie asked.

'Well – yes. Some,' Carter said, though he hadn't. Timmie was looking at his hands.

Hazel talked of what they would do in the next days. Her office had made her a present of a week off, without pay, even though they were swamped with work as usual. She wanted to go to the Museum of Modern Art with him and Timmie, maybe tomorrow or Sunday. Then next week they must go shopping and buy Carter 'millions of things'. She liked going with him to buy his clothes, and Carter had always been pleased with her choices, and in fact he didn't like to buy as much as a tie without her. Then there were theatres, and a ballet company she had been waiting to see with him. Carter must meet Jeremy Sutter and his wife, who wanted to have them to dinner. And the people in Locust Valley, the Elliotts, had invited them for any weekend they chose in December.

'I've got to look for a job at some point,' Carter said.

'Don't even think of a job till after Christmas, darling. Nobody looks for a job at this time of year. Anyway, we're rich.' She took a bite of salad and smiled at him.

She was right, they were well off, Carter realized. In prison, being well off, quite well off, hadn't meant a thing. Now it suddenly did: the stereo set in the living-room, the furniture and books in the house, the freedom to take a trip to Europe if they chose, to send Timmie to a good prep school when he was thirteen or fourteen. Carter looked at his pretty wife and felt in a glow of happiness.

Hazel had bought a pair of pyjamas for him, though she said she had kept the best pairs of his old ones. He put on the new blue ones. Timmie had gone to bed around 10 with a solemn 'Good night, Daddy,' and no speeches about being glad to have him back, which was fine with Carter. Timmie was behaving the way he ought to, Carter thought, the way he felt, which was bound to be a little funny and shy and even suspicious and resentful: Carter knew he had caused Timmie a lot of shame. He had had no time to look at Timmie's constructions, because they had played music after dinner, Prokofiev and Mozart, whose string chords had been as rich in their way as the duck *à l'orange*, and after one side of each record, he simply had not been able to take any more.

There were two thick red books on the chest of drawers, and Carter crossed the bedroom to see their titles. They were law books. Sullivan's, of course. What were they doing in the bedroom? What were they doing in the house? Carter was vaguely ashamed of his rise of jealousy. If it were warranted, if there were anything between them, wouldn't Hazel have hidden the books? Then Carter found himself staring at the bed. If Sullivan had had an affair with her, he thought, he could kill Sullivan with pleasure. His thumbs began to hurt. He was clenching his fists. Carter went to the box of pills on the table by the bed. The pills were called Pananod, and Carter took about six a day. Dr Cassini had given him a prescription for some more on a blank piece of paper signed by him, and said if he was refused the pills, any doctor would give him a prescription for them. Dr Cassini had no personal prescription paper with his name and address on it, of course.

'Why aren't you in bed?' Hazel said when she came in. She was in a pale-yellow nightgown, barefoot, her hair loose.

'I was wandering around looking at everything,' he said.

'Aren't you tired?'

He got into bed with her. She put the light out. To embrace her was almost painful. And tears rolled out of his eyes like thawing ice. He was back home again.

13

The first two companies to which Carter applied for a job in January turned him down, the second admittedly because of the prison record, and Carter thought the first turned him down because of it, too, though they did not give this as a reason. Carter had been prepared for it, of course. There might be ten more such rejections, even twenty. Hazel wanted him to get a reference from the company he had worked for when he had last been in New York, but Carter was against it: their logical question would be, why didn't he use his last employer's reference, and where had he spent the last six years?

Timmie was back in school after the Christmas holidays. Hazel left the house every morning at 8.20 in order to be at her office by 9, and Carter sat around the house writing answers to the long advertisements for engineers that he found in the Sunday *Times* and *Herald-Tribune* and sometimes in the dailies of those papers. He went to a doctor twice a week, Dr Alexander MacKensie, who had been Hazel's doctor since her teens. He had also known Carter since he had been married to Hazel. Carter got liver extract and Vitamin C shots from him. He found himself much more tired since leaving prison, and he had had a cold since mid-December. The doctor said he was run down from a bad diet, and that after a month or so he should be feeling much better and putting on weight. The doctor also renewed his prescription for the Pananods, which he had been unable to obtain with Dr Cassini's piece of paper. The doctor asked him about the pain in his thumbs, and Carter said it had lessened in the last four years, but it was still there, enough to be annoying, practically enough to keep him awake at night unless he took something for it.

'Does your wife know it's this bad? She didn't say it hurt that much,' said Dr MacKensie.

'I suppose I didn't tell her it was this bad,' Carter said. 'She knows I still need pills.'

'You've been taking these Pananods for some time?'

'About a year. Before that I was on morphine. For four years or so in prison.'

Dr MacKensie frowned and shoved out his under lip. 'I saw the signs of it – when you had the paper on your hands. Also in your eyes.'

Then why hadn't he mentioned it, Carter thought, on the first visit, when he had balanced the two sheets of paper on the backs of his hands? Or when he had looked into his eyes with his light? 'Well, I don't take it now.'

'How much did you used to take per day?'

'Maybe eight grains. Sometimes less.' And sometimes more, he thought. He had taken what he needed. Twelve grains a day was considered the requirement of the average addict, Carter knew.

'You're bound to have had addiction symptoms, if it went on that long.'

'Yes, but not serious ones. I tried stopping it now and then. Two months at a time here and there, I didn't take any morphine. No shots at all for the last eleven months I was in prison.' He looked the doctor in the eye.

'But these have opium in them, the Pananods. It's the same thing,' said the doctor.

'They don't feel like morphine.'

Dr MacKensie smiled without amusement. 'Don't take more than four a day if you can help it.'

Many evenings, Hazel helped him by typing up his three-page résumé, which he included with each letter applying for a job. Her typing was much faster than his. Carter had the letter he had requested from Drexel. It said that Carter's work for the company had been of the 'finest calibre' and that his detention had been 'for reasons never satisfactorily proven'. It was a careful letter, meant to be shown to future employers, but Carter could not make himself send it. Hazel said he should have at least fifty photostats made of it to include with his résumé.

'The letter's too vague,' Carter said. 'To put it mildly. It sounds like somebody trying to apologize for me and not sticking his neck out much doing it.'

'But you're not getting anywhere like *this*.' Hazel turned around from the typewriter.

It was after midnight, and they were both tired. Carter had not been mentioning prison in his last several applications. He had in his first few, saying that he had served six years on a charge of embezzlement of which he was not guilty. If anyone were interested in hiring him, he thought, they could make some inquiries and find out the story for themselves – not that it would necessarily influence them in Carter's favour. Or, if they believed in the efficacy of the prison system, they could assume that six years had washed away his sins and criminal impulses, and that he would be as good or better than the next man now. Hazel had disapproved of his mentioning prison at all.

'Every employer wants to know what a man's last job was. All right, Triumph. What a name!' he said, smiling. 'That was six years ago. What've you been doing for the last six years? Well, sitting in prison. If I don't say it in a letter, I'll have to say it when they interview me. I bet the whole field is on to me now. One company tells the other. Watch out for Philip Carter.'

'All right, I'm not suggesting you hide anything. I just say include Drexel's letter. He was your last boss, after all.'

'Drexel can drop dead.'

Drexel did just that at the end of January, thus precluding any more favourable letter he might ever have written about Carter. He had been retired for two years, and he died of a stroke in his home near Nashville, Tennessee.

By mid-February, Carter was sending photostat copies of Drexel's letter with his job applications.

Hazel was going to keep her job, because she liked it, not because they needed the extra money. She told Carter not to be anxious. 'Six weeks are nothing to spend looking for a good job.'

Carter made an effort to play with Timmie in his room in the afternoons, if Timmie hadn't too much homework. Carter made an oil-pump model with one of Timmie's construction sets, which he thought Timmie rather treasured, as he did not dismantle it after a week as he usually did other constructions. Timmie still seemed a little formal with him, and remote. A few times, Carter noticed Timmie looking at his thumbs instead of the pieces that Carter was handling or talking about. Carter knew that Hazel had told Timmie something about his thumbs, because she had written him that she had, but it had been so many years ago, Carter had forgotten what she said. Carter asked her.

'I said you'd had an accident in prison.'

'It won't be very long till he guesses,' Carter said. 'He's growing up. You may as well tell him.'

'Why, darling? Let it go. I don't want you to tell him, either.'

'He's not a numbskull. He'll guess it.'

Hazel sighed and said nervously, 'Darling, let it go. Please.' She was brushing her hair at the dressing-table.

They were both about to go to bed. Carter realized he had spoken in a bitter tone and regretted it. They would be lying in bed in five minutes, and she would not be quite the same tonight. Every night, when Hazel lay in his arms, she gave him the feeling that he was the most important person in the world, that she adored him. This kept him alive as much as the beating of his own heart. It would not be quite like that tonight, because she had not liked the bitterness in his tone.

He stooped beside her and put his arm around her hips. 'You're right. I'm sorry, darling. I'll let it go.'

14

It was about a week later that Carter saw Gregory Gawill. Gawill had been waiting for him, obviously, though he said, on the side-walk a few doors from Carter's house, 'Well, Phil! What a surprise!' and he pretended that he had just been walking along the street. 'You live here?'

'Yes.' Gawill could have found that out simply by looking in the telephone book, Carter thought, and he no doubt had.

'Long time no see. How long have you been out?'

'Oh – three or four months.' The years had changed Gawill a little, too, and for the worse, Carter saw. He was heavier and coarser. But his clothes still had their flashily prosperous look.

'Well, how about a drink? Or a coffee, if it's too early for a drink?' He slapped Carter's arm.

'I'm on my way to the post office.' Carter gestured with some letters he had in his hand.

'I'll walk with you. You're not working now?'

'Not just yet,' Carter said.

'I might be able to put you on to a couple of things.'

Carter gave a non-committal grunt.

'Seriously, Phil, one of the firms we're supplying is looking for an engineer. In Long Island. I could find out what kind of salary they're –'

'I wouldn't want to work in Long Island.'

'Oh.'

Carter had no need to go to the post office, his letters had stamps on them, but because he had said he had to go, he bought two dollars' worth of five-cent stamps and a few airmail stamps at a window. Gawill was still hanging around.

'Well, Greg, I've got to be off.'

'Oh, come on. You haven't got five minutes for a coffee? I had something I wanted to tell you. Something I think would interest you.'

Carter disliked the idea of sitting anywhere with him, and at the same time he was curious. It might be worthwhile, he thought, to find out what Gawill was thinking these days. 'All right.'

They went into a bar on a corner of Twenty-third and Third Avenue. Carter ordered a beer, Gawill a Scotch and water.

'I suppose you're seeing a lot of David Sullivan?' Gawill asked, rubbing his big nose with a finger.

'Not a lot.'

'That crud. He sticks his neck out so far, one of these days he's going to get it. So far he's been getting away with murder. It won't last for ever.' Gawill's resentment was strong and real. He might have been mumbling to himself. 'Nosing into my business.' Gawill chuckled and looked at Carter. 'Well, you see how far it got him. Nowhere. He couldn't pin anything on me, no matter how hard he tried, and he sure tried.'

Carter sipped his beer.

'I'll never get over his pretending to be trying to help you, when he was fooling around with your wife. I don't see how you can get over it, either. I don't see how you can even bear to see the guy – socially.' He lifted his angry eyes to Carter.

'Let it go, will you, Greg?'

'But you are still seeing him, aren't you? – My God, a man who follows your wife all the way up to New York – Well!' Gawill shifted. 'I'm not blaming your wife. A woman gets lonely, okay. So does a man. It's the false friend bit.'

Carter could have hit him. 'Would you stop talking about my wife?'

'All right. But he had an affair with her for four solid years. I don't think you know that, and you ought to know that.'

'That is not true.'

Gawill leaned across the table and poked with his forefinger. 'It is true. Wake up, Phil. Maybe your wife won't – She doesn't want to tell you, naturally. Sullivan wouldn't tell you, either, he'd go on pretending to be the best friend you've got in the world. What a friend, ha!'

Carter's heart was beating faster. 'Is that the interesting thing you had to tell me?'

'Frankly yes. I hate to see a man be a goon. Sullivan's making a goon out of you. He sets himself up as a friend of yours, when for Christ's sake you've got every reason to beat him up or even kill him.'

It was the bitterness that gave Gawill away. So much bitterness couldn't come because Sullivan had had an affair with Hazel, or because Sullivan might be a false friend, but because Sullivan had done Gawill some damage. 'I can understand you're not very fond of Sullivan, because he knocked you out of a couple of jobs, didn't he?'

'Ah-h. Tried to. He just made a mess, nothing else. Just an unpleasant stink here and there. The stink came from Sullivan, not Gregory Gawill.'

Carter smiled a little, and saw that Gawill didn't like the smile. 'Well, Greg, I'll be going on. Thanks for the beer.'

Gawill looked surprised. 'When'll I see you again? – Listen,

Phil.' He frowned. He stood up and caught Carter's right arm. 'You think I'm telling you a lot of crap about Sullivan and your wife, don't you? You think I'm exaggerating, maybe. All the time she was going to school in Long Island, and heading straight for Sullivan's apartment when she got out in the afternoon? I had a couple of guys keeping watch on Sullivan, just like he had on me. I know what went on, with your wife using his keys to get in, and then leaving his place just before six to go home and fix the kid's dinner, maybe.' Gawill shook his head in disgust, then gripped Carter's sleeve harder. 'And I can tell you something else, too.'

'Come on, Greg, let go.' Carter pulled his arm away and went off.

'It's still going on,' Gawill yelled after him.

Carter walked quickly, and when he finally looked around to see where he was, he found he was way over on the East Side at Avenue A. He turned around and walked towards home. It's all a lot of lies and exaggerations, Carter said to himself. A child could see through Gawill.

15

February fourteenth was Hazel's birthday. Sullivan had asked them to cocktails at his house, and then they were to go with eight or ten other people to a Japanese restaurant. Carter left the house that day shortly after Hazel and Timmie, eager to pick up his present for Hazel, a silver-backed brush and comb and mirror, at a shop on Fifth Avenue. They were antiques. He had found them only last week, after much searching of the city for what he wanted, and the initialling, he was told, could be finished only by the fourteenth. He was at the shop by 9.30 a.m., expecting to be told that the set would not be ready until afternoon, but it was there and done: H. O. C. in graceful letters. The letters struck him as a trifle large, but they were not large enough to inspire him to have them changed and make the present late. The brush and comb and hand mirror went into a white box, bedded in tissue. Around this went a red ribbon, and then the box was slipped into a white paper bag with gold printing on it and handed to him. Carter went out and strolled down Fifth Avenue. He bought two dozen red roses, and took them back to the apartment.

By now the post had come, and Carter had two more

rejections, one from Trippe Industrials in the Chrysler Building, which Carter had held out some hope for. The letter said that the position had been filled since his application. Carter bit the inside of his cheek in shame. He remembered that he had included Drexel's letter in the Trippe application.

Late that afternoon, Hazel called. The train she was supposed to meet at 4.20 p.m. was going to be an hour late, and she wouldn't have time to come home and dress before Sullivan's party. Could Carter bring her black dress – the one with the zipper in back, not the side – and she would dress at Sullivan's?

'I'll just take it in another room and put it on. I can't go like this. I'm in a skirt and blouse.'

'Sure, Hazel. I'll bring it.'

'And my gold scarf. It's a long one like a stole, I don't know if you know it. Bright yellow. It's in the third drawer of the chest, third from the bottom.'

'Okay.'

'Thanks, darling.' Her voice had become soft and low, in a way Carter knew well. 'How are you?'

'Well – I wish you were coming home. I'm okay.'

She explained that the two children who were arriving were on her case load, and she couldn't ask anyone else in the office to meet them.

He hung the dress she wanted on its hanger on the door of the front hall closet, so that he could not possibly forget it, then went for the scarf. The drawer was full of folded delicate-looking slips, stacks of scarves, stockings. As he reached for the yellow scarf, his hand struck something firm behind them. They were his letters from prison, all on identical paper, a single thick sheet folded in half, then in thirds to fit the prison's windowed envelopes. Hazel had put them in bundles of thirty or so with a rubber band around them, and then had stacked these and tied them all together. He put his hand out and laid his palm flat on the two-foot-long row of them. In doing this, his fingers touched another row behind them, half concealed by some of her clothes. Another row as long as the first.

'Good God,' he said.

It was enough to fill six books, he supposed. Gibbon could have written *The Decline and Fall* in that amount of prose, or Cervantes *Don Quixote*, and all he had done was write a lot of griping or lovesick letters. But it was the idea of all the time they meant that overwhelmed him. Was it any wonder the world did not forget it, either? Carter looked at the photograph of Hazel and him in the silly party costume. He stared hard at it, then closed his eyes and turned away with the scarf.

He was not in a good mood when he set out for Sullivan's apartment. He had shaved and dressed carefully to please Hazel: his new dark-blue suit, the dark-blue and dark-red tie she liked best, a white shirt, black shoes. Everything he had on, nearly everything he owned now, was new. He carried her dress and scarf in the white bag her silver set had come in. Timmie had also been disappointed when he came in at 4.30, because his mother was not coming home, and Carter made a rather unsuccessful attempt to say something cheerful. He had said to Timmie that they would wake him up when they came home and they would have a little party. Timmie had bought a white slip with brown embroidery for Hazel, quite an expensive item, Carter thought, for a boy with a three-dollar allowance and a taste for sodas, but Timmie had refused Carter's offer of ten dollars a few days ago. The present had been bought when Carter offered. That afternoon, Timmie solemnly went to his room and got his present for Hazel, already wrapped, and put it beside Carter's presents and the roses on the hi-fi. Timmie was going to his friend Ralph Underwood's house for dinner.

Sullivan welcomed Carter at the apartment door. There was a din of conversation from the living-room behind him. 'Well,

well, the fashion plate again,' Sullivan said. 'Come in. Where's Hazel?'

Carter explained why she would be late, and Sullivan took the bag from Carter and carried it into his bedroom while Carter hung his coat. Then he went into the living-room, greeted the four or five people he knew – the Elliotts were here, Jeremy Sutter and his wife Susan, a pleasant middle-aged man named John Dwight, who was a friend of Sullivan's. Some of these introduced him to the others, not a single one of whose names stuck with Carter. He was too aware of all of them staring at him, because he was so recently out of prison. Although Hazel and David had once said, 'The new people you meet don't have to know a thing about it,' that wasn't the way things worked. The word got around, somehow.

This was only the third time that year that he had seen Sullivan. He knew that Hazel was deliberately not inviting him, or not accepting Sullivan's invitations that possibly Sullivan extended over the telephone to Hazel in her office, because she knew he did not want to see much of him. This decrease in their social exchanges had made no change in Sullivan, Carter thought, on the few occasions when they had seen him. Tonight he was confident and smiling, circulating smoothly among his guests, seeing that their drinks were all right, that everybody had a cheese canapé while they were still hot. Sullivan had a taste for Greek and Roman marble pieces, and here and there in a book-case was a marble head, a marble foot, a vase, a fragment of a Greek inscription. He had bought these on a trip to Greece, he said. His rugs were orientals.

'How's the job situation?' Sullivan asked.

'Nothing yet. Still trying,' Carter said as casually as he could.

'That fellow Butterworth isn't back yet. I called up yesterday about him.'

Butterworth worked for a firm of engineers that Carter had heard of – Jenkins and Field. Butterworth was in California on business. Sullivan had said several times that he thought Butterworth could get Carter into the firm, but Butterworth just wasn't around to do it, and had begun to seem to Carter like someone who didn't exist.

Carter was relieved when Hazel arrived. She greeted everyone, met the new people in her easy, graceful way, without insisting on changing her clothes first, as many women would have done, Carter thought. He watched with pleasure the faces of the men who had not met her before, watched the way they all jumped up from their chairs, no matter how deeply sunk in them they had been, because Hazel was a pretty woman. When Hazel came to Carter he was smiling a little, but it was a real smile, his first that day.

'Happy birthday, darling. How are you?'

'Bushed, but I'll feel better out of these clothes. Timmie okay?'

Carter nodded, as dazed as the men who had just met her, and then she disappeared.

Sullivan followed her.

Carter sipped his second drink.

When Sullivan came back, after about two minutes, he beckoned to Carter and said in a low tone, 'I heard some news today via a very long grapevine. Gawill is back up north. Working or connected with some pipe company in Long Island. His boss is a man called Grasso who owns some crummy apartment houses in Long Island, a slum landlord, it sounds like. Slum landlords always have a couple of sidelines.'

Carter felt only a quick warmth in his blood at Gawill's name, then indifference. 'Well?' Carter shrugged and took a gulp of his drink.

'He knows you're out.'

'Oh? – He's working for a pipe company? Not for smoking, I presume.'

'Ha! No, the pipes they put underground. Gas and sewage and such.' Sullivan dragged the words out drily. 'I was interested that he's taken the trouble to know you're out. Or find out. It wouldn't surprise me if he tried to get in touch with you.' Sullivan looked at Carter.

'Why?'

'I dunno. But I thought I'd warn you. I don't imagine you want to see him.'

'No, I don't.' Hazel was just coming in then, and they both turned to her.

Carter would have liked to stay by Hazel's side for the duration of the cocktail party, but he forced himself to mix with the others. Sullivan stayed near Hazel, however, or she near him, it was hard to tell which. They looked absolutely at ease together, Carter thought, as if they always had something to talk about, which was probably only natural since they had spent so much time together while he was in prison. Nearly as much, he realized with a sudden shock, as he and Hazel had spent together before he went to prison. Just seven years for him versus six for Sullivan. Sullivan was leaning on the back of the easy chair in which Hazel was sitting, listening to her and nodding seriously, and now and again Hazel glanced up at him with a look quick and brief, but it seemed to Carter of such intimacy and familiarity that it was obvious that they had slept together and many times. He'd ask her tonight, Carter decided, simply ask her if she'd ever slept with him. Then he realized that he was feeling his drink, and that he must not ask her that question on her birthday, or maybe any other day. He had no doubt that Hazel loved him. But he also had no doubt that Sullivan was in love with her.

At the Japanese restaurant, they drank warmed saki. They sat on cushions around a long low table, and once more Carter was separated from Hazel, who was once more beside Sullivan.

'Et pour vous, monsieur?' said the man on Carter's left, holding the napkin-wrapped bottle of saki.

'Oui, avec plaisir,' Carter said, and held his little cup.

'Vous parlez français?'

'Oui.'

And from then on they spoke French, and Carter talked to no one else. His name was Lafferty – Carter asked him his name, with apologies for not having remembered it when he was introduced – and he had worked for two years in Paris for his firm, which sold bottling machinery. They talked about the French character, the joys of life in France, the ravages of unhappy love affairs.

'Each separation,' he said, 'each parting, strikes a blow and takes something away, as the sea does when it hits a cliff. A man can stand just so many, like a cliff. One day he is small and thin, and then he is nothing, finished.'

Mr Lafferty was not talking about hopeless love affairs, just separations. This semi-poetry from a businessman was a pleasant surprise to Carter. Or perhaps what he was saying sounded better and more profound in French. Or perhaps it was that talking with Mr Lafferty reminded him of happy moments with Max. Then in a pause in the conversation, as Mr Lafferty spoke in English to a woman on his left, Carter looked over and saw Sullivan laughing heartily – yet the laugh was still restrained in volume, suitable and proper to the environment, just like Sullivan – and Sullivan touched Hazel's shoulder, pressed it, before he let it go. Carter wondered if Sullivan had ever made a mistake in his life, ever done anything on impulse that he regretted? And suddenly, Carter remembered his uncle and aunt lecturing him when he was about fourteen for letting things slip through his fingers. A tennis racquet once, that he had lent to a school friend. A trenchcoat. A dinner-suit when he was in college. No, he wasn't very efficient or practical or well organized, like Sullivan. Finally, his supreme act of carelessness, signing the receipts for Wallace Palmer, which had netted him six years in prison. To be so trusting was stupid. Sullivan would never have been like that. He had the lawyer's mind: don't make a move unless your interests are covered. Then Carter realized, and it was as if a bullet hit him, that he had also trusted Hazel with Sullivan. Suppose he had been a sublime idiot there, topping even his Wallace Palmer folly?

Hazel suddenly looked at him. 'Phil! Are you okay?'

His face must be pink, he knew from its heat. He pushed his palm against his forehead nervously. 'I'm all right,' he said. He hated Sullivan for looking at him, too. He reached for a glass of water and found there wasn't any. But by that time, Hazel wasn't watching him. Carter drank his saki.

'What did David give you?' Carter asked when they got home that evening. Hazel had the white bag with her other clothes in it, and the bag was heavier. Carter had carried it from the car up the stairs.

'A book that I wanted. It's Aubrey Menen's book on Rome. I haven't opened it yet.'

Carter had supposed Sullivan's present would be something more personal than a book.

Timmie woke up and came in in his pyjamas. He threw his arms around Hazel and said, 'Happy birthday, Mummy!'

'Thank you, darling. My goodness, it looks like Christmas,' she said, looking at the presents on the hi-fi. 'And what wonderful roses! Which of you do I thank for that?'

'Both.' Carter smiled at his son.

Hazel loved the brush and comb and mirror, and she did not think the initials were too big. Carter had also given her candy and soap and handkerchiefs. They had a nightcap while she opened the presents, and Timmie had a glass of chocolate milk.

He could not sleep that night. The liquor he had drunk might as well have been benzedrine. And his thumbs ached. He longed for a needle full of morphine. Around 3 a.m., he got up gently and went into the bathroom to take one of the Pananods. Then he came back in the dark.

'Darling – you can't sleep?' Hazel said.

It was suddenly unreal to Carter, Hazel's voice in the darkness, the room in which they both were, presumably, the whole evening, Sullivan, Max. Yet Max seemed more alive and real than any of the rest of them, even himself. 'No,' Carter said tentatively, as if he replied to a question in a dream, just to keep the dream going.

'Put on the light.'

He put on the light and blinked. It did nothing to dispel the unreality.

'Sit down, darling. What's troubling you?'

He sat down on the edge of the bed. 'Sullivan.'

'Oh, darling.' She closed her eyes and frowned, turned her head away for a moment. 'Phil, if it'll make things any easier – we don't have to see him any more.'

Her tone sounded as if that would be a nearly superhuman sacrifice, but she would make it. 'No, I wouldn't want you to do that,' he said, but not in the light tone he tried for, and he saw her expression change to wariness.

'Then – I think it's time you stopped making scenes, don't you? Like tonight?'

'I didn't know I made a scene.'

'I thought you were going to explode – in the restaurant – just because David touched my shoulder once. Everybody noticed it. You looked as if you hated him.'

So she was aware of the shoulder-touching too. 'I don't think everybody noticed it. That's just not true.'

'And you hardly said good night to him. That's not very nice, considering he was the host and took us all out to dinner – in my honour.'

'But I did say good night to him.' Carter remembered, though, that he hadn't thanked him.

'I think you're behaving rather childishly.'

Carter stood up, suddenly angry. 'I don't think you're behaving like a wife.'

'Just what are you talking about?' Hazel sat up.

'I'd just like to know one thing,' Carter said quickly. 'Did you have an affair with him while I was in prison?'

'No! – Shut the door. I don't want Timmie to hear this charming conversation.'

Carter pushed the door shut. 'I think you did, that's why I ask.'

'Ridiculous,' she said, but he saw her waver and give ground.

'I can tell it!'

She gave a long, shuddering sigh. Then she reached for a cigarette. Her hand was shaking as she held her lighter to it. 'I think it may help,' she said, not looking at him, 'if I tell you I did have an affair with him. It lasted all of three weeks. Or rather two weeks and four days to be perfectly exact.'

Carter felt breathless now. 'When?'

'Four years ago. More than that. It was a few weeks after the second rejection, the Supreme Court second rejection.' Now she looked at him. 'I was very unhappy then. I didn't know what I should do with my life – or what would become of yours. I loved David in a way, yes. But the affair didn't help and I felt worse. I felt ashamed of myself and I broke it off. I couldn't even see David – for about a month afterwards.'

He was still barely breathing, standing motionless. 'Now at least I know.'

'Yes, you know. You know that I'm sorry about it. You know that it can't happen again.'

'Why can't it? Why do you say that?'

'If you think it can, then you don't understand. You don't understand *me*.'

'I'm beginning to,' he said. 'Why can't it?'

She didn't answer, only looked at him.

'You say you loved him. Do you still love him?'

'Aren't I here with you?'

'Yes, but if I weren't here, weren't in the picture?'

'Oh, Phil –'

'I asked you a question. If I weren't here.'

'Since you ask, yes. If you weren't here – if you died in prison, for instance, the way your friend did, then yes, I'd undoubtedly have married David. Timmie likes him, too. He's easy to be with, easier than you're becoming lately.'

Carter tore off his pyjama top. He went to the closet, winced for an instant as his eyes fell on the costume party photograph, which he felt like tearing up, then jerked the cord of his pyjama pants.

'Where are you going?' Her voice was alarmed.

'Out for a walk.'

'At four in the morning? – Phil, you're not going to do something crazy like go to see David, are you?'

'I'm going out for a walk, Hazel, I have to.' He was dressed in a flash, doubling his shirt over and not bothering to button it. He walked out of the bedroom, left the door open, and got his overcoat from the front closet by feeling for it in the dark. Then he opened the front door and went out, started to close it, then opened it on an impulse and listened. It was like part of the bad dream coming true, the clicking of the telephone dial as Hazel dialled Sullivan's number on the bedroom extension. To warn him? To have a comforting chat? Carter might have stood there in the dark and perhaps heard what she said, something of what she said, but he could guess it, anyway. He closed the door and went down the steps. There was nothing to do on such a night but walk.

He walked until the dawn came up, and it did him a great deal of good, the walk and watching the dawn. He would say to Hazel, 'I'm glad you told me, and we don't have to mention it again, as far as I'm concerned.' Or something like that. Or maybe it was better to make no speeches at all.

16

A couple of mornings later, Carter found a letter from Gawill in the box downstairs. Somehow he knew it was from Gawill before he opened it. It was a small white business envelope with no return address, the handwriting tall and thin and a little wobbly. Then Carter noticed the Long Island postmark, barely legible. Carter was on his way out to buy a couple of things Hazel had forgotten on her shopping list, but he climbed the stairs again to read Gawill's letter in the apartment. It said:

Dear Phil,
    I feel like finishing what I started to tell you. I had my men watching Sullivan's apartment and the apartment he had before that on Fifty-third Street. I guess you know about Fifty-third Street when your wife was plainly living with him. I'm talking about the four years after that. Even your son ought to know about it, because kids aren't so dumb. I had the feeling you didn't believe me the other day about any of this, and considering what I've put up with from Sullivan that's annoying. Maybe you don't know that your wife went twice (maybe more, I mean we saw her

twice) to Sullivan's apartment in the last *month*? Do you think I'd be putting this all down on paper if it wasn't true? Did your wife tell you she saw Sullivan twice in the last month by herself? I bet she didn't. Is he still stringing her along, saying he'll get a job for you or something like that for a little attention she might give him? Probably. That's like Sullivan. It's still going on, Phil. Wake up. Proof you want, I guess. Okay. I've got the notes of my boys and I've got a tape record of conversations Sullivan had with your wife – I wasn't after those but they came in. They happened about six months ago, some later. You are welcome to hear them when you want. I can also have one of the boys snap her picture going in his house any time *now* if you want it.

I don't like anybody to think I'm a liar. Address at top of paper in case you want to get in touch with me. All the best,

Greg

'One of the boys', as if Gawill had a paid staff. Gawill had delusions of grandeur. He glanced at the multi-numbered, Jackson Heights address again, plus the telephone number, then he tore the letter up and stuck it in the garbage pail among the breakfast orange rinds.

David Sullivan telephoned that afternoon around 3 and said that his friend Butterworth was back in New York, and that Carter ought to call him for an appointment.

'There's something else I want to talk to you about, Phil. Are you free today around six?'

'Sure, David. Want to come over here?'

'I'd rather talk to you alone. Would you mind coming to my place?'

Carter said he would come. He felt uneasy after he had hung

up. Was this going to be another confession? A confession perhaps of a four-year affair? He forced himself to go briskly to the
telephone directory – which Hazel preferred to keep on the floor
of the hall closet, because she thought it unsightly in the living-
room – look up the number of Jenkins and Field, Inc., and call
Mr Butterworth.

Mr Butterworth sounded very friendly, and they made an
appointment for Friday at 10 o'clock.

Hazel usually got home just before 6, and Carter told Timmie
to tell her that he was going to David's and ought to be back a
little after 7.

'Mummy's not going?' Timmie asked.

'No. David just wants to talk to me about something. A job,
I think. Tell Mummy that.'

'Can I go?'

Carter turned at the door. The boy's eagerness hurt him.
Timmie was very fond of Sullivan. 'Why, Timmie? It's not going
to be any fun – just talking business.'

'Well, if it's just for an *hour*,' Timmie said, still pleading.

'No, Timmie. Sorry. It's business, and I've got to take off now
or I'll be late.'

Carter took a taxi to Sullivan's house. He rang the bell
marked Sullivan, and went in when David pressed the release
button. Sullivan was on the third floor and he had the floor
through. As in his and Hazel's house, there were only three other
apartments in the building.

Sullivan greeted him at the door, took his coat and asked if he
would like a drink.

'I suppose. Thanks. Not too strong.'

Sullivan went to the bar-cart in a corner of his living-room.

Carter waited, watching him.

'I had a phone call from Gawill,' Sullivan said, handing Carter
his drink. He also had a drink for himself. 'A very nasty phone

call. He said he'd had a talk with you.' Sullivan looked at him. Tenseness made his narrow face look thinner. He was also pale.

'Yes. It was a nasty little talk we had, too.'

'He told me about it. Listen, Phil –' Then he stopped, and stared into the fireless fireplace as if he were trying to gather up his thoughts or his courage. 'Hazel called me – late Monday night. Her birthday. She was pretty upset. She said she told you – about us.' Sullivan turned and looked at Carter.

'Yes, she did.'

'She told you the truth. I'm sorry, Phil –'

'Oh, it's over, it's over,' Carter said impatiently. 'I think Hazel can weather it. Or all of us.'

'I'm sure you can,' Sullivan said solemnly. 'But I understand Gawill told you something else. Something that's not true. Something about its lasting four years.'

'Yes.'

'That isn't true.'

Carter only looked at him, but Sullivan was waiting for him to say something, to say he believed him. 'Well, I didn't tell Hazel I saw Gawill.'

'I know. She –' Sullivan stopped.

She would have told me, Carter knew Sullivan had started to say. Carter took a big gulp of his drink. Then he tried to control his anger. Sullivan might not be the picture of virtue, but Gawill was a lot worse. 'I didn't believe Gawill,' Carter said.

'Good.' Sullivan's shoulders relaxed visibly. 'It's a hell of a nasty story and it's insulting to Hazel.' He stood a little taller, as if he were Hazel's champion.

Was four years so much nastier than three weeks, Carter wondered? He supposed so.

'You're taking all this very well, Phil,' Sullivan said.

Was he? Carter shrugged. 'I love Hazel. And anyway – I

suppose this isn't the Victorian Age any more, is it?' As soon as he said it, he felt it was.

'There's nothing Gawill won't stoop to. I don't think this is the end by any means. Especially if he sees it doesn't get results.'

'What do you mean by results?'

'Gawill hates my guts, as I've told you. He'd love you to beat me up – or worse. He'd love you to make a big stink and drag my name around – you know, in the firm where I work. You may think stories like this can't hurt a professional man today, but they can.'

Carter saw that Sullivan was mainly concerned about himself, his career. It seemed contemptible. 'Well, I'm not going to do that,' Carter said. 'Gawill himself might, I suppose.'

'Yes, he might. I don't know what he's waiting for. Well, he was waiting to see you, of course. Do you know what he told me?' Sullivan said with a short laugh. 'He told me you were blind mad when he told you about – told you that it had gone on for four years. Said you threatened to kill me.'

Carter watched him carefully.

'I'm beginning to think I'd better hire a bodyguard.'

Sullivan said it as if he meant it. Carter realized that he was not much interested in the subject, in Sullivan's physical safety. He realized something more, that he wished Sullivan *were* out of the picture. In a prison, Carter thought, in the jungle law of a prison, if a man knew that another inmate had slept with his wife, that inmate might be found mysteriously dead in a corridor one day.

'Why are you looking at me like that? You don't believe me?' Sullivan asked.

'Well, yes, I suppose I do.'

'You see, Phil, you've got an interest in this, too. Gawill would love to get one of his tough boys to kill me – and somehow pin it on you. I've said that before. Look at what he's doing now, trying to work you up to it. You see that, don't you?'

'Yes, I see that.'

Then there was a silence, while Sullivan frowned and strolled around the room, as if he were going to say something else. Carter sat down. He felt somehow quite secure. It amused him to see Sullivan anxious about his life. It was something new to Sullivan. It would not have been new to Carter. 'Did you hear from Gawill today, by any chance?'

'No. Why? Did you?'

'No,' Carter said calmly, and flicked his cigarette ash into a tray.

Sullivan was staring at him, as if he were afraid to ask any more questions. Obviously, Sullivan was afraid Gawill had said something more to him. And Carter thought it very likely that Gawill had called up Sullivan today or yesterday and told him that he had sent an informative letter to Philip Carter.

'All this mess stirred up,' Sullivan said, 'because I was trying to –' He shook his head. 'I might as well not even have tried. It didn't give me all that satisfaction just to take Gawill down a few rungs. That's all I did.'

Sullivan was trying to say his life was in danger, because he had been trying to get him out of prison. But why keep repeating it, if it were true? And Sullivan's activities hadn't shortened Carter's sentence by a single day.

'I don't expect to have any more conversations with Gawill,' Carter said, getting up.

Sullivan asked him about Butterworth, and asked him to give him a ring after the interview on Friday and tell him how things went. Then Carter left.

Carter told Hazel that Sullivan had wanted to brief him for the Butterworth interview.

'You're looking more cheerful tonight,' Hazel said. 'I hope it goes like a dream on Friday.'

'A dream,' Carter repeated. He was standing in the kitchen,

watching her pour meringue on top of a lemon pie. She wore an apron, a tweed skirt, a short-sleeved white blouse, and her hair was tied back with a thin black ribbon, and a few hairs had slipped out at one side. Carter remembered watching her in their kitchen in New York years ago, then in Fremont, now here. He frowned. His vision now was a little sullied, because he knew she had been with Sullivan. It wasn't his moral sense that was disturbed, Carter thought, just his image of Hazel as some dazzling goddess, invincibly strong, who could do no evil. He could weather it, just as he had said to Sullivan. No whining, no Victoriana. It was a blotch, but so had prison been a blotch – a long one, not to mention the Whitey incident in the raid. He bore scars from prison. Now Hazel bore this.

Her brows went up a little, questioningly, as she looked at him, then she turned away to do something else. In the past weeks, she had asked him a few times, 'What's the matter, darling?' or 'What are you thinking?' but he had not always been able to tell her, or hadn't wanted to. It was not always that he was thinking something definite, Carter knew, when the odd expression came on his face. His face had simply changed in six years, and Hazel wasn't used to it. But once he knew he had troubled her by answering, 'I'm thinking the whole world is like one big prison, and prisons are just an exaggerated form of it.' And then, try as he had that night, he hadn't been able to make clear to her what he meant. There were rules and regulations in the non-prison world, too, he had meant, and at times they did not seem to make sense, except as products of fear, made to assuage fear. Sometimes he felt they held together an even madder world than prison that lay just underneath, in everybody's mind. Without the rest of the world to tell a man when to sleep and eat, when to work and stop, without everybody else who was doing these things to imitate, an individual might go insane. That evening he had believed it because he felt it, and even still he partly believed it, but Hazel had not, and the more he tried to be clear about it, the fuzzier the idea sounded.

'Darling, don't forget the Elliotts this weekend.'

'No.' He vaguely remembered. They were going to Long Island Friday evening after Hazel got off from work. Roger Elliott was an investment counsellor, and Hazel had given him most of their money, which was very well placed now in blue chip securities. Priscilla Elliott, who was about thirty, stayed at home and took care of the two children, both younger than Timmie, and painted portraits and landscapes as a hobby, competently but dully. Their house was huge and extremely permanent looking on its broad green lawn. Sullivan was not coming this weekend to the Elliotts', Carter remembered. That was one good thing about it.

The next day was Thursday, and Carter had nothing in particular to do. He supervised the cleaning girl, Sandra, who came on Thursdays from 1 to 4, more carefully than usual, thinking Hazel would be pleased that he remembered to tell Sandra to wipe the kitchen shelves and clean the medicine cabinet shelves. Sandra never paid full attention to Hazel's notes.

The telephone rang just before 3, and it was Gawill. He said, 'Hi, Phil. Well, I guess you got my letter.'

'Yes.'

'I thought it deserved an answer, don't you? – A telephone call or an answer?'

'Did it?'

'Come on, Phil. Are you afraid to hear the tapes?'

Carter felt suddenly angry. 'I am not afraid to hear your tapes or any tapes –' He left it dangling, not wanting to say 'about Hazel' or to say her name to Gawill.

'All right, when're you coming over? Tonight?'

'I'm not free tonight. How soon are you home from work?'

'Around six.'

'I'll be there. Wait – the address.' Carter took it down.

Listen to the tapes or whatever Gawill had, and get it over with, he thought. Gawill probably had nothing.

17

At 5.40 he took a taxi to Gawill's complicated address in Jackson Heights, and was let out in a street of gloomy red-brick buildings, all alike, all sitting at an obtuse angle to the street but touching one another, and all about eight stories high. Gawill's downstairs hall was full of baby carriages and there was a smell of cooking. He took the elevator to the sixth floor.

'Hello, Phil,' Gawill said affably as he opened the door. He was in shirtsleeves, a cigarette in his mouth. 'Come on in.'

Carter went into a living-room full of cheap, newish furniture which, like the painting reproductions on the wall, managed to have no personality whatsoever. Gawill offered him a drink. Carter tossed his topcoat on one end of an ugly green sofa. There was a hall that led to another room. 'Are we alone or is somebody else here?'

'Oh, we're alone. Thought you'd rather be.' Gawill came back from the kitchen with two drinks. 'I've got what you're interested in right here.' He moved to the round coffee table in front of the sofa. On the coffee table lay, between two laden ashtrays, a worn brown-paper envelope with an untied string. It bulged. Gawill sat down on the sofa. 'These notes,' he said, pulling out a messy handful. 'Well, like I said, they're mostly on Sullivan, but they've got a few times and names of other people, times when they came to see him, I mean.'

After a little more of Gawill's mumbling, Carter said, 'I wish you'd just hand me what's pertinent and let me see it.'

'Here, for instance, June twenty-seventh, *three* years ago, "Mrs Carter arrived four thirty-five p.m., left at six." That's at Sullivan's, when she was going to school in Long Island, telling your son, I suppose, she didn't get off from school till five or so, because she kept it up pretty regular. Here we have again, "Mrs C. arrives four thirty-five, leaves six twenty."' He fumbled in the notes. '"S. enters house nine fifty p.m. with Mrs C. She leaves midnight, S. puts her in taxi." *One* year ago.' Gawill leaned forward to hand Carter the note.

Gawill produced six more. The latest time Hazel had left his apartment was at 2 a.m., and that had been with two other people, when Sullivan had been giving a party.

'But you know, *lateness* don't matter,' Gawill said with a smile.

Carter had to smile, too. 'I don't see anything to get excited about – in anything you've got here.' Carter felt bored and vaguely angry, but the anger, he realized, was anger with himself for having bothered to come here.

Gawill looked surprised and disappointed. 'You don't. Well, maybe you'd like to hear the tapes.' He got up and went to the closet near the front door. He dragged out a heavy-looking box, then still another box from behind it. The second box was full of rolled tapes, two long rows of them – long, if Gawill didn't know what he was looking for, and he didn't seem to. He stooped by the tape box, murmuring, 'Got into Sullivan's house twice, once to put the machine in, once to take it out. Let's see here. Marchand –' He put it back and pulled out another. 'More Marchand. Another of my chums,' he said with sarcasm.

Carter drew on his cigarette. Gawill was a mental case, a

paranoid, Carter thought, and Sullivan's investigations must have added a lot of fuel to the fire. Carter looked again at the sordid heap of notes on the sofa cushion. How many other dirty brown envelopes did Gawill have on his other persecutors? And how much money had he paid to get all this junk? Enough to keep him half broke, evidently, and in a cheap apartment.

'Ah, here they are,' said Gawill. 'Sullivan –'

It took him several minutes to put the tape on the machine. Carter listened, smiling, to the first few incomplete conversations between Sullivan and his cleaners' delivery boy, who had come with a suit but without a white dinner jacket that Sullivan had expected. A door slammed and there was silence.

'Come on, Greg, speed it up,' Carter said.

'Can't speed it up, you'll miss something,' said Gawill, hunched avidly over his machine on the floor.

Sullivan making a restaurant reservation on the telephone. For two at 9 o'clock.

'We put the machine right near the telephone,' Gawill put in.

Another long pause.

'Wait,' Gawill said, and speeded up the tape until it struck voices, then went back. Hazel was arriving at Sullivan's.

'How are you, darling,' Sullivan said.

'Fine, and you?' Hazel replied. 'What a day!'

'I had to make the dinner at nine, because there was nothing at eight,' Sullivan said. 'Okay, honey?'

'I don't mind. Gives us a little more time. I wouldn't mind taking my shoes off.'

Sullivan laughed a little. 'Do that. Get you a drink?'

'No, thanks. Not yet.'

'Darling.'

Maybe they kissed, maybe they didn't. The silence sounded like it to Carter.

'Get that,' said Gawill.

155

'Oh, come on. Why didn't you put it in the bedroom if you were trying to prove something?' Carter said with a laugh.

'Timmie going to be all right?' Sullivan asked.

'He's staying the night with one of his school friends,' Hazel said.

'Ah-h, great,' from Sullivan.

Their two voices faded away and vanished.

'Get *that*,' Gawill said. 'This tape is last *October*.'

Carter knew Hazel's voice, her moods. She had talked to him in the same way many times.

Gawill clicked the machine off. 'Timmie staying the night with one of his school friends.' He nodded meaningfully.

Carter opened his shaky hands. 'He does that every now and then, if we've got a late night somewhere.'

'Ah, come on. You weren't born yesterday,' Gawill said.

Carter smiled wryly. No, he wasn't. And the tape was last October. He could see the date on the spool himself, unless Gawill was faking the date.

Gawill seized his glass and fixed him another. 'You ought to let me tip you off some late afternoon when she's with Sullivan, and you go over and –' Gawill set the drink down firmly on the coffee table.

'And?'

'Ah – throttle him right in his bed.'

Carter's forehead felt cool with perspiration. 'I think you hate him much more than I do. You'll beat me to it.'

'I think you ought to do it. You've got the moral right.'

Carter laughed. 'Come on. The honour is yours.'

Gawill studied his face.

Carter finally looked down at his glass. He passed his fingers over his moist forehead. The faint sweat reminded him of withdrawal symptoms in the prison ward.

'How about a shot?' Gawill asked. 'I've got some in the bathroom. Horse.'

Carter sat back, took a long time to answer, but he knew what his answer would be. 'Why not?'

'It's not in the bathroom, but I'll get it,' said Gawill, going off briskly like a good host, going into his bedroom down the hall.

Carter stood up. He heard Gawill in the bathroom now. He went in.

Gawill had the box on the floor, a cardboard box about two feet square with some forty ampoules laid in compartments in cotton on the top layer of the box. If the box were full, Carter thought, there were at least two hundred and forty ampoules in it.

'Each one is ten grains,' Gawill said, laying a hypodermic needle on the edge of the basin. 'Dunno if you want a whole one.' He smiled genially and went out of the bathroom.

Carter moved automatically, and the stuff was in a vein in his forearm in a matter of seconds, though the ampoule and the new square needle were different from the prison ward equipment. He took slightly more than half the plastic ampoule. Where did Gawill get all the stuff, Carter wondered, and thought it would be undiplomatic to ask. But it was a lucrative business and explained why Gawill could hire private detectives, or crooked facsimiles. Carter looked and saw that there were at least six layers of ampoules, and at a modest price on the junkies' market, the box was worth six thousand dollars. Carter walked back into the living-room.

'If you want a couple of shots to take home,' Gawill said, nodding towards the bathroom, 'help yourself.'

Carter smiled. 'No, thanks, Greg.' The shot was going through his veins, strong and familiar. Carter sat down comfortably in an armchair.

Gawill got up and handed him his drink. Carter no longer wanted it or needed it, but he took it.

'Seriously, Phil, you're the person who could erase Mr Sullivan and go scot-free – legally speaking,' Gawill said quietly.

Carter frowned and laughed. 'With a prison record behind me?'

'A man has the right to –'

'Doesn't that particular law apply only in Texas?'

Gawill subsided and rubbed a hand across his mouth. 'We could always make it look as if one of my friends did it. And then they wouldn't have – you see – so what could the law do there? You might be suspected, but –' Gawill paused.

Gawill wasn't making sense, but Carter imagined himself delivering a sidewise blow to the front of Sullivan's throat, Alex's blow to kill. 'I should think I would be suspected, if I did it,' Carter said, looking at his wristwatch. A quarter to 7. Hazel would be wondering where he was. He hadn't left any note at home. 'Or even if I didn't,' he added.

'Think it over, Phil. We could work out something. You've got cause. You won't stop their affair until you do, you know.'

Carter kept calm. But he felt scared, and his heart was beating faster. It was like a lot of moments in prison, when he had been physically threatened, or just before a blow of some kind really landed – the way he had felt sometimes with his back turned to Squiff in Max's cell. 'I think I'll leave the job to you,' Carter said, getting up.

'Oh, no, I'm leaving it to you.'

Carter laughed.

So did Gawill. Gawill got up and reached in his hip pocket. He pulled out his wallet and took a photograph from it. 'A present for you. The date's on the back.'

Carter took it. It was a photograph of Hazel, back view, hatless and in a coat, going up the steps of what looked like Sullivan's Thirty-eighth Street house. Carter turned it over and read, 'Jan. 4th 4.30 p.m.' Carter said, 'She works till five thirty usually.'

Then, interrupting Gawill's interruption, 'I've called her many times in her office just after five. I know.'

'Sullivan's supposed to, too. They can arrange things now and then, though. Love will find a way, like they say. You can't just deny that photograph, can you?'

Carter shrugged and tossed the photograph down on the coffee table. Hazel was in the dark-brown coat with black fur collar and cuffs that she had worn to work most days this winter. Carter felt sickish.

'All right,' Gawill said, clapping his shoulder. 'You know it's true. All right, I'll race you for the pleasure of wasting Mr Sullivan, but I think you'll win.'

'Good night, Greg.' Carter walked to the door.

Gawill was there first and opened it for him. 'See you again, Phil.'

Hazel was in the kitchen when Carter got home.

'Hi,' she called. 'Where've you been?'

He crossed the living-room floor and stood near the kitchen door. 'Just out,' he said. 'Taking a walk.'

She glanced at him, then looked back at what she was doing – opening a package of frozen peas.

He could have turned away then, since she wasn't pursuing the questioning, but he kept looking at her, could not take his eyes from her for several seconds. She looked over her shoulder at him again, and then he turned. Carter hung up his overcoat, then started into the bathroom. He looked through the open door of Timmie's room. Timmie was lying on his stomach on the floor, doing his homework, a place he preferred to his work-table. Carter saw that his right hand was bandaged.

'Hi, Timmie. What happened to your hand?'

'Oh – fell on the playground playing handball this afternoon.'

'Oh. A scrape? Is it bad?'

'No, it's a cut. I hit a piece of glass or something, but it's not bad.' Timmie did not look up as he said that.

159

Carter hesitated a moment, then went on into the bathroom. He washed his hands with soap, then he washed his face. He felt quite well. Hazel might be having an affair with Sullivan now – she was quite a busy woman these days – but the heroin made him feel very well, as if the world were still right side up. It was a strange comfort to Carter, too, that Gawill knew about the affair, had always known, and yet obviously it hadn't turned his world upside down, hadn't shocked him too much. Gawill even had a bit of humour about it: *love will find a way*. Yes, it would take more than his coming home from prison to interrupt the course of true love.

He went back into the kitchen and said, 'Like a drink before dinner?'

'No, thanks. Have one yourself.'

'No, thanks.'

She was making something in a casserole with salmon and peas. She looked at it in the oven, then closed the oven door again. 'Where were you really just now?' she asked.

Carter blinked at her challenge, but he kept perfectly calm. She was acting as guilty as Sullivan, he thought, and of course for the same reason. 'Out for a walk,' Carter said, rather challengingly himself, before he thought what he was saying. But he let it stand. He turned and walked into the living-room.

18

'David's told me quite a lot about you already,' Butterworth said, but he continued to read the résumé that Carter had brought with him.

Butterworth sat behind a large desk on which were some blue-prints and a model of what looked like some tool-making machine. Butterworth looked about forty-five, but he was quite bald except for a fringe of black hair. His mouth was soft, not in the sense of being weak but of being gentle, and Carter was oddly reminded of Hazel's mouth when he looked at it. Jenkins and Field were consulting engineers, and Carter had gathered that his job would be to handle some of the work that Butterworth was too busy to do. Butterworth was often sent to other cities, and some of this work would fall to him, if he got the job. The job paid fifteen thousand a year, with a month's vacation in summer.

'Well, Mr Carter, the position is yours if you'd like to take it,' Butterworth said.

'Thanks. I think I would.'

Butterworth glanced over his shoulder at the closed door. 'David told me about your ... time in prison down South. I understand it was none of your fault. The guilty one was the man who died.'

Carter nodded and said, 'Yes.'

'Terrible thing,' Butterworth murmured. 'But I wanted to tell you that I know about it, we all know about it here and – we all know David, I know him better than the others, and if David says you're a good man, you're a good man, as far as I'm concerned.' He smiled, awkwardly, as if he were unused to smiling. 'I think even real – jail-birds might be given a second chance sometimes. Most people aren't willing to. And you're not that, I realize. I think you'll do better work for us if you know we know about it and we're not having any – lurking reservations about you.'

Carter walked out of the office in a quiet glow. He went into the first telephone booth and called Sullivan. 'Hello, David. I just wanted to thank you. I got it.'

'Oh, great, great,' Sullivan's smooth tenor voice said. 'When do you start?'

'Monday morning.'

'I've got to go now, somebody waiting to talk to me. Congratulations, Phil, and I'll see you very soon.'

Hazel was delighted that he had got the job, and that evening at the Elliotts' they toasted it in champagne. The Elliotts insisted on bringing out a bottle of the best from their cellar after dinner. Timmie had a glass, too, and Carter thought his son looked at him with a new respect that evening, because he had a job like other kids' fathers. But the job had come through Sullivan. Timmie knew that, too. One up, one more up for Mr Sullivan.

Carter could not get to sleep that night. Hazel had been tired, and she slept soundly beside him in the double bed in one of the Elliotts' guest-rooms, where they had spent other nights. There was a mournful wind outside. He put on his suit over his pyjamas without making a sound, and went downstairs. Carter walked out on the lawn. The wind made him less nervous when he could face it.

The tops of the tall maples and the hickory sycamores nodded and swayed, like the heads of exhausted people being tortured and buffeted. He stared at the house and thought it very strange that he had been invited here. The evening seemed strange, too, like something that had either not really happened, or that had happened years ago.

'Phil?'

Hazel's voice caught him by surprise. It sounded as if she were right beside him. Then he saw her pale figure in her nightgown, small in the tall window in the right upper corner of the house. He suddenly felt he did not know her. It shocked him and frightened him. It was like the wind, blowing his identity away. But he walked automatically towards the house, looking up at her.

'What's the matter, darling?' she asked, softly, as if she were afraid of waking other people in the house.

Awkwardly he waved to her, in an effort to be reassuring. She really belongs to Sullivan, he thought suddenly. He didn't know her at all. He stopped, limp as a rag, nothing.

'Are you all right?'

He stared at her. 'I'll be up.'

19

Sullivan was invited for dinner on the Tuesday of Carter's first week at Jenkins and Field. Hazel made an effort with the dinner – cold cucumber soup, a complicated veal and bacon and grated cheese dish, asparagus with *hollandaise* sauce, and a lemon soufflé for dessert. She was in a good mood.

'Ah, my favourite dish. You're wonderful,' Sullivan said to her. He had strolled into the kitchen with his first drink.

Carter had known somehow that he would say just those words, though Hazel hadn't said anything about the veal dish being his favourite. Hazel was cooking as if she enjoyed it tonight. She always cooked as if she enjoyed cooking – just tonight a little more so. And Timmie had brightened up, too, with Sullivan.

'How long are you going to be at this?' Sullivan asked Hazel.

'What do you mean? This?' She was slicing radishes.

'Ye-es. I don't have to have my radishes turned into little tulips. Are you going to sit down with us?'

'He's so unappreciative!' Hazel laughed and glanced at Carter.

'Galley slave,' Sullivan said, and beckoned to Carter to come into the living-room.

Timmie trailed after them, and Carter saw Sullivan look at

him. Timmie, who was concentrating on Sullivan, looked embarrassed for a moment, then at a very slight nod from Sullivan retreated back to the kitchen, hands in the pockets of his new long trousers. Sullivan had him well trained, Carter thought. He couldn't have done that with his son.

'Have you heard any more from Gawill?' Sullivan asked. His voice was low.

'No.'

'Good.' Sullivan turned, frowning slightly, towards the kitchen. 'I didn't mean to shoo Timmie off, but I didn't want him to hear it, either. Well, let's hope he shuts up. At least to you.'

'And you?' Carter said.

Sullivan smiled. 'I'm still here. No, I haven't had a peep in some time – except the phone call I told you about.'

'And – what were the peeps? In the past?'

'Well – for one thing, I think I was shadowed a few times.' Sullivan looked down at the ashtray where he was mashing out a cigarette. 'I'm sure Gawill wanted me to know I was being shadowed. Around my house. Wanted to scare me a little, you know.'

'I'm not sure I get the purpose of that,' Carter said.

'To scare me off his back. This was when I was asking about him in a lot of hotels in New York. Four or five years ago, you know. I haven't noticed any shadowers for – oh, maybe a year.'

Carter didn't believe the 'maybe a year'. 'Had you shadowed,' Carter said, 'when Gawill himself was still in Fremont with Triumph? And then when he was in New Orleans?'

'Yes. Oh, I'm sure for a modest fee or some other kind of favour, he had a guy in New York loiter across the street from my house, then follow me for a couple of blocks – if I was walking somewhere.' He shrugged. 'Not pleasant, but I never got worried enough to mention it to the police.'

Why not, Carter thought, because he didn't want to disclose the fact that Hazel was visiting him a lot? Carter put his drink down and folded his arms. Then his thumbs gave simultaneous throbs, and he relaxed his hands. 'Does Hazel know about the shadowing?'

'No,' said Sullivan. 'I didn't want to make her worry.'

Or stop her from coming to his house, Carter thought. 'You don't think you're being shadowed now?'

Sullivan smiled at Carter. 'Now that Gawill's up here himself, maybe he feels he doesn't need to hire any shadowers.'

Carter smiled, too. 'You mean Gawill's doing the shadowing himself? The watching?'

'If so, he's discreet. I haven't seen him. You'll tell me, won't you, if you hear anything more from him?'

'Yes. Too bad you have to be still so concerned.'

'He's my enemy. It pays to know what your enemy is doing or even thinking.'

Neither said anything for a few moments. Sullivan had already asked him how his new job was going, and Carter had told him reasonably well. It was going to be paper work for the next two weeks, then a trip to Detroit for two or three weeks. Sullivan had showed no surprise or interest in the fact he would be away for a few weeks, or at least he had not betrayed any.

Then Hazel and Timmie came in, and Hazel and Sullivan talked of other things, the new watercolour that Priscilla Elliott had painted and given to Hazel because she liked it. It was now framed and hanging between the two windows that gave on to the street. They talked of Europe in July, but even this Carter couldn't or didn't join in, though it was he who was going and not Sullivan. Timmie was keen about the trip and asked Sullivan if there were soccer games in July in Rapallo, the town where Hazel wanted to spend some time.

'Rapallo,' said Sullivan, 'is a pretty small town for a stadium. I think you'd better depend on Genoa for a good soccer game.'

And Timmie sat down on the hassock, looking a little wistfully at Sullivan, as if he were suddenly realizing that Sullivan wasn't going to be with them, that his father was, and his father didn't know much about soccer.

Sullivan called the dinner a masterpiece, and Hazel beamed. And so did Timmie. And Carter kept hurting his thumbs that evening, gripping a knife or a cup handle too hard, until pain finally made him jittery. Carter decided that he ought to see a specialist and have an operation. That was about 10.15 p.m. An hour later, when Sullivan was leaving, he had changed his mind again. After all, the specialist Hazel had made him go to had said that after they pared the bone and the gristle down, got the joints possibly to fit, there would still be bad articulation and possibly pain, too.

'Happy, darling?' Hazel said to him, smiling.

'Yes,' he said, and put his arms around her and kissed her neck. He held her tight. She felt very solid in his arms, and yet something was not there that had been. Was it gone from Hazel or from him? Or both?

20

Hazel had to go to an office dinner in the following week. It was to be held in a hotel on Fifty-seventh Street, and since there were to be a lot of speeches afterwards on subjects that Hazel thought Carter would find dull, Hazel had suggested that she go alone. Carter agreed. He had some homework to do for Jenkins and Field.

'I'll take Timmie out for an early dinner, and then he can go to the movie on Twenty-third he's been wanting to see,' Carter said. 'It's a western or something.'

'Then you'll pick him up?' Hazel asked. 'I don't want him wandering into a drugstore late at night and having three sodas.'

Timmie had augmented his soda intake lately. Three at a sitting were nothing unusual for him.

'I'll find out when the show lets out and pick him up,' Carter said.

They had that conversation at breakfast. Carter found out there was a show at 6, 8 and 10, and thought Timmie ought to go to the 8, after their dinner. He telephoned at 5 o'clock and told Timmie he would be home by half past 6, a little later than usual, and they'd go out to dinner then.

Carter took a downtown bus after work, and got off at Thirty-eighth Street. All day, he had thought about Sullivan, and he felt tonight was a good time for a short talk that Hazel need not know about. He wanted to ask Sullivan outright what was going on, and if Sullivan told the truth, so much the better, and if he lied, Carter thought he would know it. And if Sullivan weren't in, that was his hard luck, but Carter hadn't wanted to make an appointment beforehand.

When he was within thirty yards of Sullivan's house, Carter saw Hazel. She saw him, too, nearly stopped, then came on, smiling at him.

'Well, hello!' they both said, almost simultaneously.

'You couldn't be going to David's!' Carter said with a laugh.

'Just what I'm doing. Taking him a book,' Hazel said, gesturing slightly with the pile of papers and books she carried in one arm, topped by her purse. 'Come on. I've only got a minute.' She started up the steps of the house.

'No, no, that's okay. I'll go on.'

She looked at him.

'I just thought I'd drop in. Nothing important,' Carter said.

'Don't be silly. If you're here –'

Carter was walking on. 'See you later,' he said, smiling and waving. He walked on to the corner like a stick man, like a man on stilts. There was no office dinner tonight. Hazel was spending the evening with Sullivan. And Carter had to admire the good face she'd put on it. If he had come up, she'd have said to Sullivan, 'Look who I just ran into. Here's the book, David,' putting down something on postnatal care of children, *faute de mieux*. 'Got to be off to that Fifty-seventh Street thing, because they have a very early cocktail hour, if I get one at all. Bye-bye.' Yes, Hazel would have carried it off very smoothly. And Carter threw his head back and laughed, thinking that Hazel might beat an early retreat tonight, suspecting he'd be standing somewhere on the street, watching to see how soon she came out.

He took Timmie to where Timmie wanted to go – a cafeteria on Twenty-third Street, where Timmie ordered five portions of various things, three desserts, and two glasses of chocolate milk. And still Timmie was slender, a little underweight for his height. He was five feet three. In another two years, Carter thought, he would probably shoot up ten inches, and all the eating was preparing for it. He took Timmie to the movies. Carter decided to go to the show, too. It provided a noisy yet somehow restful background to his own thoughts, and he had not the faintest idea of the story when it was over.

Hazel was not home when they got back. Carter got Timmie to bed, or at least in bed with a book, with a promise that he would read no longer than fifteen minutes.

'I'm going out for a while,' Carter said. 'Mummy should be home any minute, but don't wait up for her, because you're supposed to be asleep.'

'Where're you going?' Timmie asked.

'Out for a walk,' Carter said. 'Back soon.' The conversation reminded him of the one he'd had with Hazel.

Carter took a taxi to Gawill's. If Gawill wasn't in, it wouldn't matter. If he was, fine. Carter didn't make the taxi wait. He got out and rang the bell.

There was no answering ring, and Carter didn't need one to reach the elevators, but he heard the grating sound of a voice through a speaking tube that he hadn't noticed before. He yelled into it:

'Hello, Gawill, it's Carter. Can I come up?'

'Oh, Phil! Sure, Phil, come on up.'

Carter went up.

Gawill had the door open for him, and was standing there. A depressing sound of dance music came from the door, and voices.

'You've got a party?' Carter said. 'Then I won't –'

'Ah, naw, no party,' Gawill said. 'Come on in, Phil.'

Carter went in, glad somehow of Gawill's welcome, though his attitude to the man Gawill introduced him to and also to the plump blonde he was with was cool. Carter hoped it didn't show.

'Phil's an old buddy of mine from down South,' Gawill said to his two uninterested friends.

The man was about thirty-five, a big, brawny fellow with shoulders that bulged under his well-cut suit. The blonde was just a blonde, a bit heavily made up, and Carter doubted if she had a regular job. There didn't seem to be a girl for Gawill, unless she was in the bedroom.

'Are you a Southerner?' the blonde asked Carter.

'No,' Carter said, smiling. She had a deep cleavage in the V of her brown silk dress, very high-heeled shoes, and there was a run in her right stocking. 'Are you?'

'Ha! I'm from Connecticut. Originally,' she added. 'Want to dance?'

'Not just now, thanks.' The girl, to Carter, was like one of the blondes on the prison movie screen, come to life and talking to him. Impulsively, he reached out and took her wrist. 'But you can sit down, can't you?'

He had meant on the broad arm of his armchair, but the girl sat in his lap. Carter was surprised at first, then he smiled. She was terribly heavy.

Gawill looked at them and said, 'Hey, what's going on here?' with a delighted smile.

'I think we're taking off here,' said the girl's boy friend, holding out a hand for her.

'Bye,' said the blonde cheerfully to Carter. 'See you soon, I hope.' Her breath smelled of Scotch and lipstick.

Carter didn't do her the courtesy of standing, but he waved. 'I hope so. Nice to have met you both.'

They had a short conversation with Gawill near the door, which Carter didn't listen to. Then Gawill closed the door on them.

'Ain't she something?' Gawill said, coming back, rubbing his hands. 'Anthony don't appreciate her.' Sometimes Gawill lapsed into the New Orleans drawl of his youth.

Carter said nothing.

'So what's on your mind tonight? – How about a shot?'

'What a good idea,' Carter said, getting up.

Gawill went off to get the stuff, and Carter stayed where he was, thinking for the second time he shouldn't know, for politeness' sake, where Gawill hid it in his bedroom. When Gawill came in again, Carter bowed his thanks and went into the bathroom and took it. He took the rest of the bottle he had started. It had a rubber cap that pressed on the plastic ampoule. Then he brought the empty ampoule into the living-room and deposited it in one of Gawill's busy ashtrays. 'Thanks very much,' Carter said.

'Late for you, isn't it?' Gawill remarked.

'Yes. Oh, well, Hazel's busy tonight. An office dinner.'

'Yeah?'

'Yeah. So she said. She's with Sullivan.'

'Ahah,' said Gawill, with no emotion at all, no triumph, no surprise.

'Yes, you're right,' Carter said. He took a breath. 'I was going to see Sullivan tonight to ask him straight to his face what he was doing with my wife, when who should I see walking in the door but Hazel herself.'

'You see?' said Gawill, and reached for his glass. He sighed. He looked tired, maybe a bit drunk. 'Well – what're you going to do about it?'

Carter had nothing to say. He even had no thoughts about it.

Gawill leaned back on the sofa and looked at Carter. 'Oh, I suppose you'll try asking her to stop, but she won't. What those two have is closer than most marriages.'

Carter frowned, looking intensely at Gawill. Then I'm the

person *de trop*, he thought. 'Then why the hell don't they say so?' Carter asked suddenly. 'What's all this beating around the bush?'

'Well, look at the advantages for both. Your wife keeps her respectability – at least with most people – she's got a husband and child, everybody thinks probably she's the picture of virtue, waiting six years for her husband to get out of the slammer. And Sullivan has the best of two worlds, he's a free bachelor and he's got a nice lay.'

The words didn't bother Carter at all now. It was true. And it was practically a relief to hear the words said.

'So what did Hazel say when you ran into her at Sullivan's?' Gawill sat up, smiling expectantly.

Carter smiled, too. 'She said she was dropping a book by for Sullivan and she was going on to dinner.'

Gawill laughed loudly.

Carter laughed, too.

'And what did you do?'

'I – I just walked on. Didn't go up.'

'Don't tell me you were *asked* up,' Gawill said.

'Yes.'

More laughter. Gawill fixed him another drink, and one for himself.

'You missed your opportunity tonight – or did you?' Gawill looked at him sidewise.

'What do you mean?'

'You should've crashed the apartment about half an hour later and caught them inflagranty as we say in N.O. Why didn't you?'

'Oh –' Carter looked down at his drink. 'Oh, the hell with it.'

They got off the subject. They talked about fishing and frog-catching, Gawill's methods of stabbing frogs after shining a light in their eyes. He had done it as a boy around New Orleans.

It got to be after 1 a.m.

Carter hauled himself up and said he had to get home.

'Oh, I don't see why you *have* to. Do you think Hazel's home?'

Carter laughed at that.

He took a taxi home. He was as quiet as possible hanging up his coat, undressing in the bathroom and putting on his pyjamas, which he kept on the door hook. Then he went into the bedroom. Hazel turned on the lamp.

'Where've you been, Phil?' she asked sleepily.

'I went to see Gawill,' Carter said.

'Gawill?' She lifted her head from the pillow. 'Why? You went after the movie?'

So Timmie had been up or waked up and told her he'd gone to the movie. 'Yes.' He realized he hadn't washed, and went back to the bathroom. He came back after a couple of minutes, carrying his suit, which he hung up in the closet. 'And what did you do? How was the dinner?'

She looked at him as if she thought he was drunk. Or perhaps it was only a wary look: the truth might come out.

She lit a cigarette, took a puff, and said, 'Fine,' on a crest of smoke.

'You're saying there was one – Oh, get off it, Haze.'

'All right. I'll get off it. I spent the evening with David. Nicer company than Gawill, I think.'

'I spent the evening with Gawill, but not in bed with him.'

'I wasn't in bed with David, either. – I can imagine the kind of stories you were given tonight – from Gawill. It's no wonder you're so aggressive.'

'Me aggressive?' Carter walked towards the foot of the bed. 'Why did you lie about the office dinner tonight? Why do you bother lying?'

'Why did you go to Gawill's?'

'To learn a little more of the truth, maybe.'

She touched her cigarette end in the tray, then stabbed it out. Her shoulders shook. She was weeping.

174

Carter shifted, embarrassed. 'Oh, come on, Haze. Tears?'

She tossed her head and sat upright again, facing him as if the momentary breakdown hadn't happened. Her eyes were not even wet. 'I miss David and I need him. I suppose I got awfully used to talking to him over a period of six years.'

'I'm sure you did,' Carter said.

'He's easy to get along with – easier than you've been lately.'

'Just what do you mean by that?'

'You've had a shot of something tonight, haven't you? Morphine? I suppose Gawill has everything. Everything slimy.'

'Yes, I had one.'

'You look exactly as you used to in prison sometimes – a kind of phoney calmness about you. A quiet drunk.'

'Your tactics tonight,' he said, 'seem to be to attack me – to cover up your own activities. You can call Gawill all the names you want, he seems to know more about you than I do. And as for phoneyness, I've had it up to here with Sullivan. That bastard can save his smiles and his good turns –'

'Like getting you a job? Close the door, Phil.'

The way she said the last words hurt Carter more than anything else she had said. She was in complete possession of herself, and thinking of Timmie's sleep, of course, thinking of Timmie overhearing some of this. Carter closed the door slowly, resting both hands on the knob, and pondered the terrible efficiency of women: Hazel running the house in Fremont and slaving in a dress shop at the same time, Hazel being quite a good mother to Timmie, Hazel going to school and getting a master's degree, Hazel keeping Sullivan happy and on the string all this time, Hazel – up to now – keeping him happy, too.

'Thanks.' She glanced at him sharply.

Carter felt then that she actually disliked him, that she disliked the person he had become after prison, perhaps. Certainly she hadn't disliked him before. He had a feeling of being swept away, annihilated physically. It lasted only a few seconds. He wiped a hand across his forehead and faced her. 'I can't deny that prison changed me. I don't think it's made me into a monster. You may not like me. That's another matter. I trusted you. Apart from the two weeks' affair you told me about, I thought you were loyal to me. If I –'

'All those fine words and you're full of morphine this minute?' She took a fresh cigarette and lit it. 'All right, Phil, I know a lot of awful things happened to you in prison – and that's why I haven't said anything to you about it and never blamed you. I imagine you had to be in a trance or *something* to stand that filthy place. I wouldn't have blamed you if you'd become a real addict. I mean a heavy one.'

Carter opened his hands. 'You're talking as if I'm an addict now. For God's sake, Hazel, this is the first – the second shot I've had since I got out of the clink!'

'Oh, the second. Yes, I think I know when you had the first. Last Thursday when you said you'd been out for a walk.' And for an instant she showed her pretty profile as she looked sideways at the night table.

'You've got the usual phobia about dope, about the awful people who take it. What's so much better about alcohol? Alcohol just happens to be legal in this country, that's all.'

'Then why isn't dope legal, too?'

'Maybe because a lot of people are making money on it.'

'You're defending dope as a social custom – like a drink before dinner?'

'All right, I'm not!'

'The pills you're taking are full of morphine. I asked Dr MacKensie about them. Timmie notices it, too. You can't even play with him the way you used to, and one would think it's easier to play with a twelve-year-old than a six-year-old.'

'Not necessarily. And Timmie hasn't been too easy – you know that – since I was out of prison. I'm not blaming him. It takes time. I realize what he went through at school because of me.'

'And do you realize what I went through, too? Do you think a woman's proud of having a husband in prison? Do you think it's easy to keep bolstering a father in a child's eyes, when he knows the father's in prison?'

'Darling, I'm aware of all that. What can I say except I'm sorry the whole damned thing happened? You're skirting around the issue.'

She was silent. She knew the issue.

'Which do you want, Sullivan or me?' Carter asked.

'I miss David. I can't seem to live without seeing him – talking to him.'

'And sleeping with him?'

She didn't answer that.

'That's part of it, isn't it?'

'It has been. I tried – I mean – sleeping with him isn't the most important part.'

'Maybe not for you,' Carter put in.

'You can't understand, I suppose, that it meant – life itself to me to be able to see him now and then just for an hour or less some afternoons, just to talk with him?'

'Gawill believes it. He's got snapshots of you going into Sullivan's house. Recent ones.'

'All right, so now you know. I hope it'll take the wind out of Gawill's sails – if he's got any sails.'

'If it means life to you, you're not going to give it up, are you?' Carter asked. 'Or were you possibly using the past tense?'

'You don't understand women. Or me. You never did.'

Carter mashed his cigarette out. 'Stop talking in clichés. I can understand your liking to talk to Sullivan, I can understand friendship. Unfortunately, I can understand a woman's inclination to add a little icing to the cake by sleeping with a good friend if he asks for it. I can certainly understand Sullivan's asking for it. What man wouldn't? Can you understand that you're married to me? Is that too difficult?'

'This happened while you were in prison. Were you so innocent in prison, I wonder? I never asked you any questions about that, did I?'

Carter smiled. 'There aren't any partners in prison. Unless you want another man, of course. Plenty of those.'

'You and Max?'

'What about Max?'

'What about Max?'

Carter felt the blood in his cheeks. 'I liked him, yes, but not the way you're talking about.'

'Never even thought of it?'

Carter's eyes narrowed and he hated her then. This was picking, petty, nasty, bitchy. 'I'm not even going to answer that.'

'Maybe that's answer enough. Anyway, Max died too soon, perhaps.'

'Cut it out, Haze, you're making things worse.'

'Oh, I'm making things worse.'

'You want to punish me – light into me about thinking? Sure it crossed my mind, maybe Max's, too. Do you want me to make some trite statement about things like that happening in prison all the time because there's nothing else? I'm not going to make it. How can you compare Max with Sullivan? Max was the pleasantest thing I had in that stinking place, nicer and better than thinking of you sleeping with Sullivan or wondering if you were. I gave you the benefit of the doubt in those days. To tell you the truth, I doped myself so I wouldn't think about you with Sullivan at all. So I wouldn't admit to myself you were sleeping with him all those years – because it might have finished me.'

'You doped yourself, all right.'

Hazel's intensity reminded him of her jealousy of Max when

178

Carter had first told her about him. She had intuitively grasped Max's importance to him – and so, of course, had he. But Max was gone, and Carter could not remember a single physical touch of him, except the afternoon Max had pushed him in the shoulder to make him lie down on his bunk. Carter had never thought, *I love Max*, and yet for a while he had been as dependent emotionally on him as on Hazel, simply because he was there. It was at once simple and complex. Carter blinked and stared at her.

'What are you thinking?' Now her beautiful face looked merely beautiful, and quite empty, like a dry field waiting for the rain of his thoughts.

'I'm thinking that all the words you used tonight – everything you've said – in such bitterness – is part of your fighting for David. You're not going to give him up, are you?'

She lay back deeper in her pillow, squirming uncomfortably. 'I don't know.'

He took a step towards her. 'I'd appreciate a little honesty. Say yes or no.'

'I can't.' Her eyes were closed.

'I want you, Hazel. I want you back.'

'I can't talk any more tonight about it.'

Carter felt baffled. 'Sullivan – He had me up in his apartment to tell me also it was two weeks and four days. Well rehearsed. He hadn't even the guts to admit the truth. Do you like men without guts?'

'All right, he's weak. I know it.'

'He's cowardly,' Carter said. 'It's still going on, isn't it?'

'Not really, not really. Let me sleep,' Hazel said, her eyes still closed, her brows frowning.

Carter gave it up for the night. He wasn't hooked on morphine, he was hooked on Hazel, he thought with a detached amusement. He hadn't presented her with any ultimatum, he realized, no 'give him up or else, or else I'll do this or that'. He hadn't thought Hazel would need an ultimatum. Carter turned from the closet, where he had just hung his robe, and looked at her. Her face was turned towards the edge of the bed, her eyes closed.

21

'Hello, Phil. Greg,' Gawill's voice said. 'How are things?'

Carter glanced around automatically in the empty living-room, though he knew Timmie was in his own room, probably with the door closed. 'Things are all right,' Carter said.

'I thought you might have had a talk with your wife – that night.'

'Nope.' Carter drew on his half-finished cigarette.

'Ah, come on, Phil. You can talk to me. There's nobody there, is there? Maybe the kid?'

'Nope,' Carter repeated.

'I know Hazel's not,' Gawill drawled in his baritone voice, Gawill the omniscient.

Hazel was a bit late tonight, but she might come in the door any minute, Carter thought. But obviously, Gawill had someone watching the house now. Carter had just come in himself. 'What's on your mind, Greg?' Carter asked.

'Is your wife going to keep on seeing that jerk? Did she make you any promises?'

Carter wanted to bang the telephone down. He only squeezed it in his left hand, wordless and angry.

'I don't know why you don't talk to me, Phil.'

'Because I really have nothing to say. Sorry.' He put the telephone down.

Then he went into the kitchen and poured a drink of Scotch, which he sipped straight. Things hadn't progressed a jot since he'd had the talk with Hazel Tuesday night. Today was Thursday. There was an atmosphere of quiet enmity between them, which Carter wondered if Timmie had noticed, and thought probably that he had. Carter was really waiting for Hazel to say something, and Hazel wasn't saying anything more. It'd be a matter of a week, maybe a little more, until another phoney engagement turned up – an evening with Phyllis Millen, or with one of the office workers going over the case loads, something – and she'd spend another evening with Sullivan. Maybe she was with him now, a bit late after one of their *heures bleues* that had begun before 5 this afternoon. Well, Hazel had delivered her answer, really, she was going to keep on seeing Sullivan and sleeping with him. If she had any serious intentions to the contrary, she would have said so by now. Hazel figured he loved her so much, he'd put up with it. That was what it amounted to.

Carter was jolted a little closer to doing what he had been thinking of doing since the Tuesday night conversation. He would talk to Sullivan. Ask him to stop seeing her, or – Or what? The law could scarcely step in and protect his rights here, throw a guard around Hazel. Carter smiled. All he had was good grounds for divorce. But he didn't have Hazel. It was a funny world.

Hazel came in, glanced at the drink in his hand and said, 'Good evening.'

'Evening. Fix you a drink?'

'Just had one, thanks. Our sociologist-at-large Mr Piers blew in today and insisted on taking me out for a drink. He gave me another sixty-page thing to get through tonight.' She slapped a stapled, mimeographed manuscript down on the coffee table, then straightened and stretched, smiling. 'Sorry. I'm stiff. Can we go out to that Chinese place tonight for dinner? Timmie likes it. I don't feel like cooking if I've got all that tonight.'

'Okay. Sure.' And Carter went in to tell the nice news to Timmie. A Chinese dinner.

But all in all, he felt a trifle better that evening than the two previous evenings, because he had come to a decision. Futile and absurd as it might be, he would ask Sullivan to stop sleeping with his wife. He'd at least get some kind of answer from Sullivan, a promise that he would, a half-promise, or a 'go to hell'. He debated telephoning Sullivan to make a definite date, and decided not to for the simple reason that Sullivan might duck it or postpone it: Carter had no doubt that Hazel had told him about their conversation of Tuesday night.

On Friday, Carter went directly from his office to Sullivan's, on the Second Avenue bus. It was raining slightly, and there was a balmy note of spring in the cool air. Carter pressed Sullivan's bell, then looked at his wristwatch: seventeen minutes to 6. He might even be too early. Or Hazel might be with him, Carter thought, and gave a grimace of a smile. He heard the release bell. Carter took the stairs instead of the small slow elevator, and at Sullivan's third floor he was nearly knocked down by a man running down the steps. The rude bump brought Carter's anger to the surface. No murmur of apology from the fellow. He went on down the steps, coat-tails flying. The door below banged.

'Oh, Phil! Phil!' Sullivan gasped. He was standing in his open doorway, wilting against the door he was clinging to.

Carter frowned. 'What happened?' he asked, walking up the rest of the steps.

'Come in.' Sullivan loosened his tie, opened his collar. 'Christ. Come in. You saved my life. – Here, let's have a drink.' He started towards the bar-cart in the corner of his living-room.

Carter closed the door behind himself. 'Saved your life?'

'Sorry, I need this.' Sullivan was lifting a glass of straight Scotch to his lips. 'That guy – You saw that fellow running down?'

'Yes.'

'One of Gawill's friends. He rang the doorbell. I didn't know who it was. I let him in. He said he came to see me about my insurance – or something.' Sullivan licked his lips. Even his lips looked white, and his face looked like death, like a man drained of blood. 'Pulled out a knife and started after me. Had me by the shirtfront.'

Carter saw that a button dangled on Sullivan's jacket, that his shirtfront was crumpled.

'If he hadn't heard your ring,' Sullivan said, 'I'd have been done for.'

Sullivan looked contemptible. This is the lily-livered swine that sleeps with Hazel, Carter thought in a flash, and walked towards Sullivan. Sullivan didn't know his intentions until Carter was right on him, and then Carter hit him a blow in the side of the neck with his hand. It staggered Sullivan badly. Then Carter blacked out, as he had in his rage in prison after finding Max dead, though he did not think of Max now or of anything. Only when Sullivan was lying on the floor, twisted, gripping his stomach as if hurt, yet not moving, did Carter really see him, and stop. Carter stood for a couple of seconds, getting his breath back, and then he spat at Sullivan, and gave him a kick that missed.

Carter went to the door and turned. There wasn't a doubt in his mind that Sullivan was dead. Now Carter saw in the seat of the armchair near Sullivan one of the Greek marble feet. He noticed it only because it didn't belong there. Then he closed the door and went down the steps. He went down at a normal rate, and was aware that his speed was normal. Who was Gawill's man, he wondered? The same brawny fellow he'd seen at Gawill's with the blonde?

On the sidewalk, he felt slightly faint for a moment, and stood and took some breaths of air. Don't think, for Christ's sake, he told himself. Don't think about what you've done. Carry it off. He thought the words, carry it off, but without attaching a meaning or any line of planning to them. He lifted his head and walked on to the corner and turned north. It was only a ten-block walk home, and he felt like walking. At a bar, he stopped and had a quick Scotch and water.

'Hel-lo, Phil,' Hazel said cheerily when he came in the door. 'Do you know what happened today? Something unbelievable.'

'What?' He tossed the *World-Telegram*, which he had just bought, down on the sofa.

'I got a raise.'

'Oh. Congratulations.'

She glanced at him, still smiling. 'And in celebration, I bought us some squabs. Saw them in a window and couldn't resist. Can you manage a squab?'

'I think so. Could you manage a drink?'

'Yes, definitely.'

And everything went quite smoothly, quite pleasantly, until just before 9 o'clock, when the telephone rang.

'Mrs Carter there, please?' asked a man's voice.

'Yes, just a minute,' Carter said. 'For you, Haze.'

Hazel came in from the kitchen, where she had been stacking the dishes, and took the telephone.

Carter lit a cigarette. He knew what it was.

'My God!' Hazel said. 'No ... No ... Certainly not ... No, I haven't.' She looked at Carter, who returned her look quizzically. 'I think three days ago, maybe four days, but I spoke to him just this morning ... Oh –' She sat down on the edge of the armchair seat. 'All right ... All right, of course. Thank you.' She put the telephone down, dropped it off the cradle with a clatter, then put it in the cradle correctly.

'What is it?' Carter asked.

'Mummy, what's the matter?' Timmie got up from the floor, leaving his books, and walked towards her.

'David's been killed.'

'Killed?' said Timmie. 'In a car?'

'He was murdered,' Hazel said in a shaking voice. 'Gawill, it must have been. Gawill or one of his friends. That slimy bastard!' She banged her fist down on the arm of her chair.

Carter brought her a straight Scotch.

She took the glass mechanically, but did not drink it. 'They said just a couple of hours ago. He had a dinner date with the Laffertys, and they came to pick him up. They got into the house, and a neighbour said he'd heard a strange noise around six like a man falling. So Mr Lafferty got the super to open the door and they found him.' Her voice grew tight with tears.

'How was he killed?' Carter asked.

'He was hit over the head with something. They think one of the Greek marble things,' Hazel said.

Carter cleared his throat. He was standing between Hazel and the kitchen. 'Do they want you to go there?'

'No. They said they might talk to me tomorrow. The Laffertys told them to call me up. They're calling all his friends, I suppose, but a lot of good that'll do when they ought to be calling Gawill.' She reached for the telephone and started dialling a number.

'The police are at Sullivan's?' Carter asked. For the first time, he thought of fingerprints. On the marble thing. Certainly on the doorknob.

Hazel didn't answer him. 'Hello, this is Mrs Carter. I wanted to tell you – I happen to know David had an enemy. Gregory Gawill. He lives in Long Island. I don't know the address. Just a minute. Phil – what's Gawill's address?'

Carter had to think a second, but he knew it. 'Seventeen eighty-eight One hundred and forty-seventh Street, Jackson Heights.'

'Seventeen eighty-eight One hundred and forty-seventh Street, Jackson Heights,' Hazel repeated carefully into the telephone.

Sicking them on to Gawill was sicking them right on to himself, Carter knew. The man coming down the stairs must have had a look at him. But Carter realized he wouldn't be able to identify the man, if he had to. He hadn't had that much of a look. He had been a little late getting home today. How was he going to explain that? 6.10 or so instead of 6. Anyway, he was going to stick to his story that he'd never been to Sullivan's apartment, unless the fingerprints made that impossible.

'It's very complicated,' Hazel was saying into the telephone. 'David always knew he was crooked, and Gawill disliked him.' She broke off, listening. 'All right ... You're very welcome. Can I call you again later tonight? Will somebody be there? ... Oh ... All right. You're welcome. Good-bye.' She hung up. 'They're going directly over to Gawill's. Not telephoning him.'

'When did it happen?'

'They think between five and seven. I said David usually wasn't home until after five thirty. It sounds as if someone followed him into his house. I don't think it'd be Gawill himself – would it?' She looked earnestly at Carter as if he would have the answer.

And she looked ravaged with grief already, Carter thought, in spite of her rather logical words. She wouldn't have the same expression on her face if something had happened to him, something fatal. Carter shook his head quickly. 'I don't know. I suppose it could have been Gawill.' Fingerprints can settle that, he started to say.

Timmie stood dazedly staring at Hazel, his mouth slightly open. Like a child whose father has just been killed, Carter thought.

'You don't seem at all shocked,' Hazel said to Carter.

'Shocked!' Carter opened his arms. 'What am I supposed to do?

Of course I'm shocked. – Are they going to call you again tonight?'

'I don't know. I don't think so.' She looked at her wristwatch. 'I'll call the Laffertys later tonight. I –' She got up slowly, one hand at her throat.

'Haze? Feeling faint?' Carter moved closer to her.

'No. Sickish. I think I'll lie down. But if the telephone rings –'

Carter nodded. 'How about some of that drink? It won't hurt you.'

'No thanks.' She went into the bathroom.

The telephone was going to ring again tonight, Carter felt sure. Carter started to put his hand on Timmie's shoulder. Timmie was kneeling by the armchair now, staring at the empty place where Hazel had been. 'Timmie, maybe you should think about going to bed, too.'

Timmie's answer was a great snuffle, then a groan of tears. He put his head down on the seat of the chair. Then suddenly he stood up. 'Turn on the radio! Maybe they'll tell who did it. The TV!'

Carter turned on the television. But he knew nothing about it was going to be on the 10 o'clock news.

22

Carter answered the telephone when it rang at half past 10.

'Detective Ostreicher here. Is this Mr Carter?'

'Yes.'

'We'd like to talk to you and your wife for a few minutes tonight, if that's convenient?' said the pleasant, crisp voice.

'Yes, of course.'

'We'll be over in ten minutes.'

Hazel was standing in the doorway in her nightdress.

'The police. They're coming over to talk to us,' Carter said.

'Did they say anything else?'

'No.'

She went back into the bedroom. Her light had not been off.

Carter emptied an ashtray and straightened some newspapers on the sofa.

The police arrived in less than ten minutes. Detective Ostreicher was a husky, blue-eyed young man who looked still in his twenties. With him was a dark-haired police officer, also rather young. Hazel came into the living-room in her dark-blue robe, and sat on the sofa. The two men sat down, after they had removed their overcoats, and each pulled out a tablet and ball-point pen.

They asked first for Carter's name, age, occupation and place of work, then Hazel's.

'Where were you today between five and seven o'clock, Mr Carter?' Ostreicher asked calmly, his pen poised. 'These are routine questions we're asking all Mr Sullivan's friends.'

'I was at the office, then I came home,' Carter said. 'I got home around six.'

'Can you tell us your exact movements? Your office is on Second and Forty-seventh, you said.'

'Yes. I took the Second Avenue bus down.'

'What time was that?'

'About – five thirty, I think.' It had been a couple of minutes earlier, Carter realized. 'The bus was crowded. I had to wait a few minutes for it. Then I got off before my stop – at Thirty-fourth Street – and walked home. Bought a newspaper –'

'Why did you get off there?'

'The bus was crowded. I thought I'd walk the six blocks.'

'You were home when he got home, Mrs Carter?'

'Yes.'

'Does that tally? He got home around six?'

Hazel nodded slowly. 'Yes.'

She could have said it was 6.10, Carter thought, if she had noticed, but maybe she hadn't noticed.

'When did you last see Mr Sullivan, Mr Carter?'

Carter turned automatically to Hazel. 'Wasn't it when he last came to dinner?'

'Yes. About ten days ago,' Hazel said.

Hazel had seen him since, and they were going to spring that business in another second, Carter thought. He rubbed his palms nervously and slowly together between his knees, his pinkish thumbs up. He sat on a straight chair.

'And you, Mrs Carter?'

'I saw him – Tuesday.'

'Tuesday evening?' asked Ostreicher.

'Yes.'

'Uh – you were in the habit of seeing Mr Sullivan when your husband was not present, Mrs Carter?'

Hazel rolled her head against the back of the armchair. 'I'm sure I know what Gawill told you, so let's not beat around the bush.'

'Is it true, Mrs Carter?'

'Some of it's true.'

'You were having an affair?'

'We were having an affair, yes.'

'With your husband's consent?' Ostreicher looked at Carter.

Carter did not change his expression, or he didn't think he did. He stared at some place in the middle of the coffee table.

'Not entirely with my husband's consent, no.'

'And you had some discussion about that – Tuesday night?'

'Yes. Late Tuesday night – when I came home.'

Another glance from Ostreicher to Carter. 'Did your husband make any threats against Mr Sullivan then or at any other time?'

'No,' Hazel said.

Ostreicher looked at Carter. 'Mr Carter, what was your honest attitude towards Mr Sullivan? Your feeling toward him?'

Carter opened his hands. 'I –' Suddenly he had no words at all. But Ostreicher was waiting. 'I knew about a short affair they had years ago. I learned just this week that it was still more or less going on.' It sounded damning, but Carter was sure Gawill had already said it, filled in the dates and the times Carter had visited him, and told him about the tapes. 'I mean – I've hardly had time to see how I feel – felt about him, have I?'

'You didn't attempt to see him, talk to him since Tuesday night? Gawill told me about Tuesday,' Ostreicher added.

'No.'

'Were you going to?'

Carter looked at him. 'I hadn't really finished talking with my wife. Finding out her intentions,' Carter said.

'I'm sorry to ask you these intimate questions, but what kind of talk did you have late Tuesday night?' Ostreicher looked from one to the other of them.

Carter was suddenly aware of Timmie standing in the hall doorway in his pyjamas, and he stood up. 'Timmie, you'd better go back to bed.' Carter walked towards him. 'Come on. We'll tell you all about it in the morning.'

'Do they know who killed David?' Timmie asked.

'We don't know anything yet. See you later, chum.' He patted Timmie's back and guided him, reluctantly, to his room and closed the door.

'What was the result of your conversation, Mr Carter?' Ostreicher asked as Carter came back.

'That – my wife admitted the affair was still going on,' Carter said. 'More or less.' He glanced at Hazel.

'And did you ask her to stop it?'

'Not exactly.'

'He asked me what I intended to do about it,' Hazel said, 'and I told him I didn't know – which was true.'

'You were in love with Mr Sullivan, Mrs Carter?' Ostreicher asked.

'I suppose so. Yes,' she said very softly.

'And you told your husband that?'

'More or less,' Hazel said,

'Had you any intention of dissolving your marriage?'

Hazel shook her head. 'We have a child, you know.'

'Yes, I know – In that case, the situation this week was in a very unresolved state.'

'I suppose so.'

Ostreicher looked at Carter expectantly.

'Yes,' Carter said.

Ostreicher turned a page in his tablet, turned a few more, looking at his writing. Then he said briskly, 'Mr Carter, we'll have to ask you for fingerprints.'

The officer in uniform was producing the proper materials from his briefcase.

Carter supposed this meant they had found fingerprints in Sullivan's apartment that were good enough to be compared with something.

'You had an injury to your thumbs when you were in prison, Gawill said,' Ostreicher remarked as he was pressing Carter's fingertips down.

'Yes.' His thumbs had hurt a lot since 6 o'clock, and Carter had taken a couple of Pananods before dinner. He dreaded Ostreicher's pressure.

'I'll let you do the thumbs – if you can give them a firm roll,' Ostreicher said.

Carter did, very firmly, so he would not have to do it a second time.

'We have a print from Mr Sullivan's apartment, but unfortunately it's not very good. It's from the marble foot that we think killed him, and the marble has a rough surface – at least where the print is. The doorknobs were too smeared to be of any help. The print we got is a middle finger – this one,' he said, pointing to the print next to the index on Carter's sheet of paper.

Carter said nothing. He knew he had struck Sullivan on the side of the neck – the first blow. Evidently no bruise had been visible, or it had been overlooked.

Ostreicher went back to Gawill. How long had Carter known him? What did he think of him? Did he think he might have been implicated in the fraud that got Carter into prison? Why had Carter gone to see Gawill on his own initiative Tuesday evening?

Carter explained that Gawill had been making accusations against his wife with regard to Sullivan, and that Carter had wanted to find out if Gawill had any proof.

'And had he?'

'Oh-h – some,' Carter said. 'Not as much as he boasted of having. You probably gathered he's a bit cracked.'

'Cracked how?'

'Paranoid. He hated Sullivan, magnified what Sullivan was doing against him – just as he tried to magnify the affair between Sullivan and my wife.' Carter felt a funny emotional rise as he said the words, and warned himself to be on his guard. How could an affair be magnified? It was either going on or it wasn't going on. 'My point is – Gawill was trying to whip me up to kill Sullivan. He was so transparent about it, he was funny. I said to him Tuesday night, "I'm not going to bother. You'll beat me to it, because you hate him much more than I do."'

Ostreicher listened attentively, so attentively he was forgetting to write, but the officer was writing. 'You're not going to bother, you said.'

'Something like that. I'm sure Gawill didn't tell you that, did he? He wants to pin this on me, I'm sure.'

'Yes, he certainly does. Well, so do you want to pin it on him.' Ostreicher smiled very slightly.

Carter looked at Hazel. Her face was tense, but her head still rested against the chair back.

'Did you ever tell Gawill you –' Ostreicher started again. 'According to Gawill, you threatened to kill Mr Sullivan. You said Tuesday night that you were going to do it.'

'Well, that's not true.' Carter took a breath. 'I'm quite sure Gawill told you that. Quite sure he wants you to believe it.' Carter looked at Hazel. 'Ask my wife – if I seemed that angry Tuesday night or if I made threats against him.' Carter got up and started for the kitchen. 'Excuse me, I'm going to get a glass of water. Would anyone else like one?'

Nobody wanted any.

'My husband certainly made no threats,' Hazel said.

Carter heard her voice distinctly. When he came back into the room, Ostreicher said:

'Were you ever in prison before this trouble down South?'

'No,' Carter said.

'And you served six years, according to Gawill.'

'Gawill has that right,' Carter said. 'Six years.'

Ostreicher glanced at the officer, who looked up. 'We'll see what the fingerprints can show us.'

The young officer nodded and said, 'Yes, sir.'

They both stood up. Ostreicher smiled. 'Good-bye, Mr Carter.' He turned to Hazel. 'Good night, Mrs Carter.'

Hazel got up. 'You'll call us tomorrow? Or can we call you?'

Ostreicher nodded. 'We'll call you tomorrow, I'm sure.'

'You'll check on Gawill's friends?' Hazel asked.

'Oh, all of them, never fear. Gawill's got a pretty air-tight alibi for tonight.'

'Yes, I was sure he would have,' Hazel said. 'I didn't bother asking about that.'

'Drinks and dinner with a couple of friends from six o'clock till ten. I spoke to them both by telephone tonight and also with the restaurant owner, but of course we'll talk to them all personally.'

'I don't think Gawill did it,' Hazel said with a bitter little smile, 'but he has an awful lot of shady friends.'

'Yes, I'm getting the idea,' Ostreicher replied. He waved a hand, and he and the young officer went to the door.

Carter let them out.

Hazel paused on her way to the bedroom and glanced at Carter. 'With the fingerprint – we might know by tomorrow, don't you think?'

Carter nodded. 'If it's good enough.'

Carter emptied the ashtray, and washed his water glass and put it away. Everything depended on whether Gawill's hired killer had spoken to Gawill this evening, Carter thought. But Gawill had probably told him not to telephone. Everything depended really, as usual, on money: if Gawill's killer had not collected, he might tell Gawill he had killed Sullivan when the news came out in the papers tomorrow. But if he had been paid in advance, he might say, 'I didn't do it, but I saw Carter coming up the stairs.' The in-between was more likely: Gawill's killer would collect his money for the killing (maybe five thousand dollars, maybe ten?) and then, if the police got on his trail and came to him, would come out with the real story: he hadn't done the killing, but he had seen Carter entering the apartment. Carter reckoned that he had either borrowed time – or a slim chance of absolution.

23

'How stupid of us not to have asked the police what number we could call,' Hazel said fretfully at the breakfast table.

There wasn't any jam on the table, and Carter didn't get up to fetch it. Both of them left part of their scrambled eggs. Only Timmie slowly and solemnly ploughed through his usual breakfast of Sugar Puffs, eggs, toast, and milk flavoured with a dash of coffee. He had questioned them at length as soon as he woke up, and the answers had not satisfied him.

There was the usual Saturday shopping to do. Carter volunteered to do it, because Hazel obviously wanted to be near the telephone. She wouldn't rest, Carter thought, until she had found out who killed Sullivan, and until the murderer was properly punished – put behind bars or executed. What had he possibly thought he could achieve by killing Sullivan? He simply hadn't thought, of course. Carter started making up the shopping list on his own. No use asking Hazel what she wanted for the weekend. Hazel went into the living-room to call the Laffertys. She had their number in her address book. While she was talking to them, Carter did the dishes. She talked a long while, and only finished as Carter was going out of the door with the wire shopping wagon.

Carter closed the door again. 'The Laffertys have anything to say?'

Hazel had no lipstick on, and her face was pale. 'Oh – they're saying he might have other enemies besides Gawill.'

'I suppose that's true – since he was a lawyer.'

'If he has, I don't know who they are. Neither do the Laffertys.' Hazel got up. She walked slowly towards the kitchen, but she might as well have been walking in the other direction, Carter thought, because she looked quite purposeless and in a daze.

'I should be back in about forty-five minutes,' Carter said, and went out.

When Carter got back, the police had called and wanted him to call them back.

'What did they say?' Carter asked Hazel. He was standing by the kitchen table, unloading two great bags of groceries.

'Fingerprints inconclusive,' Hazel said.

Carter frowned. 'How inconclusive?'

'The one they have isn't very definite. Could be a lot of people's or something.'

They were going to check him more closely on what he had done on Friday between the office and home, Carter supposed. Carter put everything away in the proper place, frozen orange juice, toilet paper, eggs, bacon, a large sirloin steak for tomorrow – bottom of refrigerator because Hazel didn't like it frozen – lamb chops, cold cereal, toothpaste, Kleenex, brussels sprouts and lettuce.

'Aren't you going to call?' Hazel asked. She was not yet dressed, sitting on the sofa looking over the *Times* that Carter had just bought. There was nothing in the *Times* about David Sullivan.

'Yes, just wanted to get the groceries out of the way.' Carter went to the telephone. Hazel had written the number firmly on the small tablet there and underlined it three times.

'Of all papers to buy, Phil. Couldn't you have gotten a tabloid at least?'

'I didn't see anything about it on the front page of the tabloids,' Carter said, which was true. There had been a plane crash in Long Island, and that had the front pages today. He dialled the number. 'This is Philip Carter,' he said to the man who answered. 'I'd like to talk to Detective Ostreicher.'

Carter was connected quickly.

'Morning, Mr Carter,' Ostreicher said. 'Thank you for calling. I suppose your wife told you about the fingerprint, it's not too good. Uh – We spoke with the secretary at your office this morning and – she said you left the office about five twenty.'

'Well – it could have been. What did I say, five thirty?'

'Yes,' said Ostreicher, and waited.

Carter waited, too.

'The girl says she knows, because she didn't leave till five thirty and then got delayed till five thirty-five or something taking letters out to mail – I mention this, because we're going to have to check on everybody's time very exactly, you see, since there's nothing else to go on. And your wife said this morning you could've come in at ten past six, she doesn't remember exactly.'

Another silence for a few seconds.

Had Ostreicher suggested to Hazel he might have been later than he said, Carter wondered, or had she come up with it herself? Hazel was watching him steadily. 'She may be right,' Carter said. 'I wasn't looking at my watch.' He might have mentioned stopping for a drink, but Ostreicher might try to check with the barman, and the bar he had stopped at was just south of Thirty-eighth Street. 'Did you want me to come down to the station or something?'

'Oh, no, thanks. We'll probably talk to you again this weekend. You'll be around? In town?'

Carter said he would be.

Carter put the telephone down and looked at Hazel. 'Asking me more about time,' he said. 'Six? Ten past six when I got home? I don't remember, do you?'

'I think a little after six. I don't remember exactly,' she said quietly. Hazel usually had something to do on Saturday mornings, letters to write, a trip to the library on Twenty-third. Now she sat with arms folded.

'I suppose I'll get on with this office stuff,' Carter said, moving towards the telephone table where the Jenkins and Field pamphlets were. They were material on the Detroit factory that he was supposed to redesign.

Hazel went into the bedroom.

And nothing happened that Saturday.

They had an invitation from Phyllis Millen to a cocktail party on Sunday, but Hazel called around 2 on Sunday and cancelled it. Hazel and Phyllis talked a long while, because by then the story was in the papers. The *Times* and the *Herald-Tribune* and the *Sunday News* all mentioned that Mrs Hazel Carter had allegedly been intimate with David Sullivan, but this piece of information had come from Gregory Gawill, according to all the papers, and Gawill was a self-avowed enemy of Sullivan. It was nice of the police, Carter thought, nice of Detective Ostreicher not to disclose to the Press that Hazel had admitted the affair herself. But it was bound to come out somehow in another day or so, and then the finger of suspicion, as all the newspapers called it (which was not pointing in any direction on Sunday, not even at Gawill), would be directed at him. Carter did not listen to Hazel's conversation with Phyllis. He went into the bedroom and sat at the desk with his office work. Carter doggedly made notes and sketchy diagrams for the Detroit architect he was to work with, not knowing if he would ever get to Detroit. He thought of Hazel telegraphing Sullivan's parents in Massachusetts yesterday afternoon. The police would have notified the Sullivans, of course, but

Hazel had wanted to send a telegram of condolence. 'You've met them?' Carter had asked. 'Oh, yes. Twice. They came down to New York one weekend when I was here in the summer, and David and I drove up to Stockbridge one time and visited them.' She had said it flatly, indifferently to Carter, and Carter had had the lost, left-out feeling he had so often known in prison when Hazel told him, a bit late, about something she had done or was going to do. He thought he remembered something about her meeting Sullivan's parents, but if she had ever told him she had visited them, he had forgotten it. Now it seemed to Carter she had the concern of a daughter-in-law about expressing her sorrow and her grief over Sullivan's death.

When the telephone rang at 10.15 that evening, Carter barely noticed, because it had rung so often. But now it was the police, Carter could tell from Hazel's taut, 'Yes . . . yes,' which he heard in the bedroom. He came slowly into the living-room.

'Of course. Very fine . . . Good.' She hung up. 'The police are coming over,' she said to Carter.

'Do they know anything?'

'They didn't say.' She stood up.

Timmie had come out of his room into the hall. 'Can I stay up, Mummy?'

Hazel pushed her hand through her hair. 'Yes. All right. Stay up in your room, if you like, but you shouldn't come in when the police are here, darling.'

'Why not?'

Hazel shook her head, and she looked about to weep from nerves. 'Because we'll tell you everything they say, I promise you.'

And about the affair, too, Carter wondered, or did Timmie already know about that and take it for granted? *What do they mean by 'intimate'?* Timmie had asked Carter as he was poring over the newspapers, and Carter had answered that it meant that

Hazel and David had been very close friends. But Timmie must know intuitively, Carter thought. Carter steered Timmie towards his room again.

'After they leave, we'll have a chocolate milk and I'll tell you everything they said,' Carter told him. He took his hand from Timmie's back, and patted his shoulder. 'See you, chum.' Carter went back into the living-room. Hazel was standing by the armchair. He put his right arm around her waist and drew her to him, in an impulse to comfort her, but Hazel pulled back.

'Sorry. I'm nervous,' she said.

She went into the bedroom.

Then the bell rang.

It was Ostreicher and the same young officer.

'Well, all day with Gawill and his friends,' Ostreicher said. 'Checking their fingerprints, too, of course.'

Carter sat tensely, listening. Ostreicher hadn't come to make him a report on Gawill, he was sure.

'What about the fingerprints?' Hazel asked.

'There's only one,' Ostreicher said with a smile. 'It could be Mr Anthony O'Brien's, it could be your husband's, it could be – what's his name? Charles Ewart.' Ostreicher looked at the police officer, who nodded. There were circles under Ostreicher's eyes.

'Christopher Ewart,' the officer said. He was not taking notes, though his tablet was on his lap, his arms folded.

Anthony was the first name of the fellow who had been at Gawill's apartment with the blonde, Carter remembered, a muscular fellow who looked like a prizefighter or a football player. It could have been he running down the stairs, Carter supposed, though he hadn't really been able to tell if the man was brawny or not under the flying overcoat. And Carter winced a little, involuntarily, as he realized that he had known, as soon as he heard Sullivan's story that night, that whoever it was running down the stairs would get the blame or at least be suspected of Sullivan's murder, somehow.

'Gawill's two friends he had dinner with Friday night,' Ostreicher said, 'are a couple of men from New Jersey. One's a Greek. They were having dinner in a Greek restaurant in Manhattan. We've seen both the men. Acquaintances of Gawill's he doesn't see very often, apparently, both with jobs and families and anyway their fingerprints are out, don't match at all.' He took a photograph about six inches square from his tablet. 'All we have, you might say – concrete – is this line here and these whorls above it. Arches.'

Carter took the photograph that Ostreicher held out to him, and Hazel got up to look at it over Carter's shoulder. It was approximately one-third of a fingerprint, a third finger, with a short vertical line running across the whorls near the outer edge. It was certainly fragmentary.

'It could be a part of thousands of people's fingerprints,' Ostreicher said. 'The fingerprint's a help, a guide. We won't bother questioning some man *without* a fingerprint like this.' He smiled briefly.

'What about O'Brien?' Hazel asked. 'Who's he?'

'A barman in Jackson Heights. Friend of Gawill's. According to O'Brien and his roommate, he came home at five p.m. Friday to his apartment in Jackson Heights, then the roommate went out about five fifteen, and according to O'Brien he stayed in till seven having a shower and a nap, then went out and had a hamburger in the neighbourhood and went to the movies. He's seen the movie, all right, but nobody can definitely say he was in the hamburger place Friday or went to the movie Friday. He could have gone Thursday. The movie was on Thursday, and O'Brien was off Thursday afternoon but working Thursday night, working Friday afternoon but off Friday night. No criminal record, by the way.' Ostreicher drew on his cigarette.

'But you suspect him?' Hazel asked.

Ostreicher cleared his throat and looked at Hazel. 'We have to question everybody, Mrs Carter. There're one or two people Sullivan knew – one of them in fact whose print this could be – that we've found, so far – shady, questionable – and remote.' He smiled in a resigned way. 'This was a murder of passion – either of the person who did it or the person who hired him to do it. Any lawyer can be hated by the man he's about to ruin, Mr Sullivan had such a case coming up, but nobody kills the lawyer for that, they kill the person who's hiring the lawyer, don't they?' Ostreicher unbuttoned his jacket. 'The situation would seem to leave Gawill – and you, Mr Carter.'

'And – what're you going to do about O'Brien's story, for instance? His alibi?' Hazel asked.

'Keep checking it,' Ostreicher said. 'Keep watching him, along with some others. Watch for the movements of money in people's bank accounts, watch the people themselves, who they see and talk to. The usual. We should have something in a couple of days,' he finished, on a more cheerful note.

'And what about the one named Ewart?' she asked.

'Ewart joined Gawill and the other two Friday night at the restaurant. Another New Jerseyite, a car salesman. I only mentioned him, because it could be his print, too. But he's got an alibi. He was getting his car serviced in New Jersey from five till nearly six. We checked with the garage. Then he went to the restaurant in Manhattan.' Ostreicher sighed and looked into space. 'Gawill could have hired somebody. We're going to look into his bank accounts tomorrow morning.'

'I doubt if he'd be stupid enough to show anything there,' Carter said.

'We'll look anyway.' Ostreicher smiled his twinkling smile. 'Mr Carter, you're right-handed?'

'Yes,' Carter said. He knew the fingerprint was of the third finger of a right hand.

'Not any stronger in one hand than the other – because of your thumb injuries?'

'No.' His left thumb hurt less, but that didn't make the hand any stronger.

'I must ask you both again,' Ostreicher said, leaning forward in his chair, 'if you had made any plan or come to any decision or agreement – even a peaceful one – about the future with you,' with a nod at Hazel, 'and you,' a nod at Carter, 'and Mr Sullivan because of the talks you had about it this past week?'

Hazel answered first. 'We came to no agreement. Maybe that's worse than coming to one.'

'Not necessarily. – I've told you, according to Gawill, Mr Carter was furious, but don't think I believe anything Gawill tells me.' He turned to Carter. 'You had no idea about talking to Mr Sullivan about the situation?'

'Well, yes,' Carter said slowly. 'I tried to see him Tuesday night, as Gawill must have told you. That was the evening I saw my wife on the sidewalk – on her way to see him.' He sat up straighter and said with an effort at calmness, 'I did want to talk to Sullivan to ask him if it was true the affair was still going on and to ask him what he intended to do about it – now that I knew about it. But I never saw him that night.'

'No. Gawill told me.' Ostreicher gave a small smile. 'You didn't try to see Mr Sullivan after that?'

'No.'

'Why not?'

'Because – seeing my wife visiting him was perhaps part of the answer I wanted,' Carter said. 'Any more talking, I preferred to do with my wife.'

'Did you? Why?' Ostreicher asked in a dull, automatic way, as if he were not interested in the answers. Or as if he didn't believe Carter's last reply.

'Because – I felt what Sullivan wanted to do or was doing,

having an affair with a married woman, was his business, but I did have a right to ask my wife what she intended to do – because she's my wife.'

Ostreicher nodded and smiled his little smile that looked like disbelief. 'What did you intend to do, Mrs Carter?'

Carter saw the troubled, tortured expression come over Hazel's face. How could one have one's cake and eat it, too?

'I honestly don't know,' Hazel said. 'I was confused Tuesday night. I suppose I would have given David up, yes.'

'But you didn't say that to your husband?'

'No. Not plainly.'

Ostreicher sighed. 'Did you discuss it with Mr Sullivan Tuesday night?'

'No,' Hazel said.

'Didn't you tell him you'd just seen your husband on the sidewalk out in front?'

Hazel shook her head quickly. 'No.' She looked suddenly at Carter. 'Don't you think you should tell Mr Ostreicher about Gawill's dope? Just the fact that he had it?'

'Dope?' said Ostreicher.

'Yes,' Carter said. 'He offered me some dope – heroin – and I took some, twice. I had to take morphine in the hospital – in prison – for my thumbs. Gawill had quite a bit.'

'How much?'

'It looked like more than two hundred plastic ampoules. Liquid form. Each held ten grains, Gawill told me.'

Ostreicher frowned. 'He hasn't got it now. We searched that apartment. – Why did you take it, Mr Carter?'

Carter drew a breath. 'It helps kill the pain in my thumbs. I also enjoy it.'

'You took it on two occasions, you said. Are you in the habit of taking it? From day to day?'

'No. The pills I'm taking do well enough, and they have a

morphine base, matter of fact.' He glanced at Hazel. 'I take about four a day, sometimes six, and I suppose that amounts to two or three grains of morphine.'

'Didn't you think it unusual that Gawill had so much dope in his apartment?' Ostreicher asked. 'I presume that's where you took it. Where did you think he got it from?'

'I did think it was unusual. But considering the people he goes with –' Carter shrugged. 'I didn't ask Gawill any questions, because that wasn't why I went to see him.'

'You didn't try to make any guesses as to where he might have got it?'

'No. I didn't care.' Carter felt the disapproval of Hazel and also of Ostreicher at that remark: the possession of heroin was illegal, and he had not only not reported it, but had enjoyed some himself. 'I was trying to get some information out of Gawill. I didn't want to antagonize him – frankly.'

'You might have mentioned it to me before now,' Ostreicher said, and looked at his colleague Charles, who was writing in his tablet. 'This opens up dope-handlers now. A messy batch and lots of 'em.' He shook his head, as if contemplating in dismay a new field of action, but he wasn't moving towards the telephone.

Carter felt that Ostreicher suspected him very strongly, had all along, and that he was so sure, he didn't have to hurry. Carter swallowed and glanced at Hazel.

Hazel was leaning forward with her arms on her knees, staring at the floor. Suddenly she looked up at Ostreicher. 'Just how long do you really think it will take to find who did it?'

Ostreicher took his time answering, then it was the same old answer, 'Maybe two or three days. Maybe even less. Let's see what Gawill's banks show tomorrow. We'll have to look into yours, too, Mr Carter.'

Carter nodded. He stood up as Ostreicher did.

'And of course we'll get on to Gawill about the dope,'

Ostreicher said. 'Grasso might know something. Gawill's boss. He really doesn't seem to have any idea Gawill planned Sullivan's murder or had anything to do with it, but maybe Gawill's just being very careful about that. Gawill and Grasso are very close – personally, I mean. Chummy.' Ostreicher rubbed his chin and stared at a wall for a moment, then looked at Carter and smiled. 'Back to work for us tonight. Got to look at Grasso's house and also O'Brien's for the dope. What kind of container was it in?'

'A cardboard box about two feet square,' Carter said. 'The ampoules were lying on cotton in layers.'

'Probably in mayonnaise jars now,' Ostreicher murmured, 'or liquid silver-polish jars.' He chuckled. 'Off we go, Charles.'

Timmie came in when the apartment door closed. Carter went to pour him the promised chocolate milk, while Hazel tried to answer his questions. The answer to the main question was still missing. But Timmie was very interested in O'Brien. Timmie sat on the sofa, holding his chocolate milk. 'Maybe they know O'Brien did it and they're just waiting for something very *definite*.'

Hazel looked tiredly at Carter. 'I don't know where else we can go with this tonight.'

Carter didn't know what to say, either. Timmie had seen tele-vision plays in which the detectives kept back what they knew until they could let it all fall with a wallop on the guilty person. That was what he was groping for now, that kind of situation. 'It's too early to tell anything now, Timmie,' Carter said.

In bed, Carter tried to put his arm around Hazel, to hold her while she fell asleep, but she twisted slowly, with the tension of someone wide awake, and said, 'Sorry, I can't. I can't stand to be touched right now.'

'Hazel, I love you.' Carter's hand tightened on her shoulder. 'Can't we just fall asleep together?'

But she wouldn't, and neither of them slept for a long while.

24

'Can we have a word with you, Mrs Carter?'

A camera flashed.

'Mrs Carter,' said the nervous-looking reporter with a smile, 'just one question. About Sullivan –'

'Just shove off,' Carter said.

There were three of them, and two had cameras.

'Don't *touch* me!' Hazel said, pulling her arm from the grip of the nervous young man.

Carter put his arm around her and they walked quickly towards Hazel's car, which was about six yards away.

'Get in. I'll drop you at your office,' Hazel said.

Carter got in. He practically had to close the door on one of the reporters' hands.

Hazel drove off.

'It's a wonder they haven't come before this,' Carter said.

'They were calling up yesterday – three or four times. I just didn't bother mentioning it.'

Carter said nothing, knowing Hazel was ashamed, angry and that she would turn her anger against him as much as the reporters, if he tried to talk to her. But after a few moments, he said quietly, 'You don't have to take me all the way to the office. We've got rid of them now.'

And Hazel swerved to a kerb as soon as she could, and stopped the car.

'Thanks,' he said, getting out. 'See you later, darling.' No use the 'Chin up', even the 'I love you', that he had an impulse to say to her. She was ashamed because her affair with Sullivan would be known now to everyone in her office, ashamed, too, because the newspapers and the radio were this morning blazoning the fact that her husband was an ex-convict.

Carter walked into his office and tensed at the sight of Elizabeth at the front desk, the red-headed girl who had told the police he had left at 5.20, not 5.30 p.m. on Friday. 'Morning, Elizabeth,' Carter said.

'Morning, Mr Carter. Uh –' She slid out from her desk and stood up. She was tall and slender, nearly as tall as Carter in her high heels. Her young face was serious and intense. 'I hope you're not annoyed by what I said to the police. They were questioning me very carefully, down to the minute. I just said what I remembered and what I thought was true.'

'No, it's perfectly okay,' Carter said, smiling slightly. 'Nothing to worry about.' He walked on to his office.

Mr Jenkins, a tall, grey-haired man, was walking down the green-carpeted corridor. 'Good morning, Mr Carter.'

'Morning, sir,' said Carter.

Mr Jenkins paused. 'Come in a moment, will you?'

Carter went with him into his office, and Mr Jenkins closed the door.

'I'm sorry about this awful trouble,' Mr Jenkins said. 'What's going to happen?'

'I don't know.' Carter looked back into Mr Jenkins' eyes. 'However – I understand the difficulties of taking me on here in the first place, so if you think it might be better if I resigned, I'm quite agreeable, Mr Jenkins.'

'Well, I wasn't thinking of that as yet,' Mr Jenkins replied, looking a bit embarrassed. 'But you're supposed to go to Detroit this Thursday. You can't if the police haven't cleared it up, can you? I presume they're still talking to you?' He looked at Carter as if in the next seconds he could determine whether Carter had done the killing or not.

'That's true. But – I thought I could write up my ideas and maybe Mr Butterworth could go in my place.'

Mr Jenkins sighed and opened his arms in an impatient gesture. 'Well, we'll see, we'll see. – Have you any idea who did this?'

Carter hesitated. 'I'd guess someone around Gawill. Sullivan's old enemy from years back. But I don't know, Mr Jenkins.'

Mr Jenkins looked at him wordlessly for a moment, and Carter knew he was thinking that Carter's wife had been 'intimate' with the man who was slain, and what an odd situation it was that the man who was murdered had recommended Carter for his job and that they had been presumably the best of friends.

When Carter had entered his own office and closed his door, it occurred to him that Mr Jenkins had not asked the obvious question, 'You're completely innocent, of course? You had nothing at all to do with this?' There could be only one reason why Mr Jenkins had not said something like that. Mr Jenkins thought he might be guilty.

Carter had been prepared for a sticky conversation with Butterworth that morning, but for some reason Butterworth was not in the office. He began to type up his notes on the Detroit factory. Again and again his mind drifted to Timmie, Timmie in his school on Nineteenth Street now, being asked questions by the kids, being stared at, being jibed at because his father had been in prison; and of course the kids wouldn't miss the story that

Timmie's mother had been sleeping with another man. Hazel had said once, 'Timmie's so much better now that we're in New York, because the kids here don't know anything about the prison business.' Now that was all going to break open again.

Carter's telephone rang just after 11.

'Mr Carter, this is Ostreicher. I wonder can you come down to the station for a few minutes? It's most important ...'

Carter told Elizabeth that he had to go out for a while, and that he might be back before lunch, but he was not sure. He wondered if she had listened to the conversation and knew he was off to see the police? Probably.

Ostreicher's precinct station was in the east Fifties. Carter walked the five blocks. He was shown by a middle-aged officer to a room down a hall.

'Come in, Mr Carter,' said Ostreicher, getting up from his desk.

In a large, file-lined office were Gawill and O'Brien and two men and a woman whom Carter did not know. Carter nodded to Gawill, who did not return the nod. Gawill was slumped sullenly in his chair with his fingers locked across his stomach.

'Mr Carter, I think you know Mr Gawill. This is Mr O'Brien, and this is Mr and Mrs Ferres and Mr Devlin. These people live in Mr Sullivan's building.'

Carter nodded and murmured, 'How do you do?' He had taken his hat off. The three people from Mr Sullivan's house were eyeing him carefully.

'Do any of you remember seeing Mr Carter in Mr Sullivan's house? At any time?' Ostreicher asked.

The woman answered first, shaking her head. 'No.'

The men also gave negative answers.

'These people happened to be in at the time of the murder,' Ostreicher said, 'and they were kind enough to come down this morning to – on the off chance they might have seen any of you going into Mr Sullivan's building on Friday evening.' Ostreicher's glance took in Gawill, O'Brien and Carter. His tone was as usual brisk and pleasant. 'It was Mrs Ferres who heard something that sounded like a body falling to the floor at what she thinks was six o'clock or a couple of minutes before. She heard nothing after that, no sound of running steps or anything.'

Carter avoided O'Brien's eyes, and he felt that O'Brien avoided his also. O'Brien was in a too bright blue pin-stripe suit, his hair shiny with brilliantine.

'Mr Carter, have you seen Mr O'Brien before?' Ostreicher asked. He was still standing behind his desk.

Carter looked at O'Brien briefly. O'Brien was staring at his own shoes now. 'I think I met him one night at Gawill's apartment.'

'When was that?'

'About ten days ago, I think,' Carter answered. Had Gawill and O'Brien denied it, Carter wondered? Their faces told nothing.

'Have you seen him since?' asked Ostreicher.

'No,' Carter said.

'Have you seen Mr Carter since, Mr O'Brien?' Ostreicher asked.

'Nope,' said O'Brien, glancing up briefly.

'Did you talk much to each other the night you met?'

O'Brien didn't answer.

'I don't think I said a thing to him,' Carter said, 'except "How do you do?"'

'Anthony didn't stay long that night, not after Phil came,' Gawill put in.

Ostreicher nodded. He turned around and opened a closet behind his desk and took something from a shelf. It was the Greek marble foot, a left foot. He placed it with both hands in the centre of his desk, watching Gawill, O'Brien and Carter as he did so. 'This is the murder weapon,' Ostreicher said. 'It was held like this, someone's hand around the narrow part on the instep here. Mr Sullivan was probably struck with the toes of this.'

Gawill stared at the foot with an air of indifference and boredom. O'Brien's eyes widened as he looked at it. His rather stupid face looked merely blank.

'Mr Carter, let me see you pick this up,' said Ostreicher.

Carter moved closer to Ostreicher's desk, and extended his left hand, changed to his right, and picked up the foot with his thumb under the arch and his fingers curved around the outside of the foot. He felt pain in his right thumb as he lifted it. His grip was not tight.

'Turn that over, please. Just turn your wrist,' Ostreicher said, illustrating with a turn of his own wrist.

Carter turned his wrist. On the bottom of the foot, on the marble peppered with time and abrasion, was a circle a good inch away from where his third finger rested, no doubt the spot where the fingerprint had been.

'Um-m,' said Ostreicher, and moved Carter's fingers until the third finger rested on the spot, then shook the marble foot to feel Carter's grip.

Carter then put the foot down on the desk.

Ostreicher glanced at him, then looked at O'Brien. 'Mr O'Brien, would you oblige?'

O'Brien got up obediently and picked up the foot from the same sole-on-the-desk position it had been in when Carter picked it up. With a thumb under the arch was the most likely way anyone would pick up the thing, because what nubbin remained of the ankle was uneven and slanting inward towards the arch side of the foot. Ostreicher turned O'Brien's hand over. O'Brien's middle finger rested on the circle, Carter saw. O'Brien had bigger hands than Carter, but Carter also realized he had taken a big hard grip on the marble that night. Ostreicher made no comment on O'Brien's grip, but turned to the three occupants of Sullivan's house.

'I don't think there's any reason for you people to stay any longer,' Ostreicher said. 'My thanks to all of you for coming down. It's been very useful.'

It had been no help at all, Carter thought. The people stirred in their chairs and got up with a slight air of reluctance, as if they were being asked to leave before the best part of the show. Ostreicher walked out in the hall with them, but immediately came back and closed the door.

'Now. Well –' Ostreicher sat sideways against his desk, and pressed his palms together. 'One of you here is guilty and we're going to find out which.'

'If you're including me, you don't know your business,' Gawill said with anger.

Ostreicher ignored him, and smiled a little at Carter. 'Mr Carter, your alibi is not exactly air-tight: You had enough time – especially if you took a taxi instead of a bus – to get to Sullivan's apartment Friday afternoon, stay five minutes or even ten, and take another taxi home. It doesn't take ten minutes to kill a man with a thing like this, does it?'

Such polite accusation was new to Carter, quite unlike anything he'd experienced in prison. 'No, of course not,' he said.

Ostreicher looked at his wristwatch, then turned to Gawill. 'Mr Gawill, any idea why your boss isn't choosing to turn up this morning?'

'No idea,' Gawill said. 'Maybe he had to go do something in one of his apartments, who knows?'

'Like make sure his dope's still there or something?' Ostreicher said, frowning, and set his strong jaw, the first sign of temper he had shown. 'He doesn't spend much time at the pipe factory, does he?'

'That's his business where he spends his time,' Gawill said.

Ostreicher turned to Carter again. 'You have found no reason, I take it, to change any of the statements you've made to me about your actions on Friday night?'

'No,' said Carter.

'Would you take off your jacket, please, Mr Carter?'

Ostreicher was moving towards his closet again. 'I'd like to give you a lie-detector test.' He was getting the machine from a shelf.

To Carter's surprise, Gawill and O'Brien were not asked to leave and he was not taken to another room. A rubber plate with a cord to it was attached to his bare chest, more rubber tied to his arm for his blood pressure, and then Ostreicher began his questioning. The time of everything, leaving the office, the bus ride, the walking, the newspaper buying, the arrival home when Hazel had been there. Then the questions in a different form: 'You didn't take a bus down to Thirty-eighth and then go to see David Sullivan Friday?' Carter did not think his heart beat very much faster. A little faster, yes. But he found himself able to answer the questions mechanically, as if he didn't care, didn't consider them very important. And that was exactly it, he thought, he really didn't care too much what happened to himself. 'You didn't say to Sullivan, "I've had enough of your two-facedness, your hypocrisy," something like that, then pick up that marble foot from one of his shelves and –'

'No,' Carter replied.

'Mr Carter, you're a surprisingly cool man – today. Cold.'

Carter sighed and looked at Ostreicher. He felt Gawill's and O'Brien's eyes on him. He had not once looked their way, though he was almost facing them.

'In your conversation with your wife Tuesday night, were you just as cold?'

'No,' Carter said.

'Did you ask her to stop seeing Sullivan?'

Carter was suddenly painfully annoyed by Gawill's and O'Brien's presence. He squirmed in the straight chair. 'I asked her if she could. Or if she wanted to.'

'You were asking her to make a choice then. "Choose me or else." Just how did you put it, Mr Carter?'

'Not that way,' Carter said, looking at Ostreicher. 'There was no or else.'

'What answer did your wife *really* give you?'

'She gave – what I said,' Carter said carefully. 'She said she didn't know what she could or couldn't do.'

Ostreicher smiled impatiently. 'That was an unsatisfactory answer from your point of view, wasn't it?'

Carter loathed the probing now. It was like Dr Cassini's steel probe, groping clumsily around in a wound for a piece of shiv blade. 'It was not as unsatisfactory as you seem to think.'

'Mr Carter, I submit that you had ample cause to hate Mr Sullivan and to want him out of the way. You had ample cause last week to become murderously angry.'

Carter sat motionless.

'What would you say if I told you that I'm going to prove you guilty beyond a shadow of doubt?' Ostreicher came close to Carter, wagging a finger.

But even Ostreicher's attack was not real, Carter felt. It was like something Ostreicher was enacting in a play. When the play was over in a few minutes, they'd start acting like themselves again, like people not connected with each other. 'I'd say go ahead and try,' Carter said.

'Ain't he a cool one,' Gawill said. 'Good boy, Carter!' And he chuckled.

Ostreicher only glanced at Gawill. Then he removed the buckled strap from Carter's chest. The machine had put a thin, jagged line around a drum on the desk. Carter did not look hard at it, and told himself he didn't care what it showed. Ostreicher looked at it, bending over his desk. Then he changed the paper.

A knock came at the door.

'Come in,' said Ostreicher.

A short, dark man, who Carter supposed was Grasso, came in. He smiled at Gawill and nodded.

'Hi,' Gawill said.

'Morning, Mr Grasso,' Ostreicher said.

'Morning,' said Grasso. He was a squat Italian with round dark eyes, expectantly lifted eyebrows, a heavy and somewhat down-turned mouth, but it was a face that summed up to no particular kind of expression, and was therefore a rather good mask, Carter supposed. Grasso probably had to dead-pan most of his way through life.

'Would you sit down, Mr Grasso? Mr O'Brien?'

O'Brien got up, removed his jacket, and sat down in the chair Carter had left. His shoulder muscles filled out his shirt and stretched it taut against his powerful deltoids. Even his waist was thick with muscle, though quite flat. A blow with half his potential force, Carter thought, might have broken Sullivan's neck.

'Now, Friday,' Ostreicher began.

Was Gawill going to be in for it, too, Carter wondered? Gawill looked still quite unnervous and a bit bored.

'I went straight from the Rainbow Bar home,' O'Brien said in a slightly adenoidal voice. 'I took a shower and had a nap. I went out about seven for something to eat. Then I saw a movie.' His voice was a colourless drone, as if he were reciting something he had learned by heart.

'Your roommate went out about five fifteen,' Ostreicher said. 'You could have hopped in a taxi and got to Manhattan in less than fifteen minutes.'

O'Brien shrugged slightly. 'Why should I go to Manhattan?'

'To kill Sullivan because you're being paid for it, maybe,' Ostreicher came back.

O'Brien looked down at the floor and rubbed his nose with a forefinger, simulating unconcern.

'You're usually at the gym Friday nights working out, you said, and so does the gym say so. Why weren't you there Friday?'

'I thought I had a cold coming on. That's why I took a nap Friday.'

Gawill had coached him on that, Carter thought.

'Is this your first killing, O'Brien?'

O'Brien did not answer.

Gawill laughed, barely audible.

'They don't remember seeing you at the hamburger place.'

'Why should they?' asked O'Brien. 'It was crowded.'

O'Brien was going to hang on to the money Gawill had paid him, if he possibly could. His steady nerve was comforting for Carter to see.

'Where did Sullivan live, O'Brien?' Ostreicher asked, and glanced at the slowly rotating drum.

'Manhattan.'

'Where in Manhattan? You know the address, let's have it.'

'I don't,' O'Brien said, looking at Ostreicher. 'Why should I know his exact address?'

'Because Gawill told you to remember it and you did!' Ostreicher said.

O'Brien took cover under a squirm and a laugh. 'Which one of us are you accusing, me or Carter?'

'O'Brien, whatever Gawill paid you – you're not going to have much time to enjoy it. If any.' Ostreicher unstrapped him.

It was a weak finish for Ostreicher, and O'Brien smiled a little. So did Gawill.

'Mr Carter, there's no particular reason for you to stay any longer,' Ostreicher said.

Carter stood up. He went to the door, turned and said, 'Good-bye.'

Ostreicher nodded, looking at Carter in a preoccupied way. 'Good-bye. Oh – You're not to leave town until you hear further from me, if you don't mind, Mr Carter. Your office said you were intending to take off somewhere the end of the week.'

'Yes,' Carter said. 'All right, I understand.' He closed the door.

No doubt Ostreicher had had some conversations, probably face to face, with Jenkins, Field and Butterworth over the weekend.

Butterworth came in in the afternoon, and asked Carter by telephone if he would come into his office. Carter went. Butterworth looked tired, a little puffy under his eyes. His manner was as gentle as ever as he asked Carter to sit down, and as he expressed his shock at the loss of his friend David Sullivan.

'I heard you spoke with the police this morning,' Butterworth said. 'They called me again this morning. Uh – Did you find out anything more?'

'No. They were also talking to Gawill and a friend of his called O'Brien,' Carter said, sliding back in his chair, locking his fingers together as Gawill had, as he leaned forward. 'They were still talking to them when I left, so I don't know what's happening.'

'Have you any suspicions? Any ideas?'

'Outside of some connection with Gawill, no. If there's a connection, I'm sure they'll find it. I don't know if Sullivan ever talked to you about Gawill.'

'Oh, yes, he did. Several times I suggested to David that he hire a bodyguard – or first of all talk to the police about the following that was going on. But good Lord, I never thought it would come to cold-blooded murder. – And of course the other business.' Butterworth leaned on his fingers and rubbed his forehead. 'I must say I was surprised at that. I take it you were, too,' Butterworth said, and looked at Carter. 'I mean – David and your wife. Or is that story true?'

'Yes. It's true. I hadn't – Well,' Carter stammered, flushing, 'I had suspected, I must admit, but I hadn't thought – I mean – that it was still going on. I think it's all a bit exaggerated, and I haven't tried to question my wife about it too much, because she's so upset by David's death.' Carter's face was still warm. And he realized that he was trying to cover up more for Hazel than himself. 'By the way, the police told me this morning that they want me to stay in town for the next several days, so I'm afraid that lets Detroit out. I've already said this to Mr Jenkins –'

'Yes, yes, I thought of that. I'll be able to go. I spent this morning arranging it.'

Carter got up.

When they went over Carter's notes around 4 that afternoon, the Sullivan affair was not mentioned.

Carter looked at the evening papers with great interest at 5.30, standing on the corner of Fiftieth and Second Avenue, waiting for his bus. Sullivan had been buried today in the family plot in his home town in Massachusetts, and there was a picture of his parents and some relatives standing by the graveside this morning with bowed heads. His father was very like Sullivan. Carter stared at their faces and tried to picture Hazel knowing them, talking to them. It was easy to imagine, and disturbing. He was glad she hadn't gone up to attend the funeral. He had hopes for some results of Ostreicher's talk with Gawill and Gawill's boss Grasso, but nothing was reported except that Salvatore Grasso had been called in for questioning by the police. There was no mention of dope or of a lie-detector test having been given to him or to O'Brien. They could have been beaten with rubber truncheons and that wouldn't have been reported, either, Carter thought. At least, O'Brien had not talked yet, or surely that would have been mentioned. Carter almost missed his bus, and jumped in just as the doors were closing.

At home, he found Hazel standing in the living-room with tears in her eyes, and Timmie in his room face down on his bed, shaking with sobs.

Carter walked towards her. 'You don't have to tell me. I know.'

She drew back a little, though he hadn't been going to touch her. 'He came home at lunch time,' she said. 'He's been here all afternoon.'

'Oh, Christ,' Carter said. He hung up his coat, then went in to see his son. 'Timmie?'

A long silence.

'What?'

Carter sat down at the foot of the bed, because Timmie was so near the edge, there was no room beside him. 'What happened today? Tell me all about it.'

'They said you're an ex-con. My dad's an ex-con, they said.'

'Well, you've had that before, Timmie, and you pulled through it, didn't you?'

Timmie drew his right leg away from Carter's touch. 'It's what they say about David,' he said with another rush of weeping into his pillow. 'They call him my uncle David. It's got a special meaning to them.'

'Come on, Timmie, don't cry any more. Let's have the rest of it.'

'Phil, do you have to make him go over it?' Hazel said. She had come to the doorway. Her face was furious.

'It's better if he talks,' said Carter.

'He's talked it all out to me. He doesn't want to go over it again.'

'Well, suppose I want to hear it?' Carter said, standing up.

'Don't you ever think about anybody else but yourself?'

'I'm thinking about Timmie, or I wouldn't be here!'

'You might have thought of him in the past.'

Carter moved towards her, and Hazel took a step back, turned and went into the bedroom. Carter went out and closed Timmie's door. 'You might have thought of him when you started your affair with Sullivan,' Carter said. 'You've got a hell of a right to throw something like that at me!'

Hazel said nothing.

'It's in the papers now and you can't face it, I suppose. Neither can Timmie. It's the affair he's upset about, not the ex-con business. He's had that before.' It was plain now why she had not gone to Sullivan's funeral. And suddenly it seemed to Carter that Timmie was literally an extension of Hazel's flesh and blood and mind, that their tears now were for the same reason: the public knew the secret that both of them had known since the affair began. Carter blinked his stinging eyes. 'Well, Hazel, it's happened. Can't we try to pick up the pieces instead of quarrelling?'

'I don't want the pieces,' Hazel said angrily.

'I'm talking about the pieces of Timmie – for instance. What did you tell him? That it was true?'

'Timmie doesn't really understand what the papers are talking about.'

Carter was suddenly angry again. 'He doesn't have to. The kids'll explain it to him in words of one syllable. Doesn't understand! You think he's retarded or something? Does he still like David, by the way?'

'Why do you think he's crying?'

'That's no answer, that's a *non sequitur*. Does he still like you?'

'Oh, shut up! Just shut up!'

Carter did. He opened the bedroom door and went back into Timmie's room. He stood looking at the back of Timmie's head for a minute, and finally Timmie raised up. His face did not look so tearful as Carter had feared. 'Timmie, we don't have to talk if you don't want to.'

Timmie frowned with a start of new tears. 'I just want to know is it all true.'

'What?'

'That – you killed David because you were jealous – and because you hated him.'

'I wasn't jealous of him. I didn't hate him.'

'Did you kill him?'

'No, Timmie,' Carter said automatically. It barely registered as a lie. If he hadn't killed Sullivan, O'Brien would have, he thought. And what had become of his conscience? Carter shook his head and blinked.

'Is it true,' Timmie asked, 'my mother and David –' He left the sentence up in the air, and his throat closed.

Carter felt suddenly weak. He swayed on his feet, walked to the door and leaned on it. 'They loved each other very much,' he said.

'Does that mean –'

Carter retreated from it. He wanted to go into the bathroom and bathe his face. But he came back and said, 'You should ask your mother about that.' He waited for a moment, and, getting no reply, went out again and down the hall to the bedroom.

Hazel was half reclining on the bed. Carter supposed she could have heard what he had been saying to Timmie, though she looked as if she hadn't heard, as if she were in no mood for listening.

'Hazel –' Carter had wanted to sit down beside her, to take her hand, but one look at her eyes and he knew it would be useless.

'What?' she asked.

He took a deep breath. 'I won't be going to Detroit this weekend.'

25

Carter reasoned that if the police could not pin the murder of Sullivan on him, it did not follow that they would pin it on O'Brien. Ostreicher might suspect both of them, but without more proof than he had, what could happen? Nothing. Nothing might happen. Police annals were full of murder cases that had never been solved. There might be a period, Carter thought, of perhaps three months when he and O'Brien and other suspects would be watched closely (the police might never really stop watching them, of course), but then the situation would cool. Perhaps by summer. Carter had not given up hope for his and Hazel's month in Europe. He had not given up hope about Hazel. She had loved Sullivan, but his death had exploded a mountain of guilt on her head. Carter reasoned that her guilt might bring her back to him, if he were patient, and he regretted his burst of temper and spite on Monday evening, regretted all he had said in anger about her and Sullivan, and warned himself not to let it happen again. There had been enough times in the past when he had sworn he wouldn't challenge Hazel about Sullivan – and then he had. His challenges had been on the right track, as it happened, and the truth was out now, but if he brought anything up again in anger, it would come under the heading of taunting, and be purposeless.

On Tuesday evening, Carter and Hazel kept a theatre engagement of long standing with the Elliotts and Phyllis Millen. It was for a play by Beckett in the Village. They had dinner at Luigi's first. Phyllis had brought her friend Hugh Stevens, a husky man in his early forties, whom Carter had seen once or twice before. The Elliotts and Phyllis avoided the murder subject and asked no questions. It was as if they were determined to make the evening a pleasant one on the surface, on the surface just like any other evening or the evening they had planned when they appointed Phyllis to write for tickets, a month ago. But Phyllis's eyes were busy on Carter's and Hazel's faces all evening, and so were those of her stockbroker boy friend. The Elliotts, to Carter, seemed extra warm and friendly to him, as if, because of his prison stint, they were broadmindedly giving him the benefit of the doubt about his innocence now. Hazel put up a good show of cheerfulness, but Carter had no doubt that Phyllis and Priscilla saw through it.

When Hazel and Carter got home, Hazel said, 'Phil, I'd like to go away somewhere for a week. I need it badly.'

'All right,' he said, thinking that she probably meant alone. 'Where?'

'Somewhere not far away. Where can one go in a week?' She shrugged tiredly, and folded her gold scarf, put it in the drawer from which Carter had got it the time she asked him to bring it to Sullivan's.

'Up in New England, maybe.' He thought of Sullivan's parents in New England, and wondered if Hazel was thinking of going there? 'What kind of place have you got in mind?'

'Some simple hotel, where I won't have to think about anything. We saw a few in New Hampshire that summer, remember?'

Carter remembered, most pleasantly. 'That's a good idea,' he said. He went into the bathroom and took a quick shower. When he came out, he asked, 'I suppose you prefer to go alone?' He preferred to know if she did, and to know now.

'No,' she said on a rising tone. Then she looked at him. She was in her dressing-gown. 'I don't prefer it. I thought we might arrange for Timmie to go, too. He's doing well with his schoolwork – up to now. I spoke to my office. I can get next week off. We could leave Friday night or Saturday morning.'

But maybe he couldn't, Carter thought. 'I'd better be able to say exactly where I'm going.'

'Yes,' Hazel said flatly, and turned to her mirror.

Carter spent his lunch hour the next day getting information about country hotels in New Hampshire. He did not want to return to the one they had been to. He telephoned Hazel in the afternoon to discuss what he had found, and they decided on one near Concord. Then Carter called Ostreicher and asked if he could go there Saturday morning for nine days.

Ostreicher agreed, provided Carter telephoned when he arrived and stayed there without moving anywhere else.

They started off Friday evening, and spent the night in a very nice motel by a lake. The motel put a cot in the room for Timmie. Carter had asked for a separate room for him at the Hotel Continental at Concord.

The Continental was a large white building or mansion set at the top of a gently rising lawn. The place was old enough to have huge rooms, and Timmie was very pleased with his big room all to himself, and immediately lined up his school-books, which Hazel and Carter had made him bring with him, on the executive-style desk between his windows. There were croquet hoops on the lawn, and a tennis court behind the hotel. The place looked promising. They had breakfast in bed the next morning, joined by Timmie, who ate his from a small table the maid had put up. Then, while Hazel washed her hair, Carter went out for a walk with Timmie. He bought Timmie a tennis racquet – the hotel had racquets for the guests, but Timmie needed a new one for school – and bought for Hazel an off-white, hand-knitted sweater from Ireland.

And that night, though she seemed in a good mood, and had even laughed and joked with him at dinner, she rejected his advances in bed. Carter hesitated, then asked in a carefully quiet tone, 'Well, Hazel, how long is this going to go on?'

'What?'

'Oh, you know what.'

There was a terribly long silence. Finally, she reached for a cig-arette from her bed table. 'Nothing is resolved yet, is it?'

He knew what she meant, but he said, 'You mean about the Sullivan business.'

'Yes. What else?'

Us, he thought. There's us, after all, just us. But she was wait-ing to see who killed Sullivan. Because it could be him.

'Do you ever have hallucinations, Phil? From morphine?'

'No,' Carter said. 'Not even in prison when I was actually taking the stuff.' Then he remembered his daydreams of Hazel and Timmie, so real he had almost been able to reach out and touch them. Had those been hallucinations? If so, they had been mostly voluntary, and the only ones he had experienced.

'Never dreams so you didn't know what you were doing?' she said. 'Walking around – doing things?'

He knew what she meant. 'No.'

They fell into an unresolved silence, just as unresolved as the Sullivan case. Hazel could have asked him outright: Did you do it when you were fully conscious, then? Why didn't she? Because she knew quite well he had? Would she be behaving any differ-ently now, if she knew he had? Carter couldn't see that she would be. In Hazel's own particular way, she wouldn't want to call any further attention to herself by announcing her suspicions and leaving him. Hazel put her cigarette out. They did not even say good night, and Hazel eventually fell asleep, Carter knew from her breathing. She would never let him make love to her until she knew, Carter thought. If he wanted Hazel, he'd have to hang it on O'Brien. Or O'Brien would have to get hung with it. That was not impossible, of course. As for scruple – had he any? O'Brien had been going to do it. Why should he scruple? To hell with O'Brien. Carter frowned in the darkness and tried to find his own conscience. Or the void that meant the absence of it. It slipped away from him. Maybe he hadn't any any more. He felt no pangs of conscience because of what he had done to Sullivan – bludgeoned him to death – only a little distaste at the thought of blood that he did not even remember, and a small jolt at the fact it had been he doing the deed. He had killed another man in prison for less reason, really less reason. That had never bothered him. Mickey Castle came to his mind. He remembered saying to himself the morning of Mickey's death, that if he'd taken the trouble to step between him and whatever it was that he rammed himself into, Mickey might not have haemorrhaged, but was he his brother's keeper? And after a couple of days, he hadn't thought about it. Was that what happened to men's consciences in prison?

Carter wanted to get up and take a walk in the moonlight, but he didn't for fear of awakening Hazel. He lay there with his thoughts turning, knowing he could not progress beyond this night, he and Hazel would not progress, though they had seven more nights to spend here. There was nothing to do but behave as pleasantly as possible, not approach Hazel again, make it as good a holiday for her as he could.

And Carter did this. His only reward was that Hazel didn't change for the worse towards him: she was still friendly, good-humoured, and the time away from New York certainly did her some good.

Carter returned to his office on Monday morning. He had explained to Mr Jenkins that, though the police allowed him to go to New Hampshire to a specific hotel, they had not allowed him to go to Detroit, which was true. Carter had felt presumptuous asking the firm for a week off, but they had granted it pretty readily, or Mr Jenkins had, and as to sacking him or not, Carter thought, they had probably made up their minds days ago, and taking a week off would make no difference in the scales. Like Hazel, they were probably waiting.

He telephoned Ostreicher Monday afternoon, and after three attempts, finally reached him.

'No real news,' Ostreicher said, 'from your point of view. We found the dope in the apartment of one of Grasso's friends. Gawill could be held or fined for hiding it for Grasso, but we're letting Gawill have a little rope just now. He's a free man,' Ostreicher said, so casually, with a sigh, that Carter suspected he wasn't. Every move Gawill made was probably being watched, and Gawill no doubt knew it. 'Unlike Grasso,' Ostreicher went on. 'Grasso's got a five-thousand-dollar fine to pay.'

'And O'Brien?' asked Carter.

'He's got heavy expenses and no money. An interesting situation.'

Carter understood. Gawill couldn't afford to pay him just now. Couldn't afford to be discovered paying him. But O'Brien had been counting on the money by now. 'O'Brien's a free man, too?'

'Oh, yes,' Ostreicher said with a smile in his voice. 'And you're back on your job, Mr Carter?'

Carter felt very uneasy when he had hung up. Ostreicher was letting them all out on strings, very long strings, to see what they would do. Ostreicher could have grilled him, Carter thought, really beaten him up the way police did hardened criminals sometimes, which was what he was supposed to be, having been in prison, or at least the newspapers implied it. People never knew, or didn't care what happened to hardened criminals whom the law suspected of new crimes. Carter thought the reason he had been spared was because he had a reputable job now, money and a wife who worked for public welfare. News of any beating-up would get around. And of course he was being watched just as much as Gawill or O'Brien, Carter thought.

Nevertheless, Carter telephoned Gawill that Monday night. He did it while he was out buying cigarettes around 10 o'clock, but when he came back into the apartment, he said to Hazel, 'I just called Gawill, and I think I'll go over and see him. So if the police happen to call, that's where I am.'

Hazel looked at him in surprise. She was sitting on the sofa, mending the knee of Timmie's new corduroy trousers, bought and torn in New Hampshire. 'Why?'

'I thought I might find out something. Gawill talks to me – sometimes.'

Hazel looked at her watch. 'What time shall I expect you back?'

Carter relaxed a little and smiled. She seemed to care if he would get back. 'By twelve, anyway. If I'm later, I'll call you – before twelve.' Carter tossed one of the two packages of cigarettes he had bought on to the sofa, said, 'Bye-bye, darling,' and went out again.

He took a taxi. Gawill had sounded rather friendly on the telephone. 'Phil? What a surprise ... Well, okay, why not?' Not too friendly, just willing to see him, which was all Carter wanted.

Gawill was alone, it seemed. The radio was on, the sofa covered with newspapers again.

'What's on your mind? Have a seat,' Gawill said.

Carter sat, after putting his overcoat over the chair arm. Gawill was waiting. 'I came to find out what you might know that I don't,' Carter said.

Gawill snorted. 'And I should tell you? As a favour?'

'You might.'

'When you did me the favour of telling them I had some dope here? I should do you a favour?'

Hazel had brought the dope up, Carter remembered. He wouldn't have. 'They'd have found out, anyway. They searched Grasso's apartment – or apartments – on their own, didn't they?'

'You said it was in my apartment that you got it. And saw it.'

'Sorry,' Carter said.

'I bet you are. Sullivan off your hands, you walking around in the clear –'

'I'm no more in the clear than you are.'

Gawill only smouldered faintly.

Carter waited for him to say, *You did it, and my boy or my friend O'Brien's getting the blame*. Gawill wasn't saying that. Carter waited. 'Isn't there a drink in the house?'

Gawill got up. 'Sure there is.' He went into the kitchen.

'Next time I'll bring you some.'

'Promises, promises.'

Carter smiled. Gawill came back with a fresh Scotch and soda, plus a half-finished glass which must have been his own.

'Thank you.' Carter sipped his drink for a moment.

Each waited for the other to speak.

Gawill spoke first: 'How're you making out with Hazel?'

'That's my business.'

'You don't seem to be boasting about anything.'

'I wouldn't boast,' said Carter.

'You'd tell me if things were very rosy. It'd show – on you.'

Carter let it go. The radio annoyed him, though it was not loud, but he didn't want to annoy Gawill by asking him to turn it off. 'When're you going to pay O'Brien?' Carter asked, the big question, and coolly sipped his drink.

'Never. O'Brien was never in that apartment. You were.' Gawill looked straight at him.

232

But from the way he said it, Carter knew he was lying. He was suddenly glad, very glad, that he knew Gawill this well, that he had known him since the rosy-nightmare days of working for Triumph, known him since his visits to the prison, learned when Gawill was lying, exaggerating or plain faking. This was a mixture of lying and faking. 'Quit your kidding,' Carter said. 'I can see through you. I know you've got to pay O'Brien. O'Brien's broke, I heard from Ostreicher today. He has a lot of heavy debts. Or expenses. Isn't he waiting for your money?'

'Ah, do you think I couldn't get money to him if I had to, if I owed him any? I'd just get somebody else to give it to him for me.' Gawill shrugged, lifting a big hand, palm up.

'No-o. Who could you trust, for instance? You'd have to explain why you owed O'Brien the money, wouldn't you?'

Gawill looked at the floor and pushed himself back farther on the sofa.

Carter wondered what was going on in Gawill's head? It was anybody's guess, since Gawill was a bit cracked. But he knew if Gawill wanted to demolish him, all he had to do was say, *I know you did Sullivan in, because O'Brien said he met you on the stairs going up when he was coming down – when Sullivan was still alive.* But Gawill wasn't saying that. Gawill said:

'If I'd hired O'Brien, don't you think I'd have paid him by now? And *if* I'd hired him, do you think anybody could ever find it out? Do you think they've found out anything now? No. Just the damned dope that wasn't even mine.'

Gawill was very angry about the dope, much more than about the O'Brien situation.

'Tailing me now as if I'm in a dope ring, and I got nothing to do with the damned dope,' Gawill said, standing up.

'Then why was it in your house?'

'Ah, I was keeping it a couple of days for Grasso. I never got anything out of it.'

233

Carter had suddenly had enough of Gawill's whining. 'Like the Triumph thing, I suppose. The chiselling there. *You* never got anything out of it.'

Gawill turned, stormy-faced. 'I didn't!' he screamed, hoarse and falsetto.

He'd trap himself with his blatant lying, Carter thought. Or with his blatant truth-telling, which he sometimes did, too. Carter set his empty glass down on the floor by his chair, and stood up. 'You never got anything out of it, not on your many weekends in New York with Palmer.'

'*No!*' Gawill screamed again, as if he were being tortured.

'I'll be off,' Carter said.

He left. He had found out what he came for. O'Brien was the only man who knew the truth.

As Carter walked out of Gawill's building, he noticed a black car parked at the opposite kerb in the dark street. It looked like a police car. Had it been there before? Carter didn't remember, and didn't care. A man was sitting in it, looking his way, Carter thought, and then a light came on in the car and the man bent, presumably to write the time of his departure. Carter looked at his own watch under the streetlight at the corner. 11.35.

Hazel was up and not yet undressed when Carter got home. She was curled in a corner of the sofa with her shoes off, reading some of her mimeographed office papers.

He smiled at her as he hung his coat in the closet. 'Well –'

'Well?'

Carter came into the living-room slowly, unbuttoning his jacket, happy to breathe the smell of home. 'Gawill hasn't paid O'Brien, doesn't know how he's going to. Of course, says he doesn't owe O'Brien anything.'

'Did you find out anything you didn't know?'

'Gawill's very annoyed because the police are after him for having dope in his house.'

'How after him? They don't seem to be doing anything to him.'

'No, they're letting him out on a string. But he'll be fined something, probably. They may be attaching what money he has now. All the more reason why he finds it hard to pay O'Brien.' Carter laughed a little. 'Also they're shadowing him everywhere, which Gawill hates. He can dish it out, but he can't take it. — There was a police car across the street from his place tonight.'

Hazel looked startled. 'That means they saw you, then.'

'Yes. That doesn't bother me. They could have had a tape recorder in the apartment tonight for all I care. I was trying to find out what Gawill knows. The police are trying to find out the same thing.'

Carter had sat down on the sofa, not close to Hazel, but she suddenly reached out and put her hand over his right hand. Carter's fingers took hers. It was the first affectionate gesture he could remember from her in weeks.

She looked in front of her. She was not about to speak, not tense or strained. It was as if the touch of her hand spoke words of love and loyalty that did not need to be said.

He set his teeth. He had told Hazel that he thought O'Brien's lie-detector test had shown some agitation, more than his own, anyway. That was true, but the remark perpetuated the bigger lie. Hazel had not taken that as conclusive, Carter thought. In New Hampshire afterwards, she had asked him about hallucinations. He was continuing to lie tonight, because he loved her. She was necessary for his own life. Was that love or was it self-interest? Carter pulled her to him, and held her in his arms.

She did not answer, but she stayed in his arms for several minutes, several wonderful minutes. At last, she pushed gently away and said, 'I suppose it's getting late.'

He did not push his good fortune that night, did not touch her again, but he felt blissfully optimistic about Hazel.

26

What were the police doing, Carter wondered, besides waiting and twiddling their thumbs? It took only so long to investigate Gawill's bank account, his sources of money, his own bank account. Were they waiting for O'Brien to get impatient for his money and attack Gawill? Too obvious, and O'Brien wouldn't risk it. The stillness of everyone, everything, got on Carter's nerves. It also got on Hazel's. The only people who seemed to be reassured by it were Jenkins and Butterworth. Carter's arrival every morning at 9 o'clock might have been to them a guarantee that he was innocent, that the police were letting him alone therefore.

'This frankly –' Butterworth said to Carter, 'seems to have been an affair between Gawill, David and –'

'Your wife,' Carter started to say for him.

'I should say Gawill and David Sullivan.' Butterworth spoke gropingly, but it was evident that he wanted to be friendly to Carter.

The police were concentrating on the Gawill-inspired motive, and O'Brien was mentioned every day in the newspapers: the police were questioning him frequently. 'O'Brien, when questioned by police officials in his Jackson Heights apartment today . . . ' Whether O'Brien still had his barman's job or not was not stated, but he was certainly not locked up.

Then on a Wednesday evening at 6 o'clock, just after Carter got home, O'Brien called him up. O'Brien identified himself at once.

'You can hang up if you hear your wife coming in,' O'Brien said. 'I'm not where I can see the house, but I know she's not there now. Mr Carter, I need some dough. Five thousand dollars.'

Carter had guessed it as soon as he heard O'Brien's voice. 'This telephone may be tapped, you know.'

O'Brien hesitated a second. 'Well? – What do you mean "may be"? Is it?'

'I don't know. – You can't handle money. The police are going to find it as soon as you get it.'

'Oh, no they won't. Not in cash. I need it – Friday – and you know the either-or part, Mr Carter.' O'Brien sounded very determined and sure of himself and almost intelligent. 'You've got it, I know. Take it out of one of your banks.'

Carter said nothing.

'I'll make a date with you on the street,' O'Brien said, slowly and distinctly now. 'Tenth Street and Eighth Avenue, north-west corner, Friday night at eleven o'clock. Got that? You turn up with the money – in fifties and hundreds – and turn up on time – or I'll talk to the police by eleven thirty. That's all, Mr Carter.' O'Brien hung up.

Carter put the telephone down. He looked automatically at Timmie's room – lightless, the door ajar. Where was Timmie? Then he went to the closet to hang his topcoat. And five thousand would be the beginning, as blackmail victims always said, and if they caught O'Brien with the second five thousand, or even with the first, they'd ask where he got it. From Carter, he'd say. And why? O'Brien would tell them that, too. O'Brien wouldn't say it was from Gawill for his job, because Gawill would brazenly and probably convincingly deny such a story. Besides, Gawill would jump immediately to the truth, that Carter had paid O'Brien to keep silent. That might expose O'Brien having been at Sullivan's house, of course, but as long as O'Brien hadn't actually done it, Gawill's intention to have Sullivan killed remained just an intention, or a plot, not a deed.

A difficult spot, Mr Carter, he said to himself. Yet he felt very cool. Very, very cool, just idea-less. Except for a naïve idea, a fantasy: he might meet O'Brien and hand him the five thousand, saying calmly, sweetly, but as if he meant it, 'Okay, Anthony, now you have it. Let this be the last of it. If you keep on playing it cool and denying everything, we'll both go free, you know. Is it agreed?' But men like O'Brien wouldn't accept that for long. He'd be tempted to ask for more soon. If O'Brien weren't sorely tempted by money, he would never have hired himself out as a killer. Carter smiled grimly, like a man who has found himself with both shoes in muck, up to the ankles.

It was 6.10. Hazel had said she might not be home until 7, as there were bits and pieces of work at the office. That might mean 8, Carter knew. Hazel's office was being quite nice. 'They're acting okay – more or less,' Hazel had said evasively when he had asked her how Ginnie Joplin, her matronly boss, and Mr Piers, the in-and-outer, and Fannie, the secretary, were behaving. Naturally, no one would come out and chastise her for immorality, not in these days, but they'd act smug and holier-than-thou, which was worse, maybe even priding themselves on broadmindedness while secretly envying her and – the awful fact remained, the worst fact remained, her husband had been in prison once and they all knew it. Though they had all met him, he'd even met Fannie once when he came to pick Hazel up, and though he appeared to be a nice-looking man, rather like everyone else, they all must be thinking now that he was a tough character underneath, and that killing someone, under these circumstances, would be nothing that would make him turn a hair. Therefore Hazel was working late, because her job was rather shaky now.

'Damn it to hell,' Carter said, and went into the kitchen to get a drink.

While he was pouring it, the door opened, and he went with his glass into the living-room, thinking it was Hazel, but it was Timmie.

Timmie glanced up shyly, and removed his cap. 'Hi,' he said.

'Hi there. Where've you been?'

'Oh, I went out for ink and I ran into Stephen. We took a walk.' Timmie smiled a little at him, chocolate syrup in the corner of his mouth. His tongue moved out and licked off the brown stain.

Carter smiled. 'Since when do you take walks in drugstores?'

Timmie hung his head as he walked towards his room, but he was smiling. He stopped and turned. 'Mummy's not home?'

'Not yet. She said she'd be a little late.'

Timmie went on. He turned his light on, but did not close the door.

Carter stood looking at the slightly open door, grateful for it as if it were a pair of open arms. Ten days ago, Timmie would have closed the door, closed his heart, his ears. This was the power of the newspapers, Carter thought, of public opinion. Timmie's schoolmates were letting up on him, and thinking now that O'Brien might have done it. Or maybe, like children, they were getting tired of the story. At any rate, they weren't badgering Timmie so much, and Timmie was feeling better. It was the wonderful thing about children, that their crises could quickly blow over, Carter thought, even Hazel's and Sullivan's affair might blow over in Timmie's mind, like Sullivan's death, which had really not clouded his New Hampshire holiday. Years from now, when Timmie knew what affairs meant, he would understand,

and it would not have blown over, really, but at twelve now, for immediate and practical purposes, Carter thought it had.

Immediate and practical purposes. Friday night. Forty-eight hours away. There was five thousand in one of their savings banks and two thousand in the other. Hazel had said about a month ago, that they should give Tom Elliott another three thousand to invest, that it was silly to have so much in a savings bank when it could be earning more invested. If he took it, he could say he'd given it to Elliott, but to buy what? There'd be no statement from Elliott about buying any stock. That wouldn't be the end of O'Brien, and it was conceivable that if the police didn't indict either him or O'Brien, O'Brien could milk fifty thousand dollars out of him. Carter smiled nervously to himself. It wouldn't go unnoticed by Hazel. He walked about the room, listening for the faintest sound that might be Hazel's step on the stairs, at the same time trying to think. He got a second Scotch and water.

If he could kill O'Brien, everything would be simple. If he killed O'Brien and got away with *that* –

It could look like the work of another of Gawill's pals. Of course. Gawill wanted him dead so he wouldn't talk, so he'd never have to pay him, either.

Tenth Street and Eighth Avenue. It was pretty far west, maybe not too well lighted, Carter couldn't remember, and they might walk farther west. Carter suddenly envisaged a policeman tailing O'Brien – O'Brien would be tailed, no doubt, unless he was clever enough to shake the tailer – and coming right up to them as the money exchanged hands. *All right, Carter. That's what we wanted to know.* Carter walked about the room.

No, no money, he thought, no matter what thoughts entered his head between now and Friday. The blackmail try, Carter thought, might even be an idea concocted by the police to see if he'd agree. The police might have been by O'Brien's side as he made the call. Carter felt a little relieved that he hadn't said he would meet O'Brien with the money. But he also hadn't said anything when O'Brien said, '... you know the either-or part, Mr Carter ...' Carter wiped the film of sweat from his forehead.

He saw no alternative but to kill O'Brien. Persuade him to walk a little farther west, where the streets got darker towards the Hudson River. Pull something out of his pocket, or pretend to, as if he were taking out the money, get O'Brien close to him, and deliver the blow that kills, as Alex used to say. Then he thought of O'Brien's gigantic size, and his right thumb began to ache. Carter collapsed in the armchair, and looked at his right hand. He was holding his thumb tightly against the index finger, ready to strike a sidewise blow. The sides of his hands were no longer calloused, and even if he succeeded, they would learn from Dr Cassini, from Hazel, that Carter knew judo. The bones in the front of O'Brien's throat would be broken. It would have to be something like a brick that he used on O'Brien. Carter got up from the armchair.

Then Hazel came in, so suddenly that Carter jumped.

Hazel smiled and closed the door. 'Didn't mean to scare you. Just me.'

He moved slowly towards her, held his right hand out, and she came into his outstretched arm, leaned against his chest.

'What a day! Hennie-Pennie and Mr Piers.' She called her boss, Ginnie, Hennie-Pennie.

'Fix you a drink?'

'Yes, please,' Hazel said.

She was tired, so Carter did the dishes after dinner, and Timmie dried them and put them away.

Carter said as he was undressing for bed, 'I've got to have dinner with Jenkins and Butterworth Friday night. They want me to meet some future client or something. I thought if you wanted to see anyone –'

'I doubt if I'll want to do anything but get to bed early,' Hazel said, her face almost buried in the pillow.

Thus he prepared for Friday.

And he also considered standing O'Brien up. O'Brien wouldn't talk immediately to the police, Carter thought, not unless he was in some overwrought and desperate condition which he didn't appear to be in as yet. He'd wait and try asking for money again. But how long could that last? O'Brien had less to lose by exposing him than by standing trial for murder. Of course, before he ever stood trial, he'd come out with the real story. The plain fact was, O'Brien had him. Carter had got no farther than this by Thursday.

He stood looking out of his window at the mist-blurred ships on the East River. A couple of functional tugs burrowed along in the water, and a rather nice-looking black and white and red freighter rode high as she moved out towards the Atlantic. On the other side of Manhattan, more beautiful ships were coming in and sailing off for Europe, South America, the Bahamas. In three months, he might be on one with Hazel. Everything at rest. Everything. Once he got over this hump. Wasn't it worth it to try to kill O'Brien? O'Brien would never let it be pinned on himself. If O'Brien told his story, and it was not believed, if O'Brien were even tried and convicted, his story would leave a fatal doubt, a fatal wound in Hazel's mind and in the minds of many other people. Even if Carter withstood all the grilling the police might give him, the doubt would remain, if O'Brien told his story well, and he would, because it was true.

On Thursday night, Carter and Hazel had Phyllis Millen over for dinner, and again nothing was said about the undiscovered killer of Sullivan, nothing about what the police were doing or might be doing. During coffee the telephone rang, and it was the Laffertys. Hazel spoke to Mrs Lafferty, then to her husband. After a moment, he asked to speak to Carter.

'Hello,' Carter said, and the memory of the conversation they had had in French in the Japanese restaurant came back to him.

Every separation takes a little away from a man ... And every murder, Carter thought.

'Well, Philip. How are things?' Lafferty asked in his genial tone, in a manner that did not demand an answer. 'What's the latest on the front? Your wife said you had company, so maybe you can't talk. But I wanted to say greetings and send you my good wishes.'

'Thanks very much. I don't know that I've got anything to say,' Carter said, his back to Hazel and Phyllis, who were in the far corner of the big living-room, and talking to each other now. 'Things haven't changed for several days. That's all I know.'

'The papers are telling everything? All there is to know?'

'Yes.' Except Gawill's rage, Carter thought, except the fact O'Brien was impatient for his payment. 'Yes, that's about it. – If anything does happen, I'm sure Hazel will let you know.'

They finished the conversation casually, and Carter returned to the table to pour snifters of brandy. His hand was very steady, rather his hands, as he used both to pour the bottle.

'Nice of them to call,' Hazel said.

'Yes. I like him.' Carter sat down.

'We must have them over. You know the Laffertys, don't you Phyllis?'

Phyllis did.

The conversation trickled on. Carter hardly listened. He looked at his son, who was finishing his plate of ice-cream. Timmie wore his best dark-blue suit, a white shirt and blue tie. The candlelight shone on his neatly combed blond hair. The phonograph dropped a new record and the Goldberg Variations began to play. Carter blinked away inexplicable tears. He took one of Hazel's Seconals that night to be sure he got to sleep.

27

By 7 p.m. the next evening, Carter had had two very slow Scotch and sodas in two different bars in the East Forties, and still the time dragged insufferably.

He called Gawill, and found that he was out. Or at least he didn't answer. What should he make of that? Were the police holding Gawill so they would be sure he didn't try to tip Carter off about the police following O'Brien tonight? But why should Gawill want to tip him off? That didn't make sense. Carter began to telephone Gawill every fifteen minutes. By 9 o'clock, it became an obsession to find Gawill at home, to go to his house even, to see if he were there and just not answering the telephone.

Carter began to be more and more sure he was walking into a police trap. He looked around him so often for someone who looked like a plain-clothes man that people began to look at him. Then Carter made himself stop turning his head.

He went abruptly into a movie on Twenty-third Street.

Now and again, he looked at his watch as he lit a cigarette. At 10.15 he could sit there no longer, and went out and walked south. At the first place with a telephone, a cigar store, he went in and called Gawill, and Gawill answered. Carter almost sighed with relief.

'Well, what's on your mind now?' Gawill asked in a vaguely annoyed way, and this was also reassuring to Carter.

He had nothing to say. 'Have you paid O'Brien yet?' he asked.

'No, have *you*?' Gawill retorted.

It was so to the point, Carter laughed a real laugh, and felt better, like the times in prison when he had laughed at fate, at the truth, at demoniacal accidents. But Gawill was deadly serious, or rather deadly bitter. That, too, was in character with Gawill and comforting to Carter. Carter sobered suddenly and said, 'Are you in a little later? I might come by and see you. I've got something to tell you.' He hung up before Gawill could say anything, and swung open the door of the telephone booth.

He began to walk rapidly downtown. *Why?* Well, he knew why. It was a kind of limping alibi for 'around 11 o'clock', and also – Gawill was a lower depth, even lower than O'Brien, as low as what he might do tonight. Carter made himself slow his walking, to save his strength, but something inside him seemed to be racing on anyway, spending his energy.

He was five minutes early at Tenth Street and Eighth Avenue.

O'Brien came up from downtown, walking casually, a folded newspaper in his left hand. He wore a hat and a trenchcoat unbuttoned with its belt dangling. He saw Carter, gestured with the newspaper, and they joined each other a few yards farther west on the sidewalk of the north side of Tenth Street. It was a darkish block, a couple of closed garages on it, the fronts of quiet, low tenements. O'Brien looked behind him.

'You weren't followed?' he asked.

'No,' Carter said.

'Did you look?'

'Yes.'

O'Brien seemed four inches taller than Carter, enormous in

the open trenchcoat, but Carter knew he was very little taller, if any. Just a lot heavier and stronger.

'Were you followed?'

'Oh, sure,' O'Brien said, looking straight ahead of him, nodding with resignation. 'As usual. But I took a few taxis. I'm not followed now. Usually, I don't bother.' He smiled slightly, glanced at Carter, and his right hand, which now held the newspaper, gestured nervously. 'You got it?'

'Yes,' Carter said. One, two, three, four, he counted off his steps. They were walking rather slowly, the way people would walk who were chatting and not in a hurry. 'One thing, O'Brien.'

'Yeah?'

'Is this the last payment, or what should I expect?'

O'Brien laughed a short, nervous laugh. 'I really don't have to tell you, do I? Okay, it's the last. – Unless I get really gone over by the cops, in which case I don't think I should get all my teeth knocked out and my nose broken for you, do you?'

The hostility barely registered on Carter as hostility. It was just something *there*, the way it had always been there in prison, among the inmates he walked beside, who might turn on him, who might have turned on him because of his friendship with Max, and who just happened never to have turned. O'Brien was slowing. Ahead of them on the left corner, across Greenwich Street, or Carter thought it was Greenwich Street, loomed the black, windowless side of a warehouse. Below it a wire fence ten feet high, a corner with a lamppost. A man crossed Greenwich Street and came walking in their direction, but on the opposite sidewalk.

'Well?' O'Brien said, stopping.

Carter looked at the man across the street, who was passing them now, paying no attention to them. He reached for the inner pocket of his overcoat, and took his hand out again, empty. 'Let's go over there,' he said, nodding towards the light.

'Why?' asked O'Brien suspiciously.

Because beside them were dwellings, where someone might stick a head out at a noise, or yell, Carter thought, and the warehouse was a deserted warehouse. 'Safer,' Carter said, starting across the street before O'Brien could protest.

O'Brien followed him, but slowly, hands in his trenchcoat pockets. Finally, there was twenty feet between them, as Carter stepped on to the sidewalk by the warehouse, and O'Brien off the kerb opposite to follow him. O'Brien looked right and left. A taxi's headlights flowed across Greenwich Street, paused at the intersection, then went on across.

Carter bowed his head with his hands not far from his chest, as if he were counting bills he had just pulled from his pocket. He stood about fifteen feet from the streetlamp, facing it.

O'Brien came up beside him, saying, 'Christ, do you have to count it again?'

Carter turned so his back was to the light, so O'Brien would not see that he had nothing.

O'Brien faced him now and bent a little to see.

Carter raised both hands simultaneously, catching O'Brien under the chin, which did nothing to O'Brien but toss his head back, but that was all Carter wanted. O'Brien came at him with a quick right, but Carter sidestepped, and slashed sideways with his left hand – between the front and side of O'Brien's throat, not where he would break any bones. It didn't seem to jar O'Brien's bulk, but it hurt him. He bent over a little, and Carter gave him another backhanded blow with his left hand, and a right to the back of the neck just below the skull. O'Brien was down on the sidewalk, and now Carter used a foot on his neck. He glanced about and saw a hunk of cement, but it wouldn't dislodge because it was part of the wire fence support. Carter slammed a foot down again on the side of O'Brien's neck. O'Brien wasn't moving. Carter might have kicked his face, which lay in profile against the sidewalk, but he couldn't, or didn't.

'Hey! – *Hey!*'

Carter ran from the voice. He ran into the first street to the left, eastward. Then he trotted lightly, not too fast, in the shadow of the buildings on the north side of the street, because a couple of men were walking towards him. Carter began to walk. Whoever had yelled would be looking at O'Brien for a few seconds before chasing after him, Carter thought. Carter crossed an avenue, not bothering to see what avenue it was. Now he was walking normally, not hurrying, he knew, though it seemed like slow motion to him. He walked southward, zigzagging eastward at every street. A trickling sensation on his right little finger made him lift his hand, and he saw blood running down. Carter sucked at the stinging place on the side of his hand. The cut felt small to his tongue. He found a Kleenex in his overcoat pocket, and held it to the cut as he walked, using the fresh blood to wipe off the drying blood on his finger. When the Kleenex was soaked, he tossed it in a rubbish basket and took his handkerchief from his breast pocket.

He was south of Washington Square. He found a parked taxi at a nightclub's kerb, and told the driver to go to Times Square. In the taxi he tried to relax, stretching his legs out, holding the wadded handkerchief against his cut.

'Where on Times Square?' asked the driver.

'Times Square and Seventh,' Carter said, just to say something.

The cut was stopping its bleeding. Carter even managed to tie the handkerchief with the aid of his teeth in a way that showed no blood on its outside. Then he paid the driver with two dollar bills that he held ready in his left hand. 'Keep the rest.'

He walked to Fifth Avenue, and got another taxi. 'Jackson Heights?' Carter asked, remembering that drivers weren't always willing to go there from Manhattan.

'Okay,' said the driver. 'Whereabouts?'

'I'll show you when we get there.'

Carter leaned forward and told the driver, as they reached Jackson Heights, to turn right, then left, and finally to stop. It was an intersection with restaurants and a bar, and Carter knew it was not more than a five-minute walk to Gawill's. He paid the driver off, then began to walk towards Gawill's. It was now a quarter to 12.

He paused in a dark street, thinking he didn't have to go to Gawill's, that he could take another taxi home – a taxi without changing half-way – but he couldn't go home just now. He felt too shaky. He couldn't even call Hazel now to tell her he'd be home soon. Carter pushed on towards Gawill's, and stopped in a liquor store, which was just closing, and bought a bottle of Johnny Walker.

I'll stay half an hour, Carter said to himself. And Gawill might be annoyed and not let him in at this hour, in which case he'd stick the bottle of Scotch at him and go. Then of course he might stay longer than half an hour. He couldn't predict. He untied the handkerchief and looked at his hand under a streetlamp. The cut was a tiny V in the side of his hand between the little finger base and his wrist. O'Brien's tooth or something had cut through some skin that looked rather calloused once it was cut. The part that had bled was deep, but very small indeed. It was not bleeding now.

Gawill did not answer his downstairs ring, but Carter took the elevator up, anyway. He rang the doorbell. After a moment, he heard Gawill's heavy tread, and Gawill opened the door in pyjamas and robe.

'You're late,' said Gawill.

'Too late? Here's some Scotch.'

Gawill smiled slightly. 'Kept your promise. Okay, come in for a nightcap.' He went into the living-room. 'What made you late?'

'Dinner with some office people,' Carter said. 'Sitting talking. You know.'

Gawill was fixing drinks in the kitchen. There was a pleasant sound of gurgling liquor from the full bottle. Carter looked around at the untidy, ugly, masculine room almost as if he liked it. Gawill came in with the drinks.

'So what did you have to tell me?' Gawill asked.

Carter lifted his glass slightly to Gawill before he drank. He drank half the glass at once. He had removed his coat. Now he sank down in the big armchair. 'You were asking me about Hazel,' Carter said, crossing his legs. 'I just wanted to say we're getting along fine.'

Gawill said nothing, but Carter could see that he believed him. 'Well – here's to it. Matrimonial bliss,' he said sourly, and drank.

Carter drank, too, and finished his.

'Musta been a dry party they gave you tonight,' Gawill said.

Carter smiled. 'Chinese dinner. Lots of tea, but –' He got up and went into the kitchen. 'You don't mind if I help myself, I hope?'

'Nope,' said Gawill.

Carter did. Under the tap, as he filled his glass with water, he washed the bit of blood from around the nail of his little finger. The V cut was dry now, and cheerful-looking, like a silly mouth, or like a V for victory. Carter took the blood-stained handkerchief from his jacket pocket, hesitated between sticking it into an empty can in Gawill's garbage pail or the incinerator chute, and decided on the incinerator. He opened and closed it noiselessly. 'Ostreicher told me something today that I think I ought to pass on to you,' Carter said as he came into the living-room again. 'They've got the material Sullivan was collecting on you and they're pretty impressed by it – as a motive for wanting Sullivan out of the way.'

'That crap again!' Gawill shouted, standing up.

'That's what they told me. A relief off my mind and a big

headache for you and O'Brien, I'd say. What're you going to do about O'Brien? Don't you think he's a danger to you?'

'Listen – f'Christ's sake,' Gawill spluttered, gesturing so that some of his drink went on the floor. 'Once and for all, I'll – *Drexel* got most of that money. Got half, anyway. He got about half and Wally Palmer the other half.'

Carter blinked. *Drexel.* That decrepit old church-goer who looked like a second Jefferson Davis, Drexel whose character was so above question, he had hardly been questioned. Not questioned at all about his own possible complicity, just questioned about the characters of his employees. Drexel, who had salved his conscience by paying Carter a fraction of his pay, and had gone on after the school fiasco to build a couple of other things in the same State. Even his deathbed, if his stroke had given him time for one, hadn't inspired a confession. Sullivan had never uttered the faintest word of suspicion against him. 'Well,' Carter said finally, feeling a little light in the head, 'it's no wonder they couldn't account for all that cash. Half of two hundred and fifty thousand dollars –'

'Drexel stashed plenty of it away.'

'Sullivan certainly didn't know that. Or did he?'

'No, Sullivan didn't know it,' Gawill said.

'Why didn't you tell Sullivan? Especially once Drexel was dead. He's been dead for months.'

Gawill sank on to the sofa again, but he leaned forward. 'I'll tell you why. I wanted to see Sullivan fail. I wanted – yeah, I wanted to kill him. You know that.'

Yes, Carter knew that. Gawill in his crazy way had wanted to keep his hatred whipped up by letting Sullivan go on looking for evidence against him. 'But you must've got something out of the Triumph deal, Greg. Didn't Drexel know you knew he was stealing money?'

'Oh, I got some crumbs. Peanuts! *Peanuts!* It was like Wally

251

was some millionaire inviting me on a holiday with him and he paid my bills in New York. On weekends sometimes. You call that getting anything?' Gawill asked rhetorically, resentfully.

Carter had to smile. 'Why didn't you gouge them for more? Palmer and Drexel, too?'

Gawill twitched, as if illustrating his memory of being unable to act.

Drexel and Palmer had had something on Gawill, of course. Probably. What else? 'Never mind, I understand,' Carter said. He looked at the telephone, and just as he did, it rang. Carter asked quickly, 'Where were you tonight, Greg?'

Gawill's hand stopped on the way to the telephone. 'Me? – I was in a bar watching a fight on television.'

'You were with me. All evening.'

'Hah!' Gawill said, nervously.

The telephone rang a third time.

'I met you in the bar. You came home first, I came a little later with a bottle of Scotch.'

'A *little* later. What's all this?' Gawill frowned.

'Answer the telephone.'

Gawill took his suspended hand away from the telephone, almost back to his lap, then reached out and picked the telephone up. 'Hello.'

Carter could hear only a burring masculine voice. He watched Gawill's face.

'Yeah? – Yeah. – Oh, yeah?' Surprised, taut-faced now, Gawill looked at Carter. 'No, I don't. – Yeah, I'll be here. Okay.' He hung up. 'O'Brien's dead.' His dark eyes seemed to grow smaller with certainty. And you killed him.'

'It's either me or you, obviously. But it better be neither of us, Greg, and we better have been together tonight. I'll tell Hazel I lied about the office dinner and came to see you. I met you in the bar. Was it a crowded bar?'

'Yes.'

'Where?'

'Jackson Heights Boulevard. Not O'Brien's. I don't know the name of it. – Yeah, Roger's Tavern.'

'Okay. – What's the matter with your watchdog tonight? Isn't there a policeman on guard downstairs?' Carter stood up suddenly and glanced at the door. He looked at Gawill. 'I didn't see a police car when I came in, but I wasn't looking for one.'

Gawill wiped his forehead, and ran a hand around his neck, inside his pyjama collar. 'Why did you kill O'Brien? Was he black-mailing you? Why?'

'Sullivan's dead, isn't he? What do you care why? Yes, I killed O'Brien. Shall I say I saw your hired man going down the steps, rushing out just as I was going *in* to Sullivan's? You don't want me to tell them you planned to kill Sullivan, do you?'

'*Jee-sus!*' Gawill squealed, and put his hands over his face, in his duped-again-I'm-tortured style.

Carter smiled at him. He lit a cigarette. 'You have no choice, Greg. Neither have I. But we can make an agreement. Somebody else killed O'Brien, someone he owed money to, maybe, but not us.'

'Jesus,' Gawill repeated more quietly, through his hands.

'Is it a deal?'

Gawill's doorbell rang.

Gawill got up and lumbered into the kitchen and pressed the release bell, lumbered in again.

'You went to the bar when tonight?' Carter asked, not knowing what Gawill's reply would be, hostile, negative or co-operative.

'Eight thirty,' Gawill said, glancing at him, and there was a helpless look in his eyes.

Carter felt the balance of his fate swing. He said in a calmer tone, 'I joined you there around eight thirty. I called you around six thirty this evening to make the appointment.' The doorbell rang on the last words. 'Were you in at six thirty?'

'Yeah,' Gawill said. He went to the door.

Ostreicher and a police officer whom Carter had never seen before came in.

'Well, Mr Carter,' Ostreicher said. 'Good evening.'

'Good evening,' Carter said.

'And Mr Gawill, ready for bed.'

'At this hour, yeah,' Gawill said.

Ostreicher and his companion did not sit down. Ostreicher managed to watch both Carter's and Gawill's faces as he said, 'Mr Carter, you probably heard the news. O'Brien was found dead over on the West Side tonight. Beaten up and dead.'

Carter said nothing, only looked at Ostreicher. He held a nearly finished drink in his right hand, his little finger under the bottom of his glass.

'Where were you tonight, both of you, around eleven o'clock? Mr Carter?'

'I was walking around Jackson Heights Boulevard around that time, I think. I'd spent part of the evening with Gawill.'

'What part?'

'From about eight thirty till – about ten thirty, I don't know.'

'Till ten thirty, then you separated?' Ostreicher asked. 'Get this, please, officer.'

And the officer hastened to get out his tablet and pen.

'We sat in a bar for a while talking,' Carter said. 'Then Gawill went off. But I wasn't finished talking, so I bought a bottle of Scotch and came over.'

Ostreicher opened his mouth slightly, but said nothing. He looked from Carter to Gawill and back again, as if he might be wishing he had thought to ask them separately where they had been. 'You, Mr Gawill, where were you?'

'I left the bar around –'

'What bar?'

'Roger's Tavern,' Gawill said, and put a cigarette in his mouth. He was also standing. 'Around ten thirty I came home, I think. I dunno. Ask the cop downstairs. He ought to know. Or are you the cop?' he asked the policeman writing, but the policeman only glanced at him and said nothing.

Ostreicher said to the officer, 'What time did he come in?'

The officer referred to another page of his tablet. 'Ten fifteen,' he said.

'And Carter?'

The officer looked again, then shrugged apologetically. 'I'm sorry, I didn't get this gentleman's time of arrival, sir.'

Ostreicher looked annoyed. 'What time did you come to Jackson Heights, Mr Carter?'

'Around eight thirty,' Carter said.

'What were you talking to Gawill about?'

'What do you think I was talking to Gawill about?' Carter said.

Ostreicher's blue eyes glinted as he looked at Gawill. 'Who did you hire to kill off O'Brien, Gawill, and how much did you pay *him*? Or not pay him?'

'Oh, let me off it!' Gawill yelled back.

'The hell I'll let you off it. Not this time. This time you'll spend a few days in the clink. And nights!'

'I dunno who killed O'Brien and I don't give a damn and you won't learn a thing from me,' Gawill replied.

Carter admired him at that moment.

Ostreicher looked bested. He turned and mumbled something to the officer, who was still writing, and the officer nodded. Then Ostreicher went over and picked up Gawill's telephone. He dialled a number, then curtly told whoever had answered to 'ask Hollingsworth to stay on'. Ostreicher hung up and turned to Carter and Gawill. 'Get your clothes on, Gawill. We're going first to the bar you were at.'

Gawill started to move, then looked at his watch. 'They're early closers. They close around twelve thirty.'

'We'll find someone,' Ostreicher retorted.

The bar was closed when they got there in the police car. Ostreicher went into a bigger bar that was still open down the street, presumably to telephone the dark bar to see if anyone would answer, or possibly to ask the proprietor's name, which Gawill hadn't known or hadn't disclosed when Ostreicher asked him. He came back after about five minutes. 'Let's go to the precinct,' Ostreicher said to the officer who was driving.

As soon as they got there, Carter asked if he could telephone his wife. Ostreicher said yes, but then rudely stayed three feet away from Carter while he called from the desk telephone, so he could hear what Carter said.

'Where *are* you?' Hazel asked.

'I'm okay,' Carter said, not smiling, but in a tone of unmistakable cheer. 'Can't talk to you now because I'm not alone, but I'm okay and I don't want you to worry.' No, not even if they beat the hell out of him tonight. He could take it, he was okay, and he'd finally be home.

Ostreicher kept them up until nearly 4 a.m., separately and alternately questioning them. Carter did not see Gawill at all after they arrived at the station. An air of defeat began to hang about Ostreicher towards 3 a.m., as surely as his questions were repetitious. Then came Ostreicher's pretence that Gawill had broken down.

'Gawill said you refused to pay O'Brien for him – even though he promised to pay you back later. But you were going to pay for this one to help Gawill out. Who were you going to pay, Carter? – We'll find out and connect you, just like we connected Gawill with O'Brien. Why put it off?'

'Why on earth should I help Gawill out?' Carter sat calmly in a straight chair, his arms folded, his legs crossed. It was a luxurious cross-examination compared to prison experiences, compared to being hung up by the thumbs. 'You're wasting your time,' Carter said quietly. He was prepared – mentally at least – to stay up the rest of the night, all day the next day, while Ostreicher slept, and all night tomorrow night, with Ostreicher again. And he was sure Gawill hadn't broken down, or Ostreicher would be putting his statements much more forcefully, perhaps underlined with a punch in the ribs. Carter felt quite secure with Gawill as a partner, in these circumstances. Gawill was out to protect himself.

'You're wasting yours. I'm not wasting mine,' Ostreicher said, reminding Carter suddenly of church services on Sunday morning in prison: *Your time here is not wasted, because you may profit by it to reflect upon* ...

Carter looked him steadily in the eye.

A little later, Ostreicher gave it up for the night. Carter was taken by an officer – who had sat with him in the intervals while Ostreicher talked to Gawill – to a cell down the hall, where grey pyjamas were laid out for him on the wall-held cot as if by a chambermaid. There was only cold running water from the single tap at the basin, but the toilet was immaculately clean, and it was a hotel room compared to the cells Carter had known in the Penitentiary. Carter still saw no sign of Gawill, but he was sure Gawill was spending the night somewhere here, too.

Nothing happened until 10 a.m., when Ostreicher appeared with two men Carter had never seen before. They were the proprietor and a barman of Roger's Tavern. Both said they had not noticed Carter in the bar, but might have missed him. They did not know Gawill by name, but recognized him by sight, as he had been in 'a few times'. Carter was present when Ostreicher confronted Gawill with the two men, because the men were then asked if they remembered seeing Carter and Gawill together.

'I don't,' said the barman, shaking his head, 'but there was such a big crowd last night watching the wrestling, you know, people would come up by themselves to get a couple of drinks and take them back to their friends, maybe in a booth.'

'You remember him buying two drinks last night any time?' Ostreicher asked, nodding at Gawill.

The barman moistened his lips and answered carefully, 'I honestly don't, but I could be wrong. I mean, there was so many people standing three deep at the bar. I don't want to say the wrong thing and get somebody in trouble, you understand. I just don't remember.'

Well done, Carter thought. A fine upholder of Mr Average Citizen's motto, *Don't get involved*.

Neither did the proprietor remember if Gawill had bought two drinks. It seemed the proprietor had spent most of the evening in a booth with three old cronies at the back of the place.

'Okay,' Ostreicher said to the two men. 'We may want to talk to you again.'

The two men were dismissed.

Then Ostreicher talked with Carter alone in Carter's cell. Carter was in his own clothes, but in shirtsleeves.

'Let's go over last night again,' said Ostreicher. 'I saw your wife this morning. She said you told her you were going to be out with some office people. Why did you lie?'

'I knew she'd worry, if she knew I was going to see Gawill.'

'Why should she worry? You'd seen him twice before.'

'Gawill's no pal of mine. He goes with a rough crowd. My wife was worried after I'd told her I saw him.'

'And why did you tell her you saw him? For what purpose?'

'To see if he'd admit he hired O'Brien. I thought – even if he lied to the police about it, I could tell if he was lying or not.'

Ostreicher's eyes narrowed. 'But what could you do about it?'

Carter looked at Ostreicher in the same sly, annoyed way. 'Isn't it interesting to find out the truth whether you can do anything about it or not?'

'Your wife said you found out – to *your* satisfaction – days ago that Gawill hired O'Brien. Why did you see him last night?' Ostreicher looked huge on the small straight chair.

Carter was sitting on the edge of his hard cot. 'I wanted some more details. How much Gawill paid or promised to pay O'Brien, for instance. Gawill never admitted to me he hired O'Brien. He denied it. But I thought he had and I told my wife I thought so. I thought if I could break him down a little more, get the sum he promised, I could get myself off the hook.'

'Oh, you admit you were on a hook,' Ostreicher said.

'Of course.'

'You're on a bigger one now. Let's say Gawill hired O'Brien, but you actually killed Sullivan. If you did, O'Brien knew that, and he was in a fine position to blackmail you. Wasn't he trying to blackmail you, Mr Carter, and you decided to kill him? And did? Didn't O'Brien make a date with you?'

'No,' Carter said.

'Last night?'

'You won't find any money gone out of my bank. Take a look.'

'There isn't any gone out of Gawill's, either. You wouldn't have taken any out, if you expected to kill him.'

'I didn't expect to kill him. He was Gawill's headache, not mine.' Carter opened his hands, then let them hang relaxed between his knees. Slowly, he reached for a cigarette, his last one, and he was aware that he looked very calm and relaxed, but he was glad Ostreicher hadn't his lie detector plastered to his chest now. Now was different from the interview three weeks ago. Now Carter cared more. *The justice I have received, I shall give back*, he thought to himself, the words burning across his brain out of nowhere, and he looked straight at Ostreicher.

'What did you order in that bar last night?' Ostreicher asked.

'Scotch and water.'

'How many?'

259

'Two, I think, maybe three.'

'Who bought them?'

'I think we each bought a round,' Carter said.

'Who went to get the drinks?'

What had Gawill said to Ostreicher? 'I bought one round at the bar, I think.'

'You think?'

'Gawill bought one, and maybe a waiter brought it, I don't know. It was crowded and noisy and a bad place to talk and that's why I went back to see Gawill.'

'After you'd dashed to New York to meet O'Brien around eleven, killed him – you dashed back then?'

Carter calmly flicked his ash on the floor. 'No.'

'Didn't Gawill know the score, wasn't that why he wasn't going to pay O'Brien, and didn't you and he agree to give you an alibi for last night if you killed O'Brien?'

Carter frowned. 'Gawill was as surprised as I was when he heard O'Brien was dead. – Why don't you check with the taxi drivers if you think I did all this dashing?'

'We've done that. Some driver may come up with the right information. Last night's drivers are mostly sleeping this morning.'

It didn't worry Carter.

'See you in a little while,' Ostreicher said, going out, closing the barred door. Ostreicher gestured, and a guard came over and turned a key in the lock.

'Can I call my wife?' Carter asked the guard.

Carter was not allowed to make any more personal calls after the one he had made, but he could call a lawyer, if he wished.

'I'll do that,' Carter said. 'Meanwhile, could you get me a package of Pall Malls, please?' He extended a fifty-cent piece through the bars.

The guard took it and went off. In about five minutes, he was back with the cigarettes and fifteen cents change. Carter then telephoned one of the three lawyers suggested by the precinct sergeant, and made an appointment for an interview that afternoon. Carter knew the bail, if there was any, would be too high for him to raise, and he was not much interested in any protection the lawyer could give him, but he wanted to engage a lawyer because it was the customary thing to do. A barber arrived to shave him at 2 p.m., and the lawyer a little later. The lawyer, Matthew Ellis, was a tall, pudgy man of about thirty with a small black moustache. He talked for twenty minutes with Carter in his cell, then assured him if no further evidence against him was discovered, he could not be held more than forty-eight hours longer. The lawyer promised to call Hazel and explain the situation to her, but he couldn't do anything about getting permission for Hazel to visit him. Carter had asked the guard, then the sergeant, that morning, if his wife could come to see him, and the sergeant had said no, probably on instructions from Ostreicher, Carter thought.

Then it was 3 p.m. Carter wondered if Gawill were being questioned all this time? If Gawill would have the wit to say what they had been talking about last night: whether Gawill had hired O'Brien or not, and Carter's anxiety about his own predicament? Or rather, it was what they should have been talking about, and what Carter had said to the police in front of Gawill that they had been talking about. Carter thought Gawill probably would have the wit. Gawill would try to make the *status quo* stay the *status quo* as long as it could. If Gawill talked, he would drag himself into a mess, a lesser mess than Carter's, but still a mess, and Gawill meant to protect himself. Much as Gawill had hated Sullivan, he had never dared strike the blow against him himself, he had got someone else to do it.

Carter lay on his back and smoked and looked at the ceiling. He used his porcelain soap dish as an ashtray. He thought of the words that had rushed through his mind as he talked with

261

Ostreicher: *The justice I have received*, etc. Well, justice was certainly the wrong word for all of it. An eye for an eye was nearer what he had felt, and yet that was not it, either, because in principle he didn't believe in that. In principle, his killing Sullivan had been an evil act, done in anger. And the fact that he felt no guilt made it worse, in principle and in fact. His killing O'Brien had been a calculated, cold-blooded act done to clear himself of an equally evil act. Carter could admit to himself that both acts were evil, and yet he felt no pangs – or very little pangs – of conscience about either of them, or both of them together. He was sorry either of them had had to happen, but then he was also sorry Hazel had had an affair, and had been continuing it, with Sullivan. Carter swung his feet down to the floor and stood up. And would there be a next victim and a next? Every time he had a grudge or a reason for wanting somebody out of the picture, would he just kill them like a savage? Carter stared at the mirror over his basin, though he was not in front of it, and the mirror gave back a reflection of the bars of his cell door. He was sure he would not kill again. He could not account through logic for his sureness, but he knew. Because if Hazel betrayed him again, somehow, with anybody else, he would prefer simply to kill himself.

The guard came to the door. 'Letter for you,' he said, sticking it through the bars.

Carter took it and opened it. It was from the lawyer, saying he had spoken with Hazel on the telephone. 'She sends her love, asks you not to worry about her and will come to see you as soon as she is allowed to.' There was a world of meaning in 'not to worry about her'. Carter smiled and a new strength surged in him.

He needed it for that evening. Ostreicher came in just after five, just after Carter had been served his supper on a tray.

'You can give it up, Carter. Gawill has finally spilled the beans,' Ostreicher said. 'He never saw you last night till nearly midnight.

You never were with him in that bar. You killed Sullivan, because O'Brien didn't. You got there before O'Brien, if O'Brien got there at all. You . . .'

Carter shut his mind to it, and finally almost shut his ears to it. He didn't believe it, didn't believe Gawill had said it. And if Gawill had, what did he have to lose now by denying the truth of it? Carter took a deep breath and pulled off his tie, unbuttoned his shirt collar: his shirt was more like a prison shirt that way. He looked at Ostreicher calmly, with the expressionlessness, the neutrality that in prison was the best expression to have, because it concealed emotion and antagonized people the least, and also conserved energy.

After half an hour, they adjourned to a downstairs room, furnitureless except for a smallish old brown desk and two straight chairs. Carter sat on one chair, Ostreicher on the other. The light overhead was not swinging, but it was bright, fixed at the ceiling under a wide green shade painted white on the underside. First, Carter's character was given a good blackening, though the blackening began in the prison days and was mostly imaginary on Ostreicher's part: the effect of association with bad company for six solid years, the demoralizing effects of morphine, which Carter had taken to as all people of weak character took to it, damaging first the structure of his brain, then his moral fibre, what was left of it. Then Carter had, in the manner of a spineless man who had already lost all pride, maintained a sick, phoney friendship with the man who was sleeping with his wife, and had also 'accepted a job from him', and finally in the manner of a criminal had let his emotions burst out in murder. He had gravitated towards Gawill, 'a fellow-conspirator' in the Triumph fraud, though Carter now denied a close friendship with him, had accepted dope twice at Gawill's house and not mentioned the dope to the police, and had at last with the coldest premeditation murdered the only man he could not trust, Anthony O'Brien. Carter had thought, said

Ostreicher, that he could trust Gawill, but there was no real honour among thieves.

And thou shalt be my rock, Carter thought, his mind turning to platitudes and clichés, too, like Ostreicher's. His rock was Hazel, cracked and damaged like himself, but still there, still quite enough to hang on to. Though I am but a shred, Carter thought tritely – and looked steadily and with his head slightly bowed, at Ostreicher.

'You're not answering anything I say, are you Carter?' Ostreicher said.

Carter spoke slowly. 'The things you are saying are not questions. What am I supposed to answer?'

'Any normal man would talk back. Deny it or admit it. You sit there like the stone-faced criminal you are.'

Carter might have smiled at that, but he did not, and it was no effort not to, it was quite normal. Guards in prison had called him the same thing, in different words, when he'd been in prison a few weeks, before the stringing-up. 'I do not admit anything you're saying, and I have nothing more to say than what I've already said.'

'Where do you think you're going to get with all this, when Gawill's already told me the *truth*?' Ostreicher's face pinkened and he wagged a finger at Carter.

'I doubt if he's told you all that, because it isn't the truth,' Carter said.

Carter and Ostreicher were in the room together until after 11 o'clock, except for twenty minutes around 9, when Ostreicher presumably went out for something to eat. Carter was hungry by 10, but said nothing about it. He was also sleepy, from the repetition of the questions and of Gawill's alleged story. Carter did not waver, really, though he found himself two or three times beginning to believe that Gawill *had* broken down and talked, but when this happened, Carter reminded himself that he had nothing to lose and everything to gain by sticking to his story, and so he did. No blows were struck, and there were no rubber truncheons in sight.

'You know what we do with people like you, Carter,' Ostreicher said as they were finishing up, Ostreicher frayed at the edges, his eyes bleary, his tie askew. 'We don't let them rest. We finish your career – what's left of it – we –'

'I'd like to see you print that story you said came from Gawill,' Carter said. He was standing up now, like Ostreicher his hands in his pockets, his right hand squeezing his rolled-up tie. 'When I get out of here, I'll look for it in the papers.'

Ostreicher showed his annoyance at that despite himself. But he made no comment.

Carter slept like a log, even though his thumbs hurt, and he had been out of pills for more than twenty-four hours.

Some time before 11 the next morning, Sunday, Matthew Ellis walked up to Carter's door smiling and said, 'Your wife's here. You can go home in a little while now.'

Carter stood at the bars, looking for her at the extreme left of the hall, towards the precinct door. A guard walked towards him, followed by Hazel. She was bareheaded. She carried something in her arms wrapped in brown paper. When she saw him, she smiled a little. Her eyes were smiling more. Her eyes spoke to him. Carter took his hands from the bars and stood up straight as the guard unlocked the door.

'Brought you a clean shirt,' Hazel said.

'Thanks, darling.' He embraced her, and tears pressed behind his shut eyes. He was reminded of his tears the night he got home from prison.

'Everything's going to be all right,' she said, quite calmly.

Something in her voice made Carter draw away and look at her, and then he realized that Hazel knew the truth, knew it all. Carter glanced at Matthew Ellis, standing in the background, and

265

Ellis nodded and smiled – Ellis who no doubt didn't know, because Hazel never would have told him.

'Want to put on the shirt first?' Ellis asked, gesturing with a finger to indicate he would be at the front of the station.

Hazel handed Carter the white shirt from the pinned brown-paper parcel, then some pills in a twist of wax paper from her pocket-book. She waited outside the cell, while he took off the dirty shirt. He broke the blue paper band from the laundry on the clean shirt, broke it with a faintly aching thumb. He wondered if Gawill was out? Or if they were going to grill him a few more days? Gawill would never talk, not to the police who could do something about what he said. And Carter felt certain, too, that he and Gawill would never try to see each other again, never say a word to each other again.

Carter took only one of the Pananods at the cell basin, scooping up water in one hand, as he had often done in prison. Then he straightened and buttoned the crisp, clean shirt – symbol of a new life. He turned to Hazel, who was looking at him. Perhaps she felt exactly as he did – she must, to be looking at him the way she was now – that they'd both made awful messes, but that there was something they could still save, and that was worth saving. They had not destroyed everything. There was plenty left, even an abundance, and everything was going to be all right. At last Carter returned her smile.

Ostreicher walked by as Carter was going out of the cell. He glanced at Hazel, then looked at Carter. 'We won't stop watching you, Carter.'

'Oh, I know that,' Carter said. 'I know.'

THE TWO FACES
OF JANUARY

Patricia Highsmith

Introduced by Hossein Amini

Patricia Highsmith draws us deep into a cross-European
game of cat and mouse in this masterpiece of suspense
from the author of *The Talented Mr Ripley*.

Two men meet in the picturesque backstreets of Athens.
Chester MacFarlane is a conman with multiple false identities,
near the end of his rope and on the run with his young wife
Colette. Rydal Keener is a young drifter looking for adventure:
he finds it one evening as the law catches up with Chester
and Colette, and their lives become fatally intertwined.

This special edition includes a foreword by the director
and screenwriter of the film, Hossein Amini.

'Highsmith is a giant of the genre'
Mark Billingham

'The No.1 greatest crime writer'
The Time

PATRICIA HIGHSMITH